SERAPH

SERAPH

JC McKENNA

for Jess

Now conscience wakes despair
That slumber'd, wakes the bitter memory
Of what he was, what is, and what must be Worse...

Milton, PARADISE LOST

1

I woke up with wet asphalt beneath me and a hunk of concrete for a pillow. The damp had seeped through my shirt, and it felt like someone had been tapping out Morse code on my lower spine with a rattan cane.

I decided that this was not a good omen for my day.

The morning light that pierced through my eyelids had left me with a dull but insistent headache, and the parts of my brain that didn't hurt felt like cotton candy. I let my inner pilot open my eyes and immediately regretted the decision, as the dull throb became a full throttle attack by what I could only assume was a miniature Panzer division. I shielded my eyes with my hands in an attempt to cut off their fuel supply. Gradually, my eyes adjusted and the light became far less offensive, despite the lingering feeling of caterpillar treads.

My body was stiff and sore, curled into a position as if I'd been trying to ward off blows or bracing for some sort of pain. I felt almost locked into the pose. Everything hurt.

How long had I been curled up like this?

I was in an alley. At least that was my best guess, as I appeared to be flanked by the ass ends of buildings. A cool breeze brushed over me, carrying with it the sickly sweet smell of hot peanut oil. Sense memory stirred. Slowly, I sat up and got a better look at my environs. I saw a white sign next to a loading dock.

LUCKY CHINA BUFFET. DELIVERIES ONLY.

Peanut oil mystery solved, and then a bell rang in the back of my skull. I was missing something important. My eyes wandered back to the sign.

Lucky China Buffet.

Home.

Lucky China meant home.

I grabbed the edge of a dumpster and pulled myself up as quickly as my body would allow. Every last joint screamed with the effort. I hung on to the dumpster a little longer until I could feel my equilibrium return.

Something inside compelled me to look down at myself.

Two legs, the something said. *Two feet. Hands. Pajamas a little shabby for outdoor wear, but at least we're not naked.*

Naked?

As soon as I got back inside, my brain and I were going to have a nice long chat. Possibly with liquor involved. *Or is it too early for that?* I realized I'd lost all sense of time. The sun was high, the air had a chill, but none of that meant much. I searched my memory for some clue as to what I'd been doing before I'd fallen asleep, but nothing beyond the initial damp feeling on my back and the piercing brightness in my eyes was coming to mind.

Shit, said the something inside. *We've gone and done it again.*

I needed to get back into my apartment.

Apartment.

Okay, I could remember that much at least. My hand, almost on its own, reached down into my pajama top and dragged out a key on a chain around my neck. A good boy scout is always prepared. Apparently.

Slowly, carefully, I stepped out of the alley and onto the street. The clock in the window of the bank across the street said 8:00—prime morning rush hour in the city, but not in this neighborhood, it seemed. The traffic of automobiles and pedestrians was sporadic. Not light, but not a stampede, either. Those who did pass by gave me no notice, or at least pretended not to notice. It said something about the atmosphere of the neighborhood I lived in. Here was a damp, barefoot hobo wandering the streets in his pajamas, and no one gave a second glance. No screaming, no ogling. No frantic calls to 911.

I stepped into the vestibule between Lucky China and a boarded up bodega and fumbled for the key again. My head was buzzing, my ears had started to ring, and I felt like the ground was going to rush up at me. I leaned up against the cool glass of the apartment building door and let the wave of dizzy pass over me.

Once the feeling of balance had returned, I shoved the key in the lock and let myself in. Still fuzzy, half dazed, I let my feet carry me via hazy sense memory towards my final destination, up one flight of stairs and then another. I climbed up to the fourth floor, resisting the temptation to crawl, and found my apartment door.

Fumbled more and rattled more—the door swung open and I fell into my living room, catching myself on the arm of a threadbare sofa as the dizzy clobbered me again. I hung my head until the spinning feeling stopped, then dragged my tired carcass toward my bedroom until I slumped over my dresser with my hands pressed down on the cool top.

With a little hesitation, I raised up my head and looked into the large mirror over the bureau. Drawn face, sharp nose. Hair dirty blond and a little longer than short, a rat's nest. Five o'clock shadow that was obviously clocking some overtime. Grey eyes a little red around the edges and baggy underneath.

I've looked better, said the voice in the back of my head. *I've looked worse, too.*

There were two pieces of paper jammed into the mirror's frame. One was an aging photograph, a portrait of the face in the mirror that looked a little cleaner and a little happier, but only just. The other was a sticky note in a neat hand that I knew wasn't mine.

Your name is Raymond Walsh, it read.

I knew that. Thank the gods. Last night's adventures hadn't created a complete tabula rasa, at least.

You are standing in the bedroom of your apartment on Wright Blvd. The phone rang.

I shook my head and turned away from my little shrine to self-awareness. I flopped down on my bed and picked up the phone on the nightstand.

"Hello?"

"I need you, Ray," said a man's voice on the other end. It sounded familiar, but it wasn't registering in my admittedly faulty memory. I decided to play for time.

"I'm flattered," I said, "but it's very unattractive when you start off sounding desperate."

"Fuck you, Walsh. It's not like you're fighting off the work lately. We've got a floater needs your special touch. There'll be a car at your place in ten minutes."

"Yes sir, Lieutenant!"

Lieutenant? Yes. Knowles, that was it. My brain was starting to catch up.

After a pause, I said, "Danny?" The name sounded somehow right. "Make it twenty. I need a shower if I'm gonna be with polite company."

"Whatever, Ray. Just bring the mojo."

Danny Knowles hung up and I headed for the shower. I stripped out of the alley-stained pajamas and took bodily inventory in the bathroom mirror. Sweat and grime, but nothing bruised. The only marks on me were the scars along my shoulder blades that had been with me for as long as I could remember, the relics of some long forgotten skirmish, of which there were, I supposed, rather many. I wouldn't know for sure. I don't remember much past the last decade, and most of that's been carefully constructed with the help of dear and clever friends so that I can have something that resembles a normal life.

Who was I before? Who knows?

Today, my name is Raymond Walsh. It says so on my driver's license.

TWENTY MINUTES LATER, I walked back out the front door of my apartment showered, shaved, and dressed much more appropriately for the hour. A uniform leaned up a against a patrol car. He nodded as he saw me and opened up the passenger door.

"Front seat?" I said as I climbed in. "It's sweet how you guys almost respect me now."

Uniform said nothing, but turned on the siren and peeled off the curb at an unhealthy speed. Ten minutes later we pulled into the parking lot of a warehouse along the river. I hopped out and headed over to where the action was, heeding the siren's call of yellow crime scene tape. There was a living, breathing Ken doll in a navy overcoat, plastic-handsome and obviously aware of it, giving orders to a uniformed posse.

"I bring the mojo," I said to the Ken doll.

"About damn time," said Lieutenant Knowles. "Your beauty regimen all square?"

"Trust me, I did you a favor."

"Like I could've smelled you over the bouquet of corpse and dead alewife," he said, cocking his head in the direction of the crime scene.

The coroner's assistant was crouched down over a corpse, male by the look of it, although it was hard to tell from the waterlogged swelling of the body.

"Rent-a-cop at the shipping warehouse called in at seven this morning," said the Lieutenant. "Victim was floating face down in the river, butted up against a pylon. Frogs fished him out about an hour ago."

The body was grey and swollen and the areas around his lips and nostrils were ragged.

The ME's assistant looked up at me with bloodshot eyes. "He's been dead about three days," he said. "Most likely he's been in the water that long, too. Long enough for the local river fauna to use him for a light snack."

I shuddered at the image and then took a deep breath.

"No ID," said Danny, "and we've got no idea how long he's been hung up on the dock here, or how long he's been following the current. I need a crime scene, Walsh. And a name, if you can swing it."

I shrugged. I didn't relish the thought of laying my hands on John Doe's nibbled up head, but it's how I make most of my living. I have a particular talent when it comes to the missing and the unknown. Cops like Danny Knowles had closed dozens of cases because they're not afraid to use my talents (although admitting that to their superiors was another story).

I knelt down beside the poor soul. The ME's assistant took one look at me and rolled his eyes.

"A little early to be bringing in the freak show, isn't it?" he asked Danny.

"I'm a closer," said the Lieutenant. "I don't like to waste time."

I shut out the banter over my head, took a deep breath to brace myself for the impending mindfuck and reached out to the corpse's head.

Dark.
Dark and suffocating.
I float now, feeling little but the cold. Even the feeling of dampness has dwindled as my body becomes saturated with polluted river.
I force myself to work backwards, floating away from this pylon

and against the flow of the river back towards the beginning of my final journey.

Faster and faster I flow upstream until I feel the shock of cold and wet against my body, the feel of rushing air replacing that shock almost instantly, until I find myself standing on a precipice looking out over the city skyline and the river that divides it in two.

I pause in this moment to gauge how I'm feeling.

Sorrow pierces my heart, a pain different from any other.

I'm flunking out of the engineering department.

Kathy's gone.

Everything hurts.

I tried talking to one of the school's counselors, but I don't think they heard me. Just handed me a prescription for antidepressants and sent me on my way. The waiting room was full of exam-panicked undergrads. No time for the lovelorn, I guess.

I crumple the prescription and Kathy's breakup note into a ball and watch it as it drops down into the rolling water below.

I always liked this bridge.

She told me she loved me on this bridge.

I hold that one perfect image in my mind and let go of the fence.

I came back to reality with a stabbing feeling in my heart and damp cheeks. I realized that I'd started crying at some point while connected to the corpse's last moments of life. I turned my head away, embarrassed, and rubbed my eyes on the sleeve of my coat. When I turned around again, I found Danny's hand reaching out to help me up.

"Who do we have?" he asked as he dragged me up to my feet.

"University student," I said. "No name, sorry. You might want to check with the engineering department, though."

"And my crime scene?"

"Suicide," I said as I tried to banish the lingering feelings of wind rush and plummet. "Let himself drop off the west side of the Sixth Street bridge."

Danny shook his head.

"Poor bastard," he said.

I nodded.

"Thanks," he said.

"I'll bill you," I said, then turned away.

"Can I have one of the boys drive you home?"

"No thanks," I said. "I need a walk in what passes for fresh air around here."

"Sure thing, Walsh. Thanks again."

"Just pay me on time."

I had a good hour's walk ahead of me. Honestly, the ride home would've been nice, but I did need some time to think. I was still feeling a little shaken by my rude awakening, so I decided to use the walk as a meditation. See if I could remember what had gone on the night before.

What had I done with my day?

Sat in my office, I seemed to recall. Actively avoided my answering machine. Chased down some past due consulting fees.

Then what?

Dinner, I thought. Then fuzzy remembrances of watching the ballgame on TV. A bourbon or two. And then?

Falling, said the voice in my head. *And then we were falling.*

Ah, yes. The regularly scheduled nightmare. An endless fall through a big, dark nothing. Now I wished that I hadn't remembered.

It's not a nightly experience, but the falling dream had been visiting me on a regular basis for as far back as I can remember, which is, embarrassingly, not that far back.

Usually, when I had the dream, I would wake up in my own bed. Sweating and screaming, sure, but in my own bed. Waking up in an alley? That didn't feel right. I was pretty sure somnambulism was not one of my hobbies, and yet the image of that alley in the morning light and the memory of that dampness against my back were not unfamiliar. I'd done it before. I think. The picture was fuzzy, but the sense of *déjà vu* was overwhelming. I'd woken up in an alley to the lingering memory of a terrible fall.

I tried to push the paralyzing feeling of the dream out of my head. It took the rest of the walk home to do it. And I succeeded. Mostly.

The early dusk of autumn had settled over the neighborhood. The neon beacon of the Lucky China Buffet called out to me through the growing dark as my stomach began to rumble. I had skipped a meal or two today. I ducked in to the Buffet and tried to drown out the lingering creepy feeling with a little pork lo mein and a helping of coconut bao. A heaping plate of greasy MSG heaven.

Back in my apartment, my appetite sated, I found myself staring out the window over a pauper's share of skyline. I knew what I'd been doing last night before things got weird. What was I doing before all that?

I sat down on the sofa, pulled out my wallet and emptied its contents onto the coffee table.

One driver's license, issued to Raymond Walsh. There was my picture on it. It felt right. Nothing weird there. There were business cards from the various police officers I'd worked with. There was Danny's card.

When had he given that to me, again?

There was another card. *Walsh Security Services.* Mine, apparently. That was my business, yes. That felt right.

Everything there felt right. I could remember it all on principle. But in actuality? Pictures of the past were a little fuzzy.

How the hell had it all gotten there? How the hell had I gotten here? In this apartment? In this city, even?

Shut up, Ray, I thought. *You're just feeling disoriented after your little adventure this morning. One good night's sleep and you'll be feeling better.*

I was probably right. Staying awake and fretting about it all certainly wasn't helping. I walked over to the kitchenette and poured myself a little nightcap.

"Ah, bourbon," I said to the empty room. "Perhaps you're just the key I need."

I walked back over to the window and took a sip of the sweet, smoky amber, enjoying every last inch of alcoholic burn down my throat.

It'll all be better in the morning, I thought, then went to lean my head against the window. The window had other ideas, however, and ceased to be solid. The rest of my body's weight followed my head, and I screamed as I began to fall, but only for a moment. The sound was soon choked off as I blacked out from the terror.

I exist in a void. There is neither light nor darkness. Nothing to be seen or felt. The terror recedes and I savor the joy of the moment.

Then without warning, the barest pinpoint of absolute darkness appears, and I can feel my body pulled in its direction. In that same instant, the sense of nothing is replaced once again with terror, this time far more intense.

The point of darkness grows as my body sails toward it. I feel as though I am being pulled, a hook set in my heart dragging me to a terrifying and alien destination.

My hands reach out into the void trying to gain a hold of something—anything—so that I might resist the pull and return to my previous state of bliss, but there is nothing to catch on to. Instead I flail, helpless. All the while the horrible darkness grows until I meet this hole head-first, the invisible hook still pulling at my chest.

The breach is barely big enough for my head. My shoulders bump up against the edges of the hole, and I find myself caught between two realities. The relentless tug continues, forcing my body through the breach, making it scream in pain. I push against the now solid edges *of this intrusion, trying to force myself back into the void, but to no avail. The hook in my heart is strong and it pulls me, inch by inch and bone by cracking bone into a terrifying new place. I let go with a soundless scream, my body now burning, as with a final, agonizing yank I am birthed into absolute, paralyzing darkness.*

The barb in my chest is yanked out, taking my heart with it and I begin to fall, endless descent, always accelerating. Every hair on my body stands on end until I feel like a million needles have pierced my skin. And still I fall, smothered in the terrifying empty.

The growing morning light pierced my eyelids and I awoke looking up into a sky framed by the ass ends of low-rent architecture. The needle piercing sensation of the endless fall still enveloped my body, but was now accompanied by the feeling of damp concrete beneath me.

The sickly-sweet smell of hot peanut oil filled my nostrils as the tingling in my skin began to recede. Slowly, I sat up. My spine was trying to argue with me over this course of action, curled as it was in a brace for impact, and with great effort I willed it into quiet. My head was filled with cobwebs and I felt hung over.

I sat up with my eyes opened and craned my neck—spine screaming all the way—trying to take in my surroundings. Nothing but dumpsters and loading docks as far as the eye could see. Above my head, I could see a small metal sign next to one of the docks—LUCKY CHINA BUFFET. DELIVERIES ONLY.

Son of a bitch! screamed the voice in the back of my head.

I felt around my neck for the comforting presence of my apartment key and found only my bare chest. I hung my head in exasperation and let the cool morning breezes wrap around my skin.

An alarm buzzer went off in my head while my hands began patting around my body of their own accord, finding nothing but skin and body hair, clammy and cold in the morning mist.

Okay, said the voice, *we're naked this time. Slightly embarrassing, but not the end of the world.*

I shook what cobwebs I could out of my skull and scrambled around the alley looking for something—anything—that would provide me with enough cover to make a quick run back inside. Thankfully, one of the line cooks had left a grease-smeared apron crumpled up on the edge of Lucky China's dock. I wrapped it around my waist in an impromptu kilt and made a dash for the end of the alley, once again thanking the gods that in this neighborhood no one thought of giving a second glance to a half-naked Viking hobo on the streets at whatever o'clock in the morning it was.

I ducked into the alcove outside my building, operating almost completely on autopilot, and took a quick look around to make sure no one was watching. Something in the foggier neighborhoods of my brain compelled me to crouch down and start prying loose one of the tiles on the ground. Underneath I found a spare key.

Somebody's a boy scout, I thought. *Hopefully that somebody's me.*

My hands and my knees were shaking, but I managed to get the front door opened and stumbled inside before I gave in to the urge to collapse against the stairwell railing. I allowed myself to rest for a moment, trying to catch my breath. With the danger of public exposure past, the terror of the preceding moments started to settle back in. The foyer was spinning around my head, and I felt my body start to tighten up into a brace for a fall that had become all too familiar. I leaned my head against a newel post and willed the room into stillness, then started to fumble my way up the stairs.

The farther up I went, the lighter my head got, until I'd reached the fourth floor landing, and my apartment door just where I'd left it. The autopilot was still operating. Hands opened doors, feet walked towards bedroom, until at last I slumped forward and caught myself on the top of my dresser and tried to regain both breath and balance.

With effort, I lifted my head only to find a face more haggard and unshaven than the one I'd seen yesterday—*had it only been yesterday?*—almost, but only almost, resembling the one in the photo still wedged in the mirror frame.

Raymond Walsh, it said.

I knew that, but so what? I knew that name applied to me, but I didn't know *why*. I took a closer look at the me in the photo. Raymond Walsh. Me. But me in seemingly happier and healthier times. Something in my subconscious poked me impatiently in the forebrain. There was something familiar about the background in the photo. I should know this place. I tried to put a name to it but was foiled in my effort to wrap my brain around this phantom.

Frustrated, I yanked the photo out of the mirror frame and tossed it angrily on the dresser top, cursing the unfairness of it all.

I knew things. I knew who I was, I knew what I did, I even sort of knew who I did what for. I just didn't have the *whys* of it all. I would have preferred full blown amnesia and not known what I didn't know.

Amnesia. There was the furious forebrain poking, again. That idea was important. Perhaps.

Again, I looked down at the photo of happy, healthy Raymond Walsh as my unconscious steered my fingers towards it and flipped it over. There in the same neat block print, it read:

(re)birthday at the welcome table

The Welcome Table. One of the city's many homeless shelters. Again, I knew *what* it was, but the why was fuzzy. Perhaps if I paid a visit, I'd get some answers.

I was somewhat relieved by the thought, but still sore and grimy. I stood up from the dresser and wobbled for a moment, still feeling light headed. I knew a shower would do me some good, so I crawled under the jet of hot water and let it sluice over every aching inch of me. As it hit my back, my spine began to burn. Hot water became acid. I started to slip and caught myself on the tile wall, looked down as I did and caught a glimpse of unmistakable red mixed in with the water that circled the drain.

Dizzy, I let myself slump onto the floor of the shower stall. Out of the corner of my eye, I saw the trail of blood leading from my bedroom into the shower.

Stay with it, Ray, said a voice in my head. *Get to The Welcome Table.*

Sure thing, I thought. *Just let me finish with the dying first.*

The last thing I saw before I blacked out was a twister of red, my own blood, rushing down the drain.

I REGAINED CONSCIOUSNESS who knows how much later with pruny skin and a massive headache. My spine didn't seem to be on fire anymore, and there wasn't any more blood running down the drain, so whatever it was that had happened couldn't have been as serious as I'd thought it was in the moment.

Slowly, I pulled myself upright and shut off the shower. I pat myself dry while my body protested every move. I tossed back a couple of aspirin, then grabbed a damp cloth and mopped up the blood on the bathroom floor. I followed the trail back into the bedroom and over to the chair in the corner where I'd shucked off the borrowed apron. Dried blood had been added to dried grease. A lot of blood. No wonder I'd felt so dizzy.

I stepped over to the dresser and turned around, trying to get a glimpse of what had happened back there, and saw practically nothing. No cuts, no scabs. All I saw were the same old jagged scars running down either side of my spine, the scars that had always been there, at least as far as my shoddy memory was concerned.

Confounded, I shaved, dressed, and headed out to get some answers.

The Welcome Table was one of the many shelters that had set up shop in the Missions. Any reasonably sized city has a place like the Missions—neighborhoods that are never planned, but come into existence out of an ever-present necessity. They're usually attached to industrial areas, with steel bars, broken glass, and graffitied plywood as the dominant architectural motifs. These places are populated by some of the worst sinners, some of the best saints, and a whole hell of a lot of the forgotten and cast-aside—the ones caught in the middle of an economic war they didn't start. Sinners and saints both looked to them as potential recruits in a never-ending battle.

Here, the Missions was once a booming industrial zone. When the Depression hit, the factory workers kept showing up, hoping against hope that their jobs were coming back. The charities and religious missionaries began setting up shop here where they were most needed, and pretty soon every poor soul in the city started showing up for their daily bread. As businesses shut down or moved on to greener pastures, the warehouses and factories emptied out and the missions and shelters moved in. The Depression ended, but the missions never went away. Their services were always in need.

There'd been some cosmetic changes over the decades. Some of the buildings got facelifts. There were more junkies, now, along with the homeless vets. More cops, too. The neighborhood's purpose, though? That never changed.

Give me your tired, your poor, your huddled masses... and I'll hide them away where you won't have to feel guilty thinking about them.

Walking into the heart of the Missions, I kept an eye open for the glass and steel structure that marked the headquarters of New Light Ministries. As it came into view I shuddered and crossed to the other side of the street. The place always creeped the hell out me. It was, however, a convenient landmark in the search for my current destination. The Welcome Table, its humble brick facade dwarfed by the slick mission across the way, beckoned me inside.

The Welcome Table felt like home. Somewhere inside was a piece of me telling me it *was* home. A comforting thought. Again, something in my subconscious steered me into the modest common space that served as the shelter's dining room. I ran my fingers over tables and chair backs, and willed sense memory to restore the missing pieces of my mind. There was coffee brewing on the kitchen's antiquated commercial stove, and it was a welcome smell. My autopilot kicked in again, and I walked straight over to the coffee urn. I tapped a generous mug of the bittersweet elixir and turned my gaze over to a tray of day-old pastries on a cart. I'd forgotten to eat again, and rotgut java and stale crullers sounded like heaven.

"About time you showed up."

I was startled mid-sip by the sound of a smoky alto voice. I just avoided spitting out my coffee as I turned to face a woman, tall and stocky, wearing jeans and chamois shirt with the sleeves rolled up. Her hair was steely grey and cut short, and she put down a tray of dirty coffee mugs on the table next to her as she walked, almost storming, up to me.

"I have been calling your office for the last two hours, Ray," she fumed. "When are you going to join the modern age and get yourself a cell..." She stopped mid-harangue. Her eyes locked onto mine, and I felt her gazing into my soul. The scowl on her face was replaced by a look somewhere between warmth and fear. "What happened?" she asked after a quiet moment.

Something inside me told me I could trust her and urged me forward.

"Woke up in an alley," I said. "Don't know why."

Her head tilted as she looked deeper into my eyes. I continued. "Know who I am and what I do," I said. "Again, don't know why."

The steel-haired woman nodded and took me by the hand. "It was bound to happen," she said. "Come with me."

I followed her without argument into a cozy office at the back of the building. She sat me down on a sofa and then walked behind a desk. She pulled out two cut glass tumblers and what looked like a rather expensive bottle of scotch. She poured about an inch of whiskey into each glass and then handed me one.

"Drink," she said.

"I'm not sure alcohol's the preferred treatment for memory holes," I said.

She placed the glass in my hand and closed my fingers around it. "Drink," she said.

I raised the glass to my lips and let the rich, peaty smell crawl up my nostrils before I took one hesitant sip. It burned sweetly as it travelled down my throat and I felt myself relaxing into the liquor. I melted into the sofa cushions and tossed the rest of the scotch back without a second thought.

The steel-haired woman smiled and poured another shot into my glass. I looked a question at her.

"Drink," she said.

"It's lovely stuff," I said, "but I'm already feeling a little too unbalanced and out of control, already."

"Balance and memory will come," she said. "First, though, you need a little lubricant. Drink. You'll thank me later."

The voice in the back of my skull urged me once again to trust her. I drank. Slowly this time. This was the good stuff, and I wanted to savor it.

As I drank, the steel-haired woman went back to her desk drawer. This time, she pulled out a velvet bag, jet black and about the size of my fist. She sat down next to me on the sofa.

"Memory's always been a bit of a problem for you, Ray," she said. She pulled the drawstrings open on the bag and reached in. I felt the hair on the back of my head stand up as she did. The voice in my head that had been urging me to trust started to sound a little panicky. "You knew you needed to be prepared for an episode like this," she said, as she pulled a piece of hematite from the bag, cool and silver black, and a little smaller than the palm of my hand.

The sight of it stirred something in me. I started to jump up from the sofa.

"I don't want to!" I said. *Don't want to what?* I thought. *Quit freaking out.*

I felt her hand on my wrist, stronger than I was expecting, and she pulled me back down to sit.

"It'll be all right, Ray."

"Ruthie, don't make me do it! Don't make me live it again!"

She smiled. "Good," she said, "you remember my name, now. That's something."

I'd stunned myself into silence. Some piece of me was waking up.

"Pick up the stone," she said. Perplexed, entranced, I nodded and let my hand close around the hematite. Something about the smooth coolness reached me. As the second belt of alcohol reached my brain, I started to relax again.

"We all need touchstones, Ray," she said. "Reminders of who we are. Some of us more than others."

I looked down at the stone in my hands.

"Not a literal stone, Ray. The hematite's a focus. A prompt."

She took my free hand and placed it flat to her temple. Something inside was still panicking, but it was muffled by a wall of quiet and alcohol.

"You made me your touchstone, Ray, in case your memories ever left you again."

She closed her eyes, and I felt myself engulfed in a wave of peaceful black.

"Remember who you are," she said, her voice echoing around me in the growing darkness.

Suddenly, I felt my eyelids pierced by daylight.

3

Daylight. Alley.

I come into consciousness with a screaming headache and my back against a brick wall. I close my eyes for a moment and try to remember how I got here, but the brick wall in my mind is even more impenetrable than the one against my body.

Slowly, I stand up and begin to take stock. Two arms, two legs. Hands, feet. Heartbeat's in the right place. I'm wearing jeans, a bit tattered, a plain white t-shirt and a short jacket, olive drab. Army? The jacket is faded, except for a small patch over the breast pocket where a name tag would have been. Anonymous jacket. No help, there.

I feel around my pockets, hoping for a wallet or some other I.D., but my luck is still short.

Here I stand. No name, no money, and no idea where I am.

I walk out onto the street with more than a little trepidation. Everything around me looks as depressed and faceless as I feel. Heavy steel bars cover windows and there doesn't seem to be much real estate that hasn't been tagged with some color of spray paint or another.

I notice wave upon wave of broken down humanity begin to pass by, all heading in the same direction. My eyes follow where they're going and are drawn to a large glass and steel building a few blocks down. Not the tallest building I've ever seen, but practically a sky-scraper in this neighborhood. The gathering army of downtrodden foot soldiers appears to be lining up outside its doors. With nowhere else to go and no one else to be, I follow.

We stand outside, my nameless comrades and I, for what feels like hours. My stomach growls, and I find myself hoping I've fallen into a bread line.

At last, the doors open and we march in, deliberate and orderly. A primly dressed missionary woman, all black skirt and sensible shoes, leads us into a large dining hall. The smell of warm bread fills the room and I have to check myself so that I don't drool all over the shiny, clean floor.

Patiently, I wait my turn in line, until I can at last accept a steaming bowl with eager hands and an enthusiastic, "Thank you," to everyone I see in the black and white uniform of the mission staff. I take a seat next to my fellow invisible soldiers and we start to dig in.

Nothing has ever tasted so good. Strike that. I've never tasted anything before this. I search my memory for any related experience, but hit wall after wall, foiled.

No moment has existed before this one.

A missionary with a blue necktie steps onto a dais at the head of the dining hall. I catch him out of the corner of my eye, mid-spoonful, and I feel my spine jolt. I look up.

"Welcome, friends," he says into a microphone. "New Light Ministries welcomes all the worlds forgotten children. Before you continue your meal, let us bow our heads for a short prayer."

The word "prayer" hits me in the gut like a brick and the jolting feeling in my spine starts to burn.

I will not trade my soul for bread, *says a voice at the back of my skull.* Certainly not with these bastards.

The fight-or-flight instinct of my reptile brain takes over higher cerebral functions—it screams out for flight, and I listen. I jump up from the long cafeteria table, knocking my soup over in the process. I run out of the mission with everyone's eyes on me. My head is filled with a piercing screaming noise. Once outside, I realize the scream is my own. I clamp my mouth shut, try to get my breathing under control and will my nervous system back into calm submission.

Back out on the streets, it is early evening, now, and chilly. The sky has taken on the strange silver color that comes before snow. I'm going to need shelter, but not here. Not with these people.

Across the way, I see another mission—brick-faced and much more modest than this New Light. A hand-painted sign over the door says simply: The Welcome Table. *I like the sound of those words. I cross the street and climb the steps inside.*

Inside is warm and there is the feeling of home about it. There are not nearly as many invisible foot soldiers gathered here, but the ones who are seem happy—or at least as happy as they can be given our shared circumstances.

A stocky woman with steel colored hair is standing at an opening between kitchen and mess hall, dishing out a rich smelling soup. Split pea with a generous amount of ham. I take a bowl from her with a grateful smile, sit down at a table and knock the whole thing back in two minutes.

Greedy, I take a second bowl when offered, along with a hunk of warm brown bread and a mug of coffee. I eat slowly this time, savoring the first full meal I can remember eating.

As I scrape up soup leavings with my bread, the steel-haired woman at the kitchen counter takes a seat across from me.

"I'm Reverend Penfield," she says holding out her hand. My body goes on alert. I shake her hand with some reluctance.

Here comes the pitch, *I think.*

"You can call me Ruth, though," she says. "Everyone does."

"I don't pray," I say, drawing my hand back.

Ruth Penfield smiles.

"Neither do I," she says. "Much."

For a moment, we sit there looking at one another, each of us sizing the other up.

"What's your story?" Ruth asks.

I breathe deep, in and out.

"Woke up this morning, found myself wandering this place."

The Reverend raises an eyebrow. "And?"

"And now you know everything I do," I say.

"What's your name?" she asks.

Again I breathe deep, looking down into my bowl.

"God only knows," I say.

Ruth smiles, more sad this time. She gets up and walks back to the kitchen, digging in a drawer. When she comes back, she's holding a small pin-backed name badge, which she pins through my jacket over the old name tag void.

"God only knows?" she says. "Well, until He starts talking, why don't you stay here for a while, help me out?"

I look up into her face. There is a kindness in her eyes along with a steely determination that matches the color of her hair. There is a voice in my head telling me that I can trust her.

I nod.

"All right, then," she says. "Let me show you to your room, Ray."

Puzzled, I look down at the badge she's pinned to my chest. Below the words "The Welcome Table" is a name in large block print.

RAYMOND

It'll do.

Months pass.

I am a fixture at the Welcome Table, Ruth Penfield's right hand man. I clean. I cook (sort of). I fix. I welcome.

I answer to the name Ray, now. It feels right. At the very least, it's nice to have something that's mine.

I get to know Ruthie, too. She's not too religious, despite the title in front of her name. She wants to make the world right, and the title opens a few more doors, even if she bought it for ten bucks on the internet. She had a military career before settling for a life in the Missions. She doesn't go into much detail about that part of her life.

We talk a lot about my past. Or we try to. My memory still butts up against a brick wall when I try to remember beyond that first day I walked in here.

Months pass.

I've become a mentor of sorts to a young man who calls himself Jinx—black clothes and black eyeliner. His attitude used to match his personal style, but he's grown almost cheerful the more he's hung around.

Weeks pass.

Ruthie and I haven't seen Jinx in days. We're trying not to fret. The foot soldiers of the invisible army are called transients for a reason. People come and go all the time. Jinx seemed to flourish with us, though.

I hope he's all right.

Occasionally, I see him in my dreams. He's in a big, empty loft, with a big window looking out onto a bridge. He's talking with a girl—dirty blonde and almost pretty. Gorgeous, haunting eyes. I can't hear what they say, but those eyes burn themselves into my waking mind.

WEEKS PASS.

The cops are canvassing the Missions looking for a kid named Martin who'd gone missing almost a year earlier after an incident at his high school and a fight at home. In the dining room, Ruth and I take a look at the photo his parents have provided. Scribble some black marker around the eyes and there was no doubt it was Jinx.

Trouble was we hadn't seen him in over a month.

That afternoon, I'm out on an errand for Ruthie when I spot those haunting eyes, along with the rest of the girl, coming out of one of the many iron-barred bodegas with a paper sack in hand.

I follow her to an abandoned tenement. To my left is a bridge across the river, the bridge in my dreams.

I run back to the shelter and tell Ruthie what I've seen. By the end of the day, we reunite a mother with her son.

The cops say I "must be psychic or something." I laugh at the idea.

A MONTH PASSES.

The cops come knocking on our door again. They want to borrow the "tall psychic dude" for another missing persons case.

Meanwhile, Ruth thinks I need some better identification than a name tag. She hands me a driver's license and a Social Security card. They are in the name of Raymond Walsh.

"How?" I ask.

"Favors were owed," says Ruth. "Best if you don't know the details."

"Why?"

"Plausible deniability," she says.

"No, why this? Why now?"

"If you can't remember the life you had, you at least deserve the life you've built now."

YEARS PASS. I see the faces of the dozens I've helped to find. Some are even still alive. I don't know how it works. I just know where people are, especially when they're in trouble.

Good job of it, too, *says a voice in my head.* Too bad you've never been able to find yourself in the process.

WHEN I AWOKE, it was well past sundown. Ruthie had turned the light off in her office and let me sleep off the psychic reboot on her couch. Bones creaking, I sat up, stretched out, and went in search of my friend.

The clock on the wall in the kitchen said it was nine in the evening. Ruth was at the stove heating up some cocoa. There were three mugs out on a tray.

"Thanks for the drink before the mental onslaught," I said.

She smiled. "Told ya," she said.

"Your idea?" I asked.

"Yours," she said. "When you started having the falling dreams a few years ago, you were worried that you'd wake up with an empty head again. So we set up the touchstone exercise. You deposited what few conscious memories you still had into—what did you call it?—'A seldom used corner of my psyche.' An emergency memory cache. Never thought we'd actually use it."

"Didn't help me remember anything beyond the last ten years, though."

"Well, no," she said. "You didn't have any memories beyond that to lay aside."

We stood there in the quiet for a moment, listening to the whisper of the big gas stove.

"I've had the dream two nights in a row, now," I said. "At least as far as I can remember."

"And your memory?" asked Ruth.

"Fuzzy but not deleted," I said. "Like I said before, I knew whats but not whys. If it happens again, I can't guarantee it won't be worse, or that I'll find you or the touchstone again."

Ruth turned off the gas and poured cocoa into the mugs.

"You know," she said, "I've never pushed you too hard about regaining your past."

"I know," I said.

"I always figured there was some trauma you weren't ready to deal with, yet."

She stopped what she was doing and looked at me.

"I sense a 'however' coming on," I said.

"However," she said, "it seems as though that trauma might be pushing its way through."

"And?"

"And it might be time to be a little more aggressive in pursuit of your past."

No! screamed the deep recesses of my psyche.

"I'll think about it," I said.

Again, we were quiet.

I looked at the mugs of cocoa Ruth had laid out.

"Expecting company?" I asked.

"Trauma and alley-naps aside, how are you feeling?" she asked. "Are you up for going back to work?"

"I could always use a job," I said.

"Good," said Ruth. "There's someone I'd like you to meet."

The television was on in the rec room upstairs. A boy—couldn't have been more than eleven, twelve years old—sat cross-legged in front of the bright glow of *Looney Tunes*, but he wasn't laughing. His shoulders were hunched, tense, and he looked ready to run at a moment's notice.

Ruthie rapped lightly on the doorframe, and the kid turned away from a whooping Daffy Duck to meet our eyes. He radiated so much fear that my own flight response started twitching.

"Did you get enough to eat?" Ruth asked the boy.

"Yeah, I'm good," he said without much conviction, a world weariness beyond his very few years seeping into his voice. "Is this the guy?"

"Ethan, this is Ray Walsh. Ray," she said, turning to me, "meet Ethan Trammler."

"Hello, Ethan."

The boy nodded a greeting with a wary look.

"Ethan arrived at the shelter last night," Ruth explained. "He has a situation that I think might require your special talents."

I raised an eyebrow in question.

"Reverend Penfield says you help find missing people."

My other eyebrow followed and I shot a glance over at Ruth. *My special talent, eh?*

Ruth did her best impersonation of an innocent bystander.

I looked Ethan in the eye. "I've been known to help the cops from time to time, yeah."

I saw his eyes bug out when I mentioned the cops, and he shot a panicked look in Ruthie's direction. She shook her head, and the kid relaxed, but only just. He looked back at me for a quiet moment, like a jockey appraising a horse, then seemed to come to some sort of decision.

"I need you to get my sister back," he said.

"You lost her?"

"No, I found her."

"I'm afraid I don't understand the problem, then."

"Apparently, Laura doesn't *wish* to be found," Ruth said.

"She what, now?" I said.

"She's a resident of New Light Ministries," she said. "Ethan's tried talking to her, but she claims she doesn't wish to leave."

My hackles went up. "Well, then, there's not much I can do," I said. "She's not missing, and I don't have any pull with New Light."

"She promised me we'd stick together," Ethan said, the barest trace of a sob entering his voice.

"Apparently, this is not the sort of thing Laura's prone to doing," said Ruth, placing a comforting hand on Ethan's shoulder. "Ethan claims that his sister is his guardian. She's sworn to watch out for him. I suspect she's being held against her will."

Might be why the place rubs me the wrong way, I thought.

"So why not go straight to the police?" I asked.

"No cops!" Ethan said, his voice rising to a wail. He jumped up, ready to run. Ruth firmed her grasp on the boy's shoulder, trying to keep him calm and in place.

Red flags had begun waving in a small parade. "Why no cops, Ethan?" I asked.

"I don't wanna go back home."

"They're both runaways, Ray. Ethan and Laura don't want to be found, just yet."

I looked sideways at my old friend. Ruth Penfield had always been a law and order gal. She knows I have ties to the police. For her to suggest working around normal channels was something of a surprise. Something more was going on.

"I can take care of myself," Ethan said, with an unconvincing tough-guy edge. "I just... I just need my sister."

The boy made a valiant effort to choke back tears. That sound, along with the pathetic look on his face, brought my inner paladin galloping to the front of my consciousness. Before the paladin could make any noble promises, however, the frightened, nameless hobo that still occupied the forgotten recess of my mind jumped out of the bushes and mugged him for his lance.

I wasn't crossing New Light's threshold again. For anyone. Ever.

"Sorry, kid. It's not my kinda job," I said, hoping he couldn't read the lie in my face.

Ethan turned away from me and back to the television, but not before I caught the abject despair in his eyes, slipping a guilt-laced stiletto between my ribs.

Shit.

The look of disapproval on Ruthie's face only twisted the knife. She tilted her head, pointing the way to her office, and I followed her down the hall. Back in her office, with the door shut, we sat there for a few moments just staring at each other. Ruth was glaring at me, and every so often she'd open her mouth to speak, then think better of it and close it again, her lips drawn into a tight frown.

I tried my best to look appropriately abashed.

Ruth reached into a desk drawer, pulled out a photo, and tossed it over to me. It was a portrait of two kids. One was Ethan Trammler. The other I could assume was the sister, Laura. They were definitely siblings, although Laura looked considerably older. She had the same round face as her brother, capped with long, wavy brown hair.

"Are you trying to guilt me into taking this job?" I asked.

"I wish you'd reconsider," Ruth said. "New Light's a shelter just like this one."

I shrugged.

"You're not living on the streets anymore," she said. "You've got a place to live and a job."

"And I'm waking up in alleys with holes in my brain," I said.

"We fixed that."

"Not the big hole that starts ten years ago," I said. I crossed my arms and willed the sofa to swallow me whole.

"Don't you dare blame me for that," Ruth said, an edge in her voice I rarely heard. "I've offered help, I've offered connections. I've told you to pursue it. Just tonight I told you that."

I looked away.

"You," she said, "are the one dodging the work."

We were quiet for a long time. After a while, I heard Ruth pull the bottle from her drawer. I looked up when I felt her standing over me as she held out a tumbler of whiskey. I took the glass, and she leaned against the edge of her desk as we drank.

"I like Ray Walsh," I said.

"I know."

"What if I breach the wall in my head and I can't be him anymore?"

"Who knows, Ray? Personally, I have a hard time believing the essence of you will be all that different. New name. New memories. Same good man, though."

I drained the scotch and stared into the cut glass pattern on the bottom.

"What if I'm a monster?" I asked, still staring into the tumbler.

"Not possible," she said.

After a moment, Ruth collected the glasses and locked the bottle back up in her desk.

"I've watched you save countless lives without a second thought to your own interests. Hell, I know you'll eventually come around and help Ethan." I opened my mouth to protest, but she gave me a look that would cow a wolverine. "Let's prove you're the man I *know* you are, Ray," she said.

"Okay," I said.

"Is there a therapist in town you haven't pissed off, yet?"

"Not likely," I said. I barely suppressed a grin.

"How about that one police consultant you've worked with?" she asked. "You know, the brunette with the legs?"

"Jesus, Ruthie, I can feel you leering from here!"

"Am I wrong?"

"Are we fixing my head or fixing you up?"

"Oh, honey, she's too young for me."

"And I'm pretty sure she's not all that fond of me," I said. "I believe the one time we were on the same case she called me..."

"...a charlatan, I know. See, she has a vested interest in fixing... quit scowling, Ray."

I stared into her smirking eyes. "Fine," I said as I stood up. "Call her."

"And Ethan?" she called out as I made my escape from her office.

"Apparently, I'll come around" I said.

"I'll haunt you till you do."

She wasn't kidding, either.

BACK AT MY apartment, with a couple of twenty-four-hour convenience store hot dogs assaulting my belly, I stared longingly at my bed. I needed to sleep. All the cues were there, but I was too amped from the day's adventures to feel tired. Instead, I went to the kitchen and poured myself a bourbon over a few ice cubes and then plopped my confused carcass down on the living room sofa.

I stared out the window for a long time while I sipped at the bourbon and tried to get my head clear. Somehow, I got to the bottom of the old-fashioned glass without feeling any more tired. Or clear, for that matter.

Fine, another snort it is.

I stood up to head for the kitchen and almost fell flat on my ass. My knees buckled, and I caught hold of the sofa in an attempt to keep myself upright, dropping the glass in the process.

Must've poured myself more than I thought.

But this was no drunken stumble. There was darkness creeping into my peripheral vision. I could feel a frighteningly familiar tug at my ribcage. Then my living room disappeared into the black as the floor fell out from under me and I began to fall.

4

I am falling, how fast I cannot tell, but the electric sensation that courses through my body hints at tremendous speed. I still drop within a vacuum, no air rushing past my skin, no howling of the wind, only the skin-prickly feeling of my every hair at attention.

I tumble, over and over, and I cannot tell up from down. Direction seems to change with each twist of my body, and still all I can sense with any certainty is that I am falling—forever, a silent howl escaping my lungs.

Then, in the periphery, a speck of light crosses my sight. I tumble so quickly I cannot view it head on, but it is there, spinning in my vision. And now, with a point of reference, my involuntary journey has a destination. A brief but futile shock of hope stabs into my consciousness, until I realize I am still falling, and the terror of the descent is replaced with the absolute dread of what might happen when my falling body, the unstoppable force, meets the immovable object that continues to expand in my vision.

Now, there is nothing but the light and my arms crossed over my head, bracing for the impact that I both dread and ache for—a messy end, but an end nonetheless.

The end does not come.

Just as suddenly as it began, my long fall stops, leaving only the remnants of electric horror arcing across my body from pore to pore. With a start, I realize that I have clamped my eyes shut in preparation for my death, and a light is piercing through the thin skin of my eyelids.

I open my eyes and let the blazing daylight resolve into lucid vision.

A lush, green field stretches out in all directions, touching the horizon wherever I look. Above me is a beautifully clear, blue sky. Perhaps it is safe now. But no. I can feel another's presence. It tugs at my ribcage much as the void has done, and I know better than to try and fight it. With caution, I walk through the grass in the direction I'm pulled. Soon, I can see a vaguely human-shaped figure up ahead of me.

I approach this other with care, and as I draw closer, I can see it is another human being, draped in a loose robe and cowl stained in a gorgeous indigo.

"Hello," I call out, raising my hand in greeting. But the blue robe does not reply. Instead, a smile spreads from underneath its cowl and I stop in my tracks. It is not, by any stretch of the imagination, a friendly smile. There are too many wolfish and hungry teeth showing. It is a smile that promises pain, a mile wide underneath the shadowed cowl and cruel. Very cruel. I am afraid if I stare too long I might fall into it, and I quickly look away out of a sense of self-preservation.

Blue robe's hands are full. The left arm cradles a large book, and the right hand grasps a sword with a gleaming, silver blade, whisper thin and deadly. The sword frightens me, but the book holds my attention even more. It looks ancient, and I can see an odd shape on its cover and the remnants of gold leaf. Despite my better judgment, I lean in for a closer look and can see a hexagonal engraving. The sides are not simple lines, but I cannot make out any more detail other than the number.

"Ray!"

I jump as I hear a voice somewhere far off in the distance calling my name. I look back towards blue robe and see that the figure has stepped to one side. A woman stands there now, also clad in the indigo robe, but with the cowl down. Chestnut curls frame a youthful face. There's something familiar, but I can't quite get my head around it. Then, the ghost of a photograph in Ruthie's hands invades my forebrain.

"Laura?" I call out, but she only smiles and turns away, stepping behind my cowled adversary and disappearing.

"Ray!"

This time I turn to look and see where the voice is coming from. It sounds closer, but I cannot locate its source.

The hairs on the back of my neck stand on end just before I hear the slight hiss of rushing air behind me. I turn back to face blue-robe and stare into that cruel smile once again. The smile has, if it's even possible, grown even wider, and the scary whisper-thin blade is now poised over my head.

I cringe, eyes closed, and wait for the inevitable death stroke.

"**G**oddammit, Walsh!"

My eyes popped open at the sound of the gruff voice. My back was resting on damp asphalt. Again. And I could smell desiccated Chinese food.

Again.

Hell.

"Before I get up," I called out to whoever was looking over me, "could you tell me if I'm dressed?"

My interloper let out an amused huff.

"Not as nicely as me," he said, "but I won't have to haul your ass in for public indecency, either."

With no little effort, I sat up. There was a living, breathing, life-sized Ken doll leaning in a loading zone doorway across from the Lucky China. He wore a cheap suit that said "thrift store" and not Saville Row.

"Wouldn't be the first time," I said, struggling to get upright. "I thought Ken was supposed to have a nicer wardrobe."

"I opted for the functioning genitalia," he said, stepping away from the loading door and holding out a hand to steady me.

"Fair trade," I said. "How'd you know where to find me?"

"Educated guess," said Danny. "If you don't answer your phone at this hour, then it's a safe bet you're sleeping back here."

So the alley naps weren't unusual? I decided to leave the more troubling question unasked.

"What can I do for you today?" *Business as usual. Nothing to worry about here.*

Lieutenant Daniel Knowles pulled me up to standing and then walked towards the head of the alley. I followed him without an invitation.

"Got a Jane Doe chilling in the ME's office," he said, opening the passenger door of his brown sedan like a chauffeur. "Identifying her's been a total bust. Thought maybe our resident fortune-teller might like a crack at the job." He swept his arm towards the shotgun seat.

"Love to," I said, settling myself into the passenger seat in Dan's car. The detective shut the door behind me and crossed around to the driver's side, opening the door and dumping himself into the automobile with little ceremony.

He gunned the engine and pulled off the curb with a jolt, tearing the car into traffic with a little more speed than was necessary or safe in this neighborhood.

We were outside the county morgue's doors in less than fifteen minutes. Danny hopped out of the sedan just as a wave of anxiety crept over me. The lieutenant opened my door and stood on the curb waiting as I sat there frozen.

"How many times have we done this together, now?" he asked.

"Dozens," I said. "Doesn't matter. I can still feel them."

He smiled, but I could see him trying to suppress a shudder. "You must be a blast at funerals," he said.

"Different story," I said. "I can walk through a cemetery without hyperventilating. But, a room full of violent and mysterious deaths? Of souls not at rest?"

This time, Danny did shudder. He stood there staring at me for a moment while he recovered, then smirked.

"Wimp."

"Says the crappy detective begging for my help year after year."

"Need a minute to get your legs under you?"

"Nah. Sooner we go in, sooner I get out."

I've walked the hallways of the county morgue more times than I care to count. Every time, it's always the same—cross the threshold, take in the overwhelming antiseptic smell, and double over from the pressure of dozens of restless souls clamoring for my attention. This time was not different, although I did manage to make it a few steps further down the hallway before succumbing to the mind-shattering headaches and my sanity's inclination to jump ship.

Danny put a hand on my back to tried to steady me.

"What are they saying?" he asked.

I took a few deep breaths and managed to get my wits about me.

"There's no talking," I said. "No one speaks unless I call on them."

The Lieutenant shot me a dubious look.

"It's more like I've just walked into a classroom," I said, "and a hundred souls have jumped into my skull, raising their hands and desperately trying to get my attention."

Danny winced at the image. "Yikes," he said.

"Tell me about it. Let's just get this done with so I can have my brain all to myself again."

In silence, Danny and I rode the elevator down to the cold storage area on the lower level. In the largest of the exam rooms, a slim woman in a lab apron was cleaning up after an autopsy, gathering instruments together and firing up the autoclave. She glanced up as Danny knocked on the door and smiled briefly as he waved at her, until she noticed me standing next to him. The smile was instantly replaced by a deeply furrowed scowl. Dr. Helen Saito was not my biggest fan. She turned away, and the Lieutenant pushed the door open.

"Danny," she said as we stepped into the lab, "you know I love your little visits, but I really wish you'd leave the traveling freak show at home."

"And good morning to you, Helen, dearest. I thought you could use a little entertainment after a hard night's dissecting."

Dr. Saito turned to face us and rolled her eyes.

"If he's here, it means you don't have any confidence in my results. It's insulting."

"Do you have an ID?" Danny asked.

Saito paused and stared at the Lieutenant, reluctant to answer. "No," she said finally, her voice hard.

"All right, then," said Danny. "Let's let Ray work his magic so we can get him out of your lovely hair."

The doctor nodded towards the center of the room. There was a body still laid out on the stainless steel table.

"I just closed up," she said. "You can have a few minutes before I send our Jane Doe back to the cooler." She pushed open the lab door. "I'll leave you three alone."

The door swung shut behind her, and it got very quiet very quickly. Danny walked over to the exam table and pulled back the sheet. The body of a young woman lay beneath it.

"Couple of kids making out under the Ninth Street viaduct found her late last night," Danny explained. "No identification, no visible marks of trauma."

I leaned in for a closer look. She had dark, wavy hair, and for a moment I thought of the girl in the photo that Ruth had given me. It wasn't her. The resemblance began and ended with the hair. Thinner face, different nose. And too old, it seemed.

"What was she?" I asked. "Twenty? Twenty-five?"

"Could be," Danny said. "Dr. Saito will know for sure."

I walked around to the head of the exam table, closed my eyes and took a deep breath.

"Okay," I muttered to myself. "Here goes."

I rested my palms on the sides of the dead girl's head and held my breath as the room dissolved around me.

Dark.

Afraid.

I've been locked in this room for two days, now.

At least I think it's two days.

He blacked out the windows and I can't tell time anymore.

I hear a scratching at the little wooden door and I skitter back into the farthest corner of the room, trying to blend in with the walls, willing myself to disappear into the corner.

The door opens, and what little light there is silhouettes two figures in the frame. Two figures. The little old pervert's brought a friend. He's probably still pissed about getting kneed in the balls. Tough.

"Be a g-good g-girl and come out," he says. "I've b-brought a friend to play."

I start to say a silent prayer. This can't go on much longer. I've fought him off so far, but he's kept me naked and hungry and in the dark for so long, now, that I haven't got much fight left.

God, help me!

The little grey pervert's guest lets out a growl—an animal sound—and I chance another look in the doorway. The new figure is human shaped, but just barely. The growl grows more insistent, and then I notice the smell—animal musk, sulfur, and something metallic. Something other. The smell hits the reptile parts of my brain and I coil to flee.

There is nowhere to run.

The animal howls.

"Ray?"

I felt concrete floor under my ass, and opened my eyes to see a hand reaching out to help me up. Danny pulled me up to standing and gave me a moment to collect myself.

"Well?" he asked.

"No idea," I said. "No idea who she is, where she's from. Nothing."

"Great," he said, in a tone that let me know he felt my lack of information was anything but.

"She was locked up in a room somewhere," I said, trying to be more helpful. "Kidnapped, maybe? There was an older guy keeping her locked up."

"How'd she die?" he asked.

"Last thing she saw was some sort of animal. I don't know, everything I saw was too much in the dark."

"Animal, huh?"

I nodded.

"Doesn't make much sense," Danny said, walking back to the table and pointing at the corpse. "There's not a mark on her. Nothing to indicate any sort of struggle or attack."

"Because there was none." The voice of Helen Saito filled the chamber as she stepped back into her lab. "Pathology shows a healthy young woman in her early twenties."

"So what was cause of death?" asked Danny

"Fright."

"Really," I said.

"Or some other form of shock," she qualified. "But it was sudden, whatever it was. Her adrenaline levels were ramped up, and there's relatively fresh scarring on the heart, typical of an infarction."

"Fright fits the last images she saw," I said.

Dr. Saito's lips hardened into a tight line while she glared at me. Danny shrugged an apology.

"Nothing else on the body to help with identification?" he asked.

"Well, I've shipped dental impressions and a DNA sample off to the state lab, but that'll take awhile."

I could see Danny tensing in frustration. Saito smiled.

"I take it he was no help," she said, pointing at me with a gloat.

"No more than you at the moment," said Danny. Saito's head snapped back at the churlish tone in his voice. Then her eyes went wide as something else crossed her memory.

"There is one other thing," she said. "There were no *visible* marks on the body, but..." She pulled a UV lamp from the back workbench and turned off the bright overhead above the exam table. "I found this."

Saito turned the girl's right arm so that her inner wrist was exposed. She held the black-light over it and pointed.

"I'll be damned," said Danny, peering over the doctor's shoulder. A fluorescent mark shone on the inside of her wrist. "Club stamp?"

"Most likely," Saito said.

"Not from any of the hot spots I know."

I walked around to the head of the table again and tried to get a better look. I felt the gooseflesh before my brain had fully processed my retinal intake. There it was, a hexagonal pattern stamped in black-light ink. In the back of my consciousness there flashed images of a whisper thin blade and a cruel smile. My knees buckled, and I caught myself on the table.

"What is that?" I managed to ask without stammering.

"Night club re-entry stamp," Danny said. "Looks like..." he peered in closer.

"Reeds," said Saito.

"Reeds?"

"Like the Egyptian hieroglyph," she said. "Six of them."

Danny and I almost bumped heads trying to see it. It was a strain, but the doctor was right. Each side of the hexagon was a single, blade-like hieroglyphic reed.

What did it mean? And why did it make my skin crawl?

"Recognize it?" Danny asked.

"I don't know," I said, hoping he didn't pick up on the fib.

"Well, I can always check in with the boys in vice." Danny stood up and moved towards the door. "Helen, do you have a photo of that mark I can take?"

"I'll send one along."

"Could I get one, too?" I asked.

"C'mon, Ray." Danny tried to hurry me along.

"No," Saito snapped.

"I can help."

"No!"

"Let's go, Ray. I'll share."

I could still feel Saito's hard eyes boring into my back as the door swung shut behind us.

"You recognized the mark," Danny said once we were safely outside.

"That wasn't a question."

"No it wasn't, but here's one. What is it?"

I took a deep breath and cleared away the memory of the near-death dream. "I honestly don't know. Something from a dream, maybe."

"But you want a second look?"

"It's bugging me, yeah."

And it was. The potluck of images, of swords and robes and reeds and dead girls and lost girls were crashing around in my head, not leaving me alone. I'd seen that shape twice now—once on the body of a dead girl, and once in a vision of Laura Trammler. For a moment I could see Laura on the stainless steel table, and had visions of a shattered Ethan and a disapproving Ruth Penfield. With that, my inner paladin regained the upper hand.

"Let me borrow your cell phone," I said.

Danny handed the sleek little candy bar over, and I dialed the number to Ruthie's office. She grunted a salutation on the other end of the line.

"Tell your little boy lost I'll get his sister back," I said. "I'll stop by later to get started."

Lieutenant Knowles gave me his best quizzical cop look.

"Got something after all?"

"Different job," I said. "But the dead girl in there's got me worried about one who's still alive."

5

It was still early afternoon as I left the morgue, so I decided to check in at my office. I needed some time to settle down before I met with Ethan again, and the place was close enough to Ruthie's where I wouldn't have to go out of my way later.

My office sat above one of those joints that charged über-usurious fees for cashing the paychecks of the faceless and disenfranchised of the city, and even deeper rates for "loans" against future pay. In the Missions, these places were a fast breeding invasive species, and despite their predatory ways they seemed to do a constant business. Ruth once caught our dear neighbors running a scam with a few of her residents and, instead of turning their corrupt asses over to city attorneys, held her knowledge over their heads for leverage as needed. They'd "sponsored" the Welcome Table's annual Thanksgiving dinner for several years, now.

A few years ago, Ruth decided I needed to work out of somewhere other than a soup kitchen, so she squeezed them once again for free rent on some office space on the third floor.

No rent and one employee. My business has very low overhead.

I don't spend a lot of time there. My main client is the police, and they know how to find me if they need me. I keep the place mostly for appearance and auxiliary storage.

I walked up to the heavy wooden door and admired the frosted glass panel with "Walsh Security Services" painted on in big block letters. Then I pushed it open.

My office has character. It looks like it belongs to a gumshoe way more hard-boiled than me. Every time I set foot in the place I feel like I should be wearing a fedora, but I can't wash off enough of my mean-streets past to pull off that particular look.

There was e-mail from Danny waiting for me as I sat down at the computer. In the time it took me to walk over here, he'd already forwarded the photo Dr. Saito had taken of the strange black-light stamp on our Jane Doe.

Enlarged, the image revealed new surprises. Full size on Jane Doe's wrist, we'd thought the sides of the hexagon were made up of the Egyptian hieroglyph that represented the papyrus reed. With the image blown up to the size of my hand, I saw we were mistaken. I zoomed in on the picture to make sure my eyes weren't fooling me. The shapes were filled in with a delicate herringbone pattern.

Feathers.

Six identical, quill-shaped feathers arranged in a hexagon. It was still no help in identifying our dead girl, or her killers, but it was better than what we had before.

I closed the picture and opened the e-mail from Ruth. There was a telephone number for a Dr. Josephine Dealy, and a terse note:

Call her. Set up an appointment. I'll hog-tie you in my office and bring her to you if you don't.

Ruthie

I'd have laughed, but I was pretty sure she'd do it.

I swallowed and dialed the number. I gave my name to her receptionist, who put me on hold for a rather impolite length of time.

Josephine Dealy was not my biggest fan. Like Dr. Saito, she held a dim view of my skills and had a tendency to belittle the value of my services to anyone and everyone in the police department who'd stop long enough to listen.

"Raymond Walsh," said an alto voice on the other end of the line. "To what do I owe the pleasure?"

Dr. Josephine Dealy sounded anything but pleased.

"Ruth Penfield seems to think you can help me," I said.

"With?"

"Recovering memories."

"Whose?"

I paused for a moment. Time to bite the bullet, Ray. "Mine," I said.

She stayed quiet for a long moment.

"I need to think about it," she said finally.

"Don't go too far out of your way," I said, a growl of annoyance tinting my voice.

"Listen," she said, "you're lucky I respect the work Rev. Penfield does in this town, or I wouldn't even have taken the call."

"She talked to you already?" I asked.

"She wanted to give me a heads up."

She would, I thought.

I sighed. "Look," I said, "why don't we meet and talk first. Somewhere not your office?"

"Like where?"

"Say, Rev. Penfield's office?"

Again, Dr. Dealy was silent.

"Fine," she said at last. "Tomorrow afternoon. We'll talk. If you can prove not to be a complete phony, I'll consider taking you on."

"Fair enough," I said as she hung up.

Won't that be fun?

I started to get up and pack it in for a visit to Ruth when the phone rang.

"Elizabeth Vincent," said Danny Knowles.

"Your senior prom date?"

"Our no-longer-Jane-Doe," he said, not taking the bait.

"Damn," I said, "that's gotta be the fastest the state lab's ever come back with a result."

"Not the state," he said. "The feds."

"Let me guess. She's public enemy number thirteen?"

"Shut up, already," he said. I could hear him shuffling papers in the background. "Elizabeth Vincent, masters candidate in philosophy at the university, stopped calling home about two years ago. Worried parents filed a missing persons report, but nothing ever came of it."

"And she's been hiding in plain sight all this time?"

"So it would seem. Got any bright ideas how?"

"It's a big city," I said.

"Easy to become invisible."

"Don't I know it." In my experience, the fastest route to invisibility is to disappear into the faceless transient army of the Missions. "I think I know where to start asking around."

Danny gave a snicker of understanding. He knew where I'd come from. "Get my present?" he asked.

"Been staring at it all afternoon," I said. "It's not hieroglyphs. It's feathers. You can tell Dr. Saito she got it wrong."

"Tell her yourself," he said. "She already hates you. So, what, we're looking for a nightclub with a bird theme?"

"Or a rave promoter with an avian surname."

"Or a giant killer pigeon. Stamp's no help. The guys in vice hadn't seen it before."

"Which leaves us where?" I asked.

"With the photo of a dead girl and a shitload of bums to canvass."

"We prefer the term 'domestically challenged,'" I said. Danny blew a raspberry into the phone. "Can the uniforms handle that part?" I asked.

"Pounding a little shoe leather's beneath the Amazing Raymond?"

"Got some canvassing of my own to do," I said, "while this client's still alive."

DINNER THAT NIGHT was courtesy of the magical soup stylings of the Reverend Ruth Penfield. What that woman could do with legumes and an aluminum pot was a bona fide miracle.

Later, we sat down in her office for an after dinner snort.

"You'll be happy to know I called her," I said.

Ruthie smiled. "Threat of a good hog-tying get to you?"

I shook my head. "She's coming here tomorrow afternoon. We want to meet with a third party before she agrees to take me on."

"I figured you might," she said. "What will you do in the meantime?"

I stopped and looked away for a moment. "I'm going to look into Laura Trammler's situation," I said.

"What changed your mind?" she asked, trying with very little success to not sound like she was gloating.

"A visit to the city morgue. Different circumstances, but a very dead girl. Could've been Laura."

"The better angels of your nature got the best of you?"

"More like my psychotic need to play the hero," I said. "It'll get me killed someday."

"So, where do you start?"

"I'm going to disturb the breakfast line at New Light tomorrow morning, see if anyone recognizes the girl."

"How about looking around *inside*?"

"I'm getting there," I said. Ruth threw up her hands in a gesture of mock surrender. "Before I do anything else, however, I want to have another chat with Ethan."

"He's in the sitting room with a book," Ruth said. "Have at it."

Ethan was curled up on the couch with an old Lloyd Alexander paperback. He glanced up briefly when I came in, but returned at once to the page in front of him. He didn't ask me to leave, so I sat down in an easy chair across from him. We sat there in a comfortable silence for several minutes until he closed up the book and set it on the floor in front of him.

"And how is the Assistant Pig-Keeper?" I asked.

"Dreaming about swords," he said, stifling a giggle. He sat there looking at me as though he were trying to see through me.

"Reverend Penfield tell you I was going to help?" I asked.

"Uh-huh."

"Wondering why I changed my mind?"

"Nope. I knew you would."

"Indeed."

"Yeah. She said you would."

Smug old bird, I thought.

"I'm going to start tomorrow," I said. "But before I do, I need some answers from you, little man."

Ethan shrugged, then nodded.

"Why are you here?" I asked.

"I needed somewhere to sleep," he said. He looked at me like I was the dumbest bunny in the pen.

"No, Ethan, why are you here in the city? You're a long way from home, aren't you?"

He nodded, but didn't say a thing.

"Why?"

"Laura said we had to." The boy was barely speaking above a mumble.

"And did Laura say why?"

Ethan shook his head, looking down into his chest.

"Look, Ethan, I can get your sister. But, I can't guarantee what happens after that. If Laura can't give me any better answers, we're going to have some problems. Ruth doesn't want any trouble for the shelter, and I don't want to be an accessory to anything."

He looked a question at me.

"I can't guarantee we can keep the police out of this once Laura's out," I said. "Understand?"

"Yes," he said, but not without some reluctance.

"Do you still want me to do this?"

I could see him weighing his options. "No cops until we've got Laura back?" he asked.

"I promise," I said, putting out my hand.

"Okay, then," he said, shaking it.

"Good. I start in the morning."

6

I tossed and turned most of the night. No nightmare this time, but what little sleep I got was fitful, at best. I got up with the sun, unable to lie down anymore. I needed to be out and about. People to meet, dragons to slay, and all. I was not, however, feeling my freshest. A quick shower, a little toast and coffee, and it was off to my first appointment of the day.

Daybreak meant the morning meal at New Light would be served soon, and I wanted to catch as many of their guests as I could while they were still out on the sidewalk. I wasn't crossing New Light's threshold until I absolutely had to, so I figured I'd be better off working the line. I had the photo of the Trammler kids that Ruth had given to me. It wasn't the best picture of the girl, but it still might help jog some memories.

The hungriest of the city's denizens began lining up outside New Light's mission by six in the morning. The mission's dining hall could seat about two hundred bodies, but there were regularly six hundred or so folks looking for a hot breakfast, so the mission had developed a pretty tight schedule of meal shifts. I'd missed the first shift, and arrived in the Missions in time for the nine o'clock feeding line.

Once again, I started feeling a dreadful, nasty chill as New Light's landmark came into view. This was the point where I usually crossed over to the other side of the street to take my refuge with Ruthie over at The Welcome Table. Today, this was not to be. Time to shove aside my personal heebie-jeebies for the sake of the greater good. I steeled myself and stepped onto the block and into New Light's sphere of influence.

In a neighborhood plagued with iron bars, broken glass, and abandoned buildings, New Light Ministries' glass and steel structure may as well have been a castle or even the gates to paradise as far as the city's invisible legions were concerned. Honestly, the place would have been right at home among the bank towers downtown. Which is, of course, part of what attracted so many of the city's forgotten to its doors. New Light was well funded and looked the part. People in need came to New Light partly because they were hoping that some of that "well off" aura might rub off on them. This morning's breakfast line was case in point. Double file, the line stretched all the way down to one end of the block, around the corner and continuing on down that side of the block. It looked like it might even turn another corner.

New Light was one of the largest recipients of corporate charity in the city, in both money and volunteers. It probably didn't hurt that a corporate suit could put in an hour's service at the mission and not feel like they'd stepped too far out of their comfort zone. New Light looked good, and it's wealthy benefactors looked good working there. It was no accident that during election season every candidate had the obligatory photo op of themselves serving up soup in their rolled up shirtsleeves.

Posers.

The only thing I hate more than proselytizers are slumming politicians. It looked like one of them might be here for his photo op this morning—or maybe it was a white-collar reprobate out doing mandatory community service. Either way, a very out of place sedan—sleek, black, luxurious—was idling quietly outside the front entrance of the mission. Even against the backdrop of the swanky building, the car looked far too awkwardly conspicuous in this neighborhood, and it was starting to draw some unwelcome attention. I didn't want the driver getting any undue grief because of some lazy suit, so I decided to do my good deed for the day. I walked over to the driver's side door and knocked on the deeply tinted window. The window's motor whirred as the tinted glass slid down, revealing an imposing figure in a black suit. His complexion was just a bit lighter than the suit, and he was all shaved head and Ray Bans.

"You know," I said, "there's a service alley around back you can park in if you want to avoid trouble."

The driver flashed me a smile that conveyed a friendly warning.

"It's okay, man," he chuckled, a slight bayou accent to his voice. "Does it look like I need to worry about trouble?"

He had a point. The guy was a bruiser, no doubt. As he reached over to close the car window, I caught the telltale outline of a holster under his suit coat. No worries, indeed. With my Boy Scout duties discharged, it was time to start rousting the locals. Photo in hand, I started working the crowd from the front of the line, asking one by one if anyone had seen Laura Trammler.

I knew I'd be pressing my luck with this tactic. In a way, most of these folks get used to being invisible, especially when they're on their own turf. Acknowledging their presence is like giving a shock to the system. Start asking questions and it might break down completely. People as a rule don't like getting involved in other people's troubles. The transient and undocumented, the invisible army, even less so. Which is all just a long way of saying that I was getting nowhere fast.

No one had seen the girl. Most could answer without even looking at the picture. Convenient. I was getting toward the end of the block and getting ready to give up when I came up to a twitchy dude, maybe in his sixties, maybe older. It was difficult to tell with the shock of gnarled grey hair that was framing his deeply lined face with kinky cords. He gave me a look like he could read every scar on my soul. It was unnerving. While he stared at me, I brandished the photo.

"Have you seen this girl around here?" I asked. "Do you know her?"

Twitchy continued to stare, looking me up, down, and sideways.

"No," he said, "but I know you."

"Really? You've spent time at The Welcome Table, then?"

"No. Nonono," he said. His shoulders and his right foot were starting to tic. "Somewhere else. Long t-time ago."

"You'll have to excuse me. My memory's not what it used to be." Dammit, Twitchy was really starting to set off my flight instinct. "I think you've got me mistaken with someone else."

I snatched the photo back and tried to step away, but Twitchy grabbed my shoulder and got in my face.

"Don't t-toy with me! I've waited a long time! I've b-been faithful! Give me a s-s-sign!"

Twitchy kept on ranting, holding on to my shoulder, but I couldn't hear a word he was saying anymore. As soon as he grabbed me, I could feel my mind slipping into some kind of liminal space—knowing I was at once on the street outside New Light and simultaneously living through the highlight reel of my increasingly bizarre dream life. I could see Twitchy's face getting in mine, but I could also see the darkness, feel the endless plummet and the pain, submit to the terror of that cruel smile and the arcing silver blade.

I fell to my knees on the sidewalk and tried to shake off the terror. My temples were pounding, and I could feel a burning sensation along my spine. All the while, Twitchy stood over me, ranting away. A hand— not Twitchy's—crossed my field of vision, offering help. I latched on to it and stood up, finding myself face to face with one of the grey-suited minions of the New Light mission. The little black name badge on her lapel read "Sister Allie" and that she as a "public liaison." New Light had sent reinforcements. That was quick.

"Is this man bothering you?" she asked, in a practiced tone of professional sympathy.

"No. No problems here. He thought I was someone else."

"Carl, leave this poor man alone," she said. She sounded like she was admonishing a five-year-old. "I'm sorry sir, Carl is one of our *special* cases." She leaned into my ear, like we were friends sharing a secret. "He thinks he's the veteran of an angelic army." I could hear her winking when she said it, putting on a show for my benefit. I stepped back to reclaim my personal space. Twitchy Carl continued to stare at me, muttering.

"Really, no trouble here, ma'am." I waved the photo in her face, just to remind her why we were both here. "Have you seen this girl?"

She took the picture and actually looked at it. I could see her eyebrows almost go up in recognition, and then the good Sister quickly recovered herself.

"I'm not allowed to talk about our residents with the public."

Resident? Gotcha! I decided to play it cool.

"Why not?"

"Many people come here seeking safe haven. We're merely looking after their best interests."

"So she is a resident here?"

"I'm sorry, sir, but I can't comment any further. If you have any more questions, I could set you up with our community relations office."

Okay, so I might have pushed the endgame a little too quickly. Sister Allie just kept right on smiling.

"Let's do that, then," I said. She turned away and radioed in to someone inside, then nodded.

"Tomorrow," she said. "You'll get a tour from someone who can answer your questions." She turned back towards the mission entrance, nodding to a couple of security flunkies as she went. My work here was done for the moment, whether I liked it or not.

As I turned to go, I found Twitchy Carl standing in my path, looking me right in the eye from between kinky grey tendrils. Damn, this guy was freaking me out.

"She ain't gonna t-tell you anythin' useful."

"Yeah, I got that, Carl. It was, uh, interesting to meet you."

"You're not f-f-foolin' me for a second, sir. Y'know that, right?"

Sir? "I'm sure I'm not. Tell you what, you keep it between you, me, and the wall for now, all right?"

I patted him on the shoulder and got the hell out of there. As I turned away from the block, I could still see the black sedan idling. Through the front windshield I could see the jovial, dangerous shape of Mr. Ray Bans. He gave me a smile and a thumbs up.

I did not feel encouraged.

7

Still feeling a little shaky, I shambled across the street to see if Ruthie had anything leftover from last night. I found her and Ethan sitting down at a table in the back corner, scooping up some leftover pea soup, so I sat down to join them. Ruth and I sat down across a table from one another, looking out over the satisfied faces of maybe a dozen men who all tucked into their bowls like it was the first meal they'd had in days. For some of them, it probably was.

Ethan never once looked up from his bowl, shoveling spoonful after spoonful of soup into his mouth. He might have stopped once, maybe, to breathe and take a sip of water. He was growing more relaxed here, but I could still sense the same tension I'd felt when I'd met him. There was a tautly wound spring inside that small frame. Ethan was ready to run at a moment's notice. I worried what little thing might trigger him.

Once he'd finished inhaling his food, Ethan stood up and collected our bowls from the table. I watched him walk over to the dirty dish tubs, where he started to chat with one of the volunteers.

"Got him well trained, already," I said.

"He's a good kid," Ruth said. "Still not responding to questions, too much. And, he woke up at least once in the middle of the night in a panic, looking for his sister. But, he's helpful, and pretty smart, to boot."

Right on cue, Ethan came back to the table in time for Ruth's compliment. As he started to sit back down, one of the front office volunteers approached and leaned in to Ruth.

"Sorry to interrupt," she said, "but there's a woman here looking to talk to you. She's been hitting all the shelters looking for a couple of missing kids—a brother and sister." She paused, and tried very hard not to look at Ethan. "I didn't say anything to her," she said. "I let her have a seat in your office and told her you'd be with her as soon as the meal was done."

As soon as the girl had said "brother and sister" I could see that spring in Ethan begin its release. By "in your office" he was out of his seat and heading for the dining room doors.

"Ethan!" Ruth had jumped up almost as quickly to call after the boy.

I held out my hand. "I'll go after him," I said. "You go see about this visitor."

Ruth nodded, and I hurried after Ethan. I chased him up the stairs and caught up to him as he rounded the corner into his room. I got a grip on his shoulder as he dropped a duffel bag onto the top of his bed.

"What are you doing?" I asked him as he turned to face me.

"She's here. I need to go."

"Who's *she*, Ethan?"

"Margaret," he said, voice dripping with disdain. "Evil, witchy Margaret."

"You don't know it's her, for sure."

"Don't care," he said, pulling away. He started to dump his meager possessions into the bag.

"Wait!" He stopped to see what I'd say next. "Before you run, take a walk with me. I know where we can listen in on Rev. Penfield's office without getting caught."

Ethan looked askance, seeming far older than his eleven years.

"We'll look in," I said. "If it's Evil Margaret, we can talk through what to do next. I can't let you run, though. If you run, I can't help you or Laura anymore."

It took a moment for my words to sink in. He got a determined look in his eyes and zipped up his duffel, but he didn't make a move for the door. Instead, he gave me an appraising look, and then a quick nod of the head.

We ducked around a corner and headed down the rear stairwell to avoid a trip past Ruth's office door. A small sitting room lay next door to the office, a *de facto* waiting area with a sliding wooden pass-through door between the two rooms. I motioned Ethan to be quiet as we stepped into the sitting area and I padded over to the pass-through and carefully slid open a crack.

I knelt down and took a look into the office. Sitting across from Ruth was a large woman. She leaned in close to Ruth such that I couldn't get a good look at her face through the mass of bottle-brassy hair that fell to her shoulders in big, fussy curls. I waved Ethan over and had him peer through, one hand on his shoulder to keep him from bolting.

He leaned in and immediately tensed. I could sense he wanted to run, but he knew he wasn't getting far with me in the room. Instead, he scuttled off to the far corner. I put my ear up to the door so I could listen in while still keeping an eye on the frightened child.

". . . been following the trail for so long, now," said a thin, contralto voice. I could hear just a touch of a patrician accent, although it sounded forced. "I just want my babies back."

"Have the local police not been any help?" I suppressed a chuckle. Ruth had her "smooth operator" public relations voice dialed up all the way.

"I've been down that road so many times," she said with a big sigh. "It's just one more missing persons case among thousands."

"How far have you come from, Mrs. Trammler?"

"Illinois. North Shore of Lake Michigan."

"The Gold Coast? You've come a long way."

"Hopefully, I don't have much farther to go."

"Well, Mrs. Trammler, I'd like to be able to tell you your journey is over," said Ruth, "but I'm not certain. One of the children looks familiar, but I'm not sure from where. Let me put the word out, and I'll see what I can come up with."

"Oh, Reverend, I can't tell you how much hope this gives me." Good Lord, this lady was pouring it on a little thick. I took a breath to try and keep my soup in check.

"Where can I reach you?" Ruth asked, smooth and smiling.

"I'm at the Plaza downtown."

"I'll call as soon as I know something."

The two stood up, and brassy Mrs. Trammler shook Ruth's proffered hand before walking out the door. Ruth sank back into her seat and her eyes cut in our direction.

"You can come out of the shadows, now, you lug nuts," she said.

I slid the pass-through open and walked through, pulling Ethan, duffel bag and all, with me.

"Sit down," she said.

"Are you gonna tell her?" Ethan asked. He sat on the sofa, but only just. His body was coiled and ready to run again.

Ruth looked the kid straight in the eye. "Do you want me to tell her?"

"She's lying, y'know."

"No, Ethan, I don't know," she said. "Why don't you tell me? Why did you and Laura run? Why don't you want to go back?"

"She's evil," he said. It was becoming his catch-all answer.

"She came a thousand miles to look for you," I said. "Looks to me like maybe she cares."

"That's not why she's here," he said. He was starting to mope.

Ruth pushed harder. "Then why?"

"She wants something."

"What?"

"I don't know."

"Then how do you know she hasn't come after you," Ruth asked, "because she loves you and misses you?"

"I don't." Ethan had begun to sob quietly. "Laura does. She wouldn't tell me. Said I was too young, that I wouldn't understand. She took me away for my own good."

"Do you do everything your sister tells you?" I asked.

Ethan was crying in earnest now. "She's my sister. She takes care of me."

Damn. I got so wrapped up in trying to get at some answers that I went and forgot my client was only an eleven-year-old boy.

"I need her!" The boy had worked himself up into a full-bore wail.

Ruth got up and picked him up off the sofa.

"C'mon, Ethan. I'm sorry we pushed you. Let's get you upstairs for some rest, all right?"

"I'm gonna see Laura tomorrow," I called out as they left the office. "We'll make it right, kid!"

Alone for the moment, I started to fret. I was going to see Laura tomorrow. I was going *inside* New Light, something I'd avoided doing for the better part of a decade. Then what? What if I freaked out again and scared Laura Trammler away? I was pretty sure I was only going to get one chance at this face to face. What if I failed?

Worse, yet—what if I succeeded? What if I walked out the front door of New Light tomorrow with Laura in tow? What then? I'd told Ethan that I couldn't guarantee anything after that, and I was right. The appearance of "Evil" Margaret Trammler had brought that reality home. Someone was looking for the pair. But why?

"Uncovered the mysteries of your navel, yet?" Ruth's voice shook me out of my reverie. "What's bugging you now?"

"You didn't hand Ethan over to Margaret," I said.

"Nope."

"Why not?"

"Didn't trust her. Something's off there, and I need to know what."

"But if she's family . . ?"

"*If* she's family, then we'll see. In the meantime . . ?"

Ruth let the question hang. We were quiet for a long time before one of Ruthie's volunteers poked his head into her office.

"There's a Dr. Dealy here to see you," he said.

The shrink.

Crap.

I felt my stomach turn and I tried to sink into the sofa cushions.

"I almost forgot," said Ruth. "Yes, show her in."

Dr. Josephine Dealy had a reputation in the police department as sterling as mine was questionable. As both a profiler and a counselor her services were almost constantly in demand. I'd worked with her in person once, about two years ago, on a serial kidnapping case. She was smart, ultra-professional, and damned attractive—jet black hair and violet eyes and what I assumed were the Platonic ideal of legs. Practically every boy with a badge, and a couple of the women, had made a run at her during that case. She'd deftly sidestepped all advances and kept right on with the job. Ultra-professional, like I said. I admired that about her.

That and her legs.

However, the chilly waves I felt emanating from her in my direction made it fairly clear that that admiration was not mutual. She'd referred to me more than once as "the bullshit artist"—although never to my face. Ultra-professional.

The temperature dipped in the office as she walked in. A grudging respect for me had not developed during our time apart. I decided that staring at her legs wasn't going to help the situation, so I willed my eyes northward and met the hard gaze of her impossibly violet ones.

"Mr. Walsh," she said, curt but not overtly hostile.

"Ms. Dealy," I said, nodding.

"Doctor," she said.

"Of course. Doctor Dealy. I'm sorry."

We stared at each other for what seemed like forever. I had an overwhelming urge to dive into her eyes. Then I remembered to start breathing again.

Down boy. She's the enemy, remember?

"You're lucky Reverend Penfield has such a sterling reputation, and that she seems to think rather highly of you," Dealy said, finally breaking the uncomfortable—for me at least—silence. "Personally, I think you're a fraud."

I smiled. "You're not completely incorrect, there."

I watched her head jerk—just a little bit. "Excuse me?"

"If you're looking for me to get defensive," I said, "or start an argument so you'll have an excuse to leave, you'll need to look a long time."

There was less of chill in the air. Ruthie was leaning back in a corner of the office, smiling at the both of us. "Told ya," she said, to me or to the doctor I wasn't certain. I could see Josephine Dealy relax as Ruth spoke.

"So you admit you're a bullshit artist, then?" she asked.

"To an extent," I said. "The psychic stuff? Real enough, although I'll be damned if I can explain it."

"But you just said..."

"That I'm a fraud, yeah. See, the psychic part may be real, but Raymond Walsh? Not so much."

And so I gave her the quick history. The ten year memory span. The amnesia. My life on the streets. The construct that Ruthie and I created named Raymond Walsh.

And the nightmares.

By the time I'd finished, Doctor Dealy was leaning against Ruthie's desk, eyes wide while she tried to keep her chin off the floor.

"That's why we called you in," I said. "I need someone I can trust to help me latch on to whatever it is in my past that's trying to break through."

Doctor Dealy stood up and straightened up her skirt. "And you trust me?" she asked.

"Not yet," I said. She started to protest, but I waved her off. "But I respect you. I admire your work."

She looked at me, mouth shut and not a little bit puzzled.

"We can work on trust," I said.

"I suppose we can," she said. "I don't have a lot of time to devote to this."

"We'll take it slow," I said. "Fit in some work where we can."

She pulled a smartphone out of her bag and started flipping through screens. "My schedule's full for the next few weeks."

"Skip the office, then," I said. "How 'bout coffee?"

"I beg your pardon?"

"Coffee. You know? Dark, caffeinated breakfast beverage. There are thirty-seven different faux-Italian words for it."

"Uh-huh." Poor thing, I think I stunned her.

"Do you start your morning with it?" I asked.

"I do."

"So do I. Perhaps we could conspire to begin our morning in the same place? Caffeinate? Talk more?"

She shook her head and got her feet back under her. "All right, Mr. Walsh. We'll give it a shot." She pulled out a small notebook and scribbled in it, then tore off the sheet and handed it to me. "Eight o'clock, there," she said.

"Looking forward to it," I said.

She looked at me for a moment, head cocked. "Okay, then," she said, and stood up.

Ruth showed her out the door and stood there watching as she left.

"Well that wasn't so bad," I said.

"Quiet!" she said with a librarian's hiss.

"Why?"

"I'm having a moment of silence for those legs."

"Ruthie!"

"And you want to share this moment with me."

"Ruthie!"

"Fine, more for me then."

"I'm going back to my office."

"Okay. Try not to sweet talk your way into a date with any more gorgeous psychiatrists on your way!"

BACK IN MY office, I dialed the lieutenant's mobile.

"Ray," he said. His voice was cheery but forced on the other end of the line. "I was just about to call. You really are psychic."

"I'm calling in a favor," I said.

"What can I do for the PD's finest consultant?" He sounded just a little too eager.

"I'm hoping you can call on the goodwill of your comrades-in-arms, do a little digging up on a woman named Margaret Trammler up in the north suburbs of Chicago. While you're at it, you can tell me if she's filed a missing persons report."

"What am I looking for?"

I gave him the abbreviated story about Ethan and Laura, and about Margaret's appearance in Ruthie's office.

"You think she's not telling the whole story?" he asked when I'd finished.

"I think Ethan's scared of her for a reason," I said. "I want to see if she checks out."

"I'm already guessing she doesn't. I'll see what I can come up with."

"You're awfully agreeable today, Danny. Usually I have to negotiate a little harder for these favors. What gives?"

"You didn't ask why I was about to call you," he said.

"I'm almost afraid to."

"How'd you like to earn another favor?"

"What do I have to do, I ask, already dreading the answer?"

"Come and meet Jane Doe number two," he said.

Swell.

8

anny Knowles and I were standing in an unlit corner underneath the Ninth Street viaduct, somewhere in the no-man's-land between the Missions and the industrial zones. It was dark out even for the early evening, and I was overwhelmed by the smell of standing water and whatever waste *du jour* had been dumped in the river this week. A small blessing, as it covered up the death stench of the corpse we were staring down at.

"White female," said the responding uniform. "Late teens, early twenties. No blood, no bruises. Looks like she just dropped dead while she was standing here."

"How long?" I asked.

"Twelve hours, maybe."

Danny thanked the officer and sent him on his way.

"I'm assuming," I said to Danny once the officer had moved on, "that this isn't random."

Danny didn't say a word, but knelt down and pulled a small UV light out of his pocket. He picked up the dead girl's wrist in a gloved hand and shone the light over it. I stepped in to take a closer look.

The invisible stamp with the feathered motif glowed under the portable black light. I shuddered as my skin gave way to that prickling electric sensation. I could feel my legs coiling to run, but I kept myself in check.

"Number two," I said, repeating Danny's earlier assertion. He nodded, his face grim.

"I don't even want to think about the possibility of what this means," he said. "But there's really only two options, as I see it. One, two random girls from the same night club—a club we can't find, mind you—met similar fates within days of one another."

"Option two?" I asked, knowing full well the answer.

"Option two's the option I don't want to think about—the stamp's not a club stamp, but a calling card."

I shuddered at the thought. "And you want me," I said, "to do my thing and hand you the former option?"

"If you'd be so kind."

I found a relatively clean patch of concrete and knelt down beside the body, closing my eyes and trying to push aside all the mental flotsam and jetsam of the day. Carefully, I reached out and put my hands to her head.

I can't see in here.

Never should've gone to that party. I'm gonna throttle Cherise when I get out of here.

If I get out of here.

I tremble at the thought.

That gross, little old creep isn't gonna let me go. I should be able to take him, but he's stronger than he looks.

The doorknob creaks, and I try to hide in the corner, in the shadows.

"No f-fair hiding," says the voice.

My skin prickles at the sound of it.

"We've g-got work to do tonight," he says. If he tries to touch me again, I swear I'll dig my acrylics into his eyeballs. Fucking Cherise.

"Imp-portant work," he says.

Again, the voice is setting off alarms.

"You're g-going to help ffff-find what I've lost."

Each word he speaks sends a jolt of electricity through my body. I'm not in the room any more. I'm not her. The stranger's words are running through my veins like ice water.

Who is he? I cannot place the voice but it's filling me with... what? Dread? No. Anger. A righteous indignation. The cold flow through my veins hits a pit within my soul. His words echo, a cavernous sound. I am still for a moment, listening to the sound fade into silence.

Then a third voice, a third presence, makes itself known.

"Not yet!" The voice is full of power. And full of fear. The force of its cry shocks me into consciousness.

I opened my eyes, but all I could see was glare for a moment before the underside of the viaduct overhead resolved itself into view. I felt damp concrete under my back. My whole body was shaking with electric aftershocks of whatever it was that had scared me off.

"What is it," I heard Danny ask, "with you and your bizarre need to sleep in damp, dark alleys?"

Little by little, my body aching, I rolled myself up to sit. The dead girl was still very much dead. Danny was leaning against a concrete column. There was no one else around. Just the three of us.

"What happened?" I asked.

"You jumped off Ms. Doe, here, and rolled over into a little nap, is all," said Danny.

I shook my head. It felt full of sand and my ears were ringing. "Did I say anything, ah, funny?" I asked.

"You didn't say a damn thing," he said. "You touched Jane for all of two seconds and then took a nap in the dirt." He was trying very hard not to be amused by my behavior. "Why? What did you see?"

Scary, bad man! my head screamed. *Someone familiar, somehow!* No, I wasn't ready to tell him that, yet.

"I've got some bad news," I said. Danny's shoulders slumped while I told him it was option number two.

IN MY APARTMENT that evening, I was a wreck—all raw nerves and jangling emotions. The ice water chill of our Jane Doe's murderer, of Elizabeth Vincent's murderer, was still boring holes in the pit of my stomach. Meanwhile, my impending date with New Light Ministries was gnawing away at the back of my skull.

I like being in control of things. When you've rebuilt a life from scratch, when your past is a big blank, then control of your present circumstances is a comfort. But someone or something was playing with my head, and I was being forced into situations I'd always tried to avoid. I was no longer in complete control.

A spontaneous Vegas getaway sounded tempting.

No. I wasn't going to run away. I could at least be in control of that. Instead of running, I dumped the last of my bourbon into a short glass and drained it in one go. It burned going down, and the hum it sent through my nerves took my mind off my troubles, if only for a moment. Long enough to crawl into bed, at least.

Sleep came in fits and starts.

I float instead of falling. I am in a square room, empty save for a chair and a cot. A window takes up most of an entire wall. Its drapes are open, and through it, I can see the skyline of the city, illuminated against the encroaching darkness of the hour. Beneath me, a young woman sits in a chair, feet flat to the floor, hands resting in her lap. Her lips are moving. I strain to hear what she is saying, but I cannot make sense of it. Perhaps she prays silently. Perhaps I am not meant to hear.

I try to will myself to float down, to get closer and hear her words, but as I do, she looks up. She looks at and through me all at once. This startles me, and I float back up and try to melt into the ceiling. Her face is unmistakable, steel grey eyes and determined lips framed in auburn curls. This is Ethan Trammler's sister. This is Laura.

As quickly as she looks through me she looks away, toward the single wooden door that lies across from the window. A blue robed figure has entered the room. It shuts the door and faces the girl.

"He is coming," he says, the voice unmistakably male—powerful and seductive. As he speaks, I can feel every particle of energy in the room focuses on him, orbiting about him. He has spoken only three words, and yet something within my own soul is drawn to this person. There is a hook in my heart, and it is tethered to him—to the power that radiates from within him.

"Are you ready for him?" he asks the girl. She nods, trembling.

"Are you well, my child?" Concern and seduction intertwine in his tone. The dream Laura nods again, barely choking out the answer.

"I am well."

"And are you happy here?"

"I am."

"And do you wish to leave us?"

"No." Her voice is resolute, now, and yet I can still hear the trembling beneath it.

Blue-robe walks past her to the window, gazing out over the city. The girl looks up, only briefly, towards the ceiling, towards my own eyes. Then, just as quickly, she averts her eyes and casts them toward the tile floor.

"Talk with him," he commands her. "Stay with him. Promise him nothing, but keep him in the room as long as you can. We will want to study him. Make certain he's the one." There is an acid tone

to the way he says "the one"—as if he doesn't believe his own words. "Do you understand?"

"Yes," she answers, pointedly not looking in my direction.

"Good," he says with a purr. In the window I can see his reflection, the image of a wide cruel smile. I jump, and the eyes of his reflection fall on me. They look right at me.

They hate *me.*

"It will be ours again, soon." With those words the tether between us tightens. The room gives way to darkness; only his reflected image remains. I cease floating and begin to fall with alarming speed into the glassy visage and his cruel, cruel smile.

As I fall, I hear a faint voice echoing.

"He has forgotten," it says.

My spine burns, and I try to fight the descent.

"He has forgotten."

I claw at the substance of darkness, but to no avail.

"He has forgotten!"

I can gain no purchase and feel only the heat of friction as my hands rake along the nothingness.

"He has forgotten!"

The cruel mouth opens and I fall in.

"HE HAS FORGOTTEN!"

I awoke to the sounds of my own screaming. My spine and hands burned, and my sheets were a tangle of sweat. Jumping out of bed, I could see the wine-red stains of blood on the sheets out of the corner of my eye. I clawed my way out of my pajama top and tried to catch a glimpse of my back in the dresser mirror. Sure enough, the jagged scars along my upper spine are weeping blood through wounds no longer open.

For a moment, baffled by the betrayal of my own body, I stood outside myself. Time slowed. There was a reason for all this. I could taste it. The answers were somewhere in these dreams, yet I felt lost in a holding pattern, hovering around the edges of the truth without ever getting near to it. My head ached physically from the metaphorical pounding it had done so often against the brick wall of dreams in recent nights. As I tried to let go of my mental exertions, my focus was broken by the odor of burning fibers. I looked down to see my night shirt, still clutched tightly in my hands, smoldering under the heat of my fingers. The impossible reality of the burning in my spine and my hands returned to the foreground of my consciousness, and I dropped what was left of the cloth, running for the bathroom. I could see scorch marks on the sheets where I'd torn them away from my body.

I turned the shower on, ice cold, and let the relief wash over me, the burning cooled, the blood cleaned away. My head ceased its nauseating spin, and I slowly began to gather myself.

I had seen Laura! She would be there at New Light tomorrow, I was certain, and there was a part of her, however small, that did *not* wish to be so. But my happy certainty was short lived, for I knew that if Laura would be there, then so would the man with the cruel smile. I was just as certain of that. He had looked right at me and I was sure he knew me, knew me in ways I did not know myself. Knew me and loathed me. The man with the cruel smile and the seductive voice had answers, and I wasn't sure I wanted them. If I ran now, I could save myself. But, the eyes of Ethan and Laura burned out into my vision from the center of my conscience.

I shut the shower off and sat down on the floor of the tub, trembling.

9

I began my day with what little sleep I'd managed to get. I hadn't been able to face my bed again after the nightmare, so had curled up on the couch and forced my eyes to shut. Sleep never returned, but I managed to rise with the sun feeling somewhat rested. Time for a little caffeine.

Coffee!

I'd almost forgot. I had a date—no, wait—*appointment* with Dr. Dealy. Over coffee. Which was, I had to remind myself, all about getting my head back on straight, and had absolutely nothing to do with staring at her legs. Much.

I knew this was going to be a lost cause before it even began, but the least I could do was keep an appointment and show up on time. That alone would go a long way toward raising her estimation of me. Wouldn't it? At the very least it seemed like a good idea to network with a sometime colleague.

Coffee it was, then.

I went to my closet and picked out the least wrinkled pair of khakis I could find, slipped into those and the one oxford collar shirt I owned, along with the corduroy sport coat Ruth had insisted I needed as part of my professional wardrobe. It was a magical jacket that somehow managed to class up almost everything I wore.

I hated it.

I found it still zipped up in the department store bag on its hanger, where it lived free from dust and wrinkles—and as far out of my sight as I could get it without actually dropping it off at some other shelter's donation bin. I lived with the fear that Ruthie would instantly know if I'd tried to ditch it and would subsequently show up on my doorstep within hours with a new one that she'd somehow permanently attach to my body.

I closed my eyes, gritted my teeth, and slipped it on.

When I opened my eyes, alternate-universe-Ray was staring at me from the other side of the full length mirror on the closet door.

I looked good. I looked like someone I might like to go have a beer with. Maybe even have a conversation with—something more substantial than, "Spare some change for a sandwich?"

I took comfort knowing that when I walked into the front door of New Light Ministries later the staff wouldn't assume that I was there to check in. Which was absolutely the reason I'd dressed up like this, yessir. Because I was not going on a coffee date. Not at all.

The place Dr. Dealy had chosen was just barely downtown—safely enough within its boundaries for her comfort, but not so far out of my way that I'd be scrambling like mad for my next appointment.

To leave the Missions and enter downtown should require a passport. They were different countries. Different planets, really. There was no gradual transition, just a sudden shift from a jungle of stained brick and shattered glass to the steep canyons between the countless glass and steel skyscrapers. In the Missions, one felt dwarfed in the presence of so much raw, bleeding humanity. Downtown, one just felt dwarfed. You could smell the wealth accumulating.

I walked into the coffee shop and was instantly grateful that I'd put on the jacket. I think the cumulative cost of the suits worn by the customers there was equal to the gross national product of Brunei. I was somewhat camouflaged, at least.

Dr. Dealy was already sitting down at one of the small tables in a back corner. I waved to let her know I was there and stood in line to place my order.

I like coffee. Let me stress that last word. I like *coffee*. Hot, black and, preferably, bottomless. No espressos. No half-caff mochas. No double Americanos with a lemon twist and a backflip. Coffee.

I was out of my element.

"Coffee," I said to the barely out of high school counter-jockey. "Big."

"What kind of... ?"

"Black. No milk, no sugar. I don't care where it comes from, I don't care who picked it or how it was prepared. I don't need its resumé. I just need it in a cup in my hand in a reasonable amount of time."

The boy with the bad crew-cut and the green apron stared at me wide-eyed and nodded, then turned to tap one of the urns behind him.

"And if I find out it's so much as breathed the same air near anything that ends in -ccino, I swear I will come back there and start smashing machinery like a Luddite."

Counter-jockey handed me a large paper cup, wrapped in a little corrugated sleeve.

"Two fifty," he said, sounding a little squeaky.

I handed him three crumpled singles from my pocket.

"Keep the change," I said.

As I turned away, Dr. Dealy was giving me the most neutral, appraising look I'd ever seen on the face of any human being.

"Feeling a little edgy?" she asked.

I tossed back a large swallow of from the cup and frowned at her.

"I like coffee," I said.

"Yes, the whole shop knows that, now," she said, waving toward the empty chair and gesturing me to sit down.

I plopped down on the hard wooden chair. The table was just big enough to set down our two cups. My leg brushed against the doctor's as I sat down, sending me into a self-conscious bubble. I contorted sideways and crossed my legs as far as the low table would let my tall frame do so. *Strictly professional*, I thought. *That's me.*

"You *are* on edge this morning," said Dr. Dealy.

"Terrible sleep," I said. "Big day ahead."

"And you managed to keep our appointment, anyway. I'm impressed."

Score!

"I figured I had nowhere to go but up in your estimation," I said. "Plus, I really like coffee."

"So you said."

We sat there in a not totally disagreeable silence for a few moments, refilling our caffeine reserves.

"Why don't we start with you telling me why *now*," she said, finally.

"Why now what?"

"You've managed to live ten years with what I'd call an alarming lack of curiosity about your past," she said. "Why start digging now? What's the impetus?"

"Well, Ruthie kinda forced the issue..."

"...but you're the one sitting here. I didn't see Rev. Penfield marching in behind you with a gun to your head."

I shrugged.

"So," she said, "again I wonder—what's driving *you* to start digging?"

I turned for a moment and watched the pedestrians on their morning commute as they drifted by the window. I was tempted to give her the flip answer, that I liked looking at her, but I imagined that would end things a little more quickly than I wanted them to.

"I've been having this dream," I said, still looking out toward the street. I couldn't meet her eyes. And then I let the whole story out: the memory of waking up in an alley ten years ago; life with Ruth at the shelter; my first vision and my new career; the resurgence of the dreams, and the waking up in alleys. I left out the vision of the man with the cruel smile. That was not an avenue I was willing to walk down with her.

When I'd finished, I drew the paper cup back up to my mouth and drained the dregs of my coffee, masking my face with the morning ritual.

"So, the answer is you," she said. "You're driving yourself to unlock the answers."

"Some part of me, at least, I guess."

"It strikes me as funny that you've spent so much time and energy looking for others as a means of avoiding finding yourself," she said.

"The irony is not lost on me."

"Something tells me this newfound interest in your past isn't what has you all worked up this morning, however."

"Yes and no," I said. "It's more to do with my current job." I explained the bare bones of the Trammler kids' dilemma to her. "Now, I've gotta pay a visit to New Light's shelter."

"And it's a problem for you?"

"It shouldn't be," I said, "but, yes. I found myself inside its walls once before, on that first morning I remember. Something in there set off a screaming alarm in my head."

"How so?"

"It's hard to explain. I was just overwhelmed by this feeling of absolute, mortal dread—then it was like there was a voice in my head screaming at me to get out while I still could."

"And you've never gone back inside?"

"Not once."

"I'm impressed. New Light practically has a monopoly on charitable work in the Missions. The fact that you've survived this long without their help is astounding."

"Ruth is not without her resources, either," I said, perhaps too defensively. "That's beside the point, though. I made a vow back then that I'd never set foot in New Light's building again. I honestly felt at the time as though my life depended on it."

"And now?" she asked.

"Now, I'm in something of a bind. I always try to see a job through to the end, but now I have to break a promise to myself to do it."

"What do you think will happen if you break that promise?"

I paused. I'd known the answer to this question for a while, now, and I didn't want to say it out loud. Dr. Dealy sat, calmly staring at me as she watched the internal struggle play out across my face. I breathed deep and looked out the window, again.

"I'm afraid," I said, "that something inside there might unlock the floodgates."

The doctor continued to look at me without speaking for a moment. "Would that be so bad?" she asked at last.

"This," I said as I pointed my thumbs at my chest, "is me. Raymond Walsh. This is what I know. This is *who* I know."

"And you don't think you'll like what you'll find beyond that?"

"I'm fairly well convinced I won't. And even if what's beyond this wall in my memory isn't so bad, I'm not certain I care."

"You're not finished being Ray Walsh, yet."

"I'm not finished being Ray Walsh, yet," I said, agreeing.

"But you're here," she said.

"But I'm here."

Doctor Dealy looked away from me for a moment and sipped her coffee.

"Ray," she said, "if you're willing to move forward, I'd like to try a little hypnotherapy with you. If you're willing."

"Right here?"

"No, of course not. In my office."

"And this'll help?"

"It'll give us a chance to try to break a hole in that wall with a little more control."

Control, I thought. *That'd be a nice change of pace.*

"When can we start?"

"Why don't you call my office later today? After you've finished your visit at New Light."

I stood up. "I'll do that," I said. We shook hands before I headed for the door.

"Try not to have any debilitating psychotic episodes while you're storming the evil castle," she called out as I stepped on to the street.

I looked back to see one of the most mischievous grins I'd ever seen on another human being.

Dammit. I was starting to like her.

10

I could see the top of New Light Ministry's glass and steel from three blocks away, its polished surface reflecting the mid-morning sun. For a moment, I was blinded by the glare and I could taste the bile that came with the dread at the back of my throat. I considered turning back. Two steps later, I walked into a welcome bit of shade and my resolve once again steeled.

The tail end of the third shift breakfast line stood outside the front door, waiting to file in. I was less than surprised to once again see a sleek, black sedan idling outside the mission. Mr. Ray Bans was still sitting in the driver's seat. It was almost welcome relief to see him there, if it weren't for the sinking feeling I had that he was there to spy on me—God only knows why. If I hadn't been so distracted by my coffee with Dr. Dealy, I would have picked up a couple of doughnuts for him. Maybe even some coffee. Y'know, just to throw him off his game.

Yeah, that'd show him.

All right, Ray, time to quit stalling. The last few morning diners were in, and there was an appointment to keep. I took several breaths to still my pounding heart, and then walked, eyes open, into the fiery furnace.

The inner lobby of New Light was just as glassy and corporate as the outside suggested. If it weren't for the general hand-me-down dress code and the patina of unwashed funk on the clientele, I could well have been standing in the lobby of an investment bank. A security team in navy blazers stood in conspicuous spots about the marble lined atrium. A garish slate and steel fountain dominated the center of the entryway, surrounded by vegetation I could only assume was of the species *genericus corporatus ficus*. Everything about New Light's interior space stood out in stark contrast to its professed purpose. If the intent of the design was to throw people off their guard, it was working.

I gathered my wits and found my way to the little reception island off to the side of the fountain.

"I'm here to see Laura Trammler," I said, as I handed my card to the woman in the navy blazer behind the counter. She dutifully tapped away at a keyboard.

"Have a seat, Mr. Walsh," she said, ordering me towards a bench with the point of a finger. "We'll have a liaison out to meet with you shortly."

I walked over to the reception area and took a seat with my back to the ugly fountain. No need to make this trip more miserable than necessary. The last of the breakfast line had made it indoors and were heading in the direction of New Light's legendary dining hall. I could see Twitchy Carl bringing up the rear, and quickly willed myself invisible.

Not, apparently, one of my superpowers.

The nervous little man looked right at me, smiled wide and began frantically waving a greeting. I shook my head and put my index finger up to my pursed lips, trying to remind him of our deal from the previous day. Twitchy stopped in his tracks and nodded in recognition. He returned the shushing signal, gave me a big theatrical nod and wink, and then tried with all his tiny will to not look at me. He moved on down the line towards breakfast, blatantly not noticing me, and then turned and gave me one last very unsubtle thumbs up as he passed out of sight. Thank God I wasn't trying to hide.

My liaison chose that moment to arrive.

"Making friends, already, I see?" said a cheery voice.

"All the time," I answered, turning around.

The woman couldn't have been more than twenty, twenty-two max. She was dressed in what I had come to understand as the standard issue uniform of the mission's staff: black pleated skirt, white blouse with name badge, and sensible shoes. This one wore the uniform well. Nice legs, that was for sure, and while the blouse was demure, the chest underneath it sure as hell wasn't. She looked at me with a TV anchorwoman smile.

"I'm sorry to say, Laura Trammler is working a shift in the laundry at the moment. If you don't mind, I'd be happy to give you a tour while you wait," she said, practically chirping without moving the smile more than necessary. "I'm Sister Sarah."

I stifled a guffaw. "And if you were a bell, you'd be ringing?"

"I'm sorry Mr. Walsh?"

"Don't mind me. I quote show tunes when I'm nervous." I could see the wires crossing behind her eyes. *Cut it out, Ray. Doesn't pay to taunt the mid-level help.* "Lead the way," I said, sighing. No one appreciates the classics.

We toured through every hidden corner of the mission, each successive section of New Light's flagship as sterile and corporate as the last. Sister Sarah had her tour patter on autopilot. I followed behind her whistling "Luck Be a Lady," but I couldn't rattle her.

"This is one of two kitchens at this facility," she prattled on. "We have a total of five throughout various locations in the city. By the end of this year, we'll have two more satellite locations opened."

"Impressive."

"Unfortunate," she said, still on script. "No matter how hard we work, the need for our services increases. One of our primary goals as an organization is to eventually make ourselves obsolete. Obviously, we're nowhere near achieving this."

It went on like that for half an hour. Sleeping quarters, dining halls, rec rooms, classrooms, the good Sister gave the impression that I was seeing everything, but I couldn't help notice as we rounded the corner on the sixth floor that one corridor was closed off, barred by a hospital style swinging door with a serious electronic lock.

"Excuse me?" I interrupted her well-memorized patter.

"Yes?"

"What's back here?" *Just curious, ma'am. Innocently curious, that's all.* The long pause for the answer told me that this wasn't usually in the script. Once again I could see those wires crossing in her eyes. She cocked her head to one side and got a look of intense concentration on her face. I could have rolled cigarettes in the furrow of her brow. I heard a vague hissing in her ear.

Interesting.

The hissing stopped and she faced me. "Staff offices," she said, a little too hastily, lest she forget her lines. "Infirmary, Bishop's residence."

"The Bishop *lives* here?" This was getting better and better.

"Oh, yes," she said, beaming. "The Bishop is very invested in the well-being of all our clients. He feels it's important to be available to the lost and the most needy."

Well, ain't he a peach? "I'll be sure to thank him personally when I see him. By the way, when do I get to meet him?"

"We're almost to the end of the tour, Mr. Walsh." the megawatt TV smile was back. "We'll finish up, and I'll take you to the conference room." As she turned around to lead the way, I caught a glimpse of the small radio earpiece she was wearing. As she moved on down the hall, I did a three-sixty as I followed behind, looking for the hidden cameras. A smoky half-globe was set back into a corner of the ceiling just behind me, almost obscured by an emergency exit sign.

Gotcha!

I gave it a wink, a grin, and a couple of finger pistols—pow! pow!—as I turned back to follow my guide. What the hell? Why not give the boys in the back room a thrill?

We headed up one last flight of stairs, where Sister Sarah led me to a long straight corridor lined with empty rooms. She led me into one where the walls had been lined with temporary shelving, overladen with books.

"There are ten rooms like this, here," she said, continuing the script. "They can be adapted for many uses. In the winter, they're emergency dormitory rooms. Right now, this one's been set up as a library with some remaindered books donated by a local shop."

"Is anything required in return for the help provided here?"

She looked at me like I was speaking Tagalog. "What do you mean?"

"Work. Washing dishes? Collecting donations?"

"Not usually, no. Some of the longer term residents may be asked to help serve food or with the laundry, but there's no work equity required from those we help."

"What about religious requirements?"

"We say a small prayer before meals," she said. Her tone suggested that she hoped this was an end to the unscripted questions.

"Do you get many converts?"

"That's not our mission."

"Anyone forced to participate?"

"No one is forced to do anything, here. Those who pray do so because they want to. These people are sincere in their faith."

"Sister, I used to be one of 'these people.'" Annoyance had started to creep in to my voice. "Most of us would have sacrificed a virgin or two to the evil lord of Tupperware if it meant a hot meal and warm bed for the night."

"Again, no one is required to pray," she said, snapping back into autopilot. She really was trying to stick to the script, the poor dear. "No one is forced to do anything they aren't comfortable with. Our mission is to provide respite and a helping hand."

"Does that include Laura Trammler?"

Again, the crossed wires were starting to show. *Look, if you want me to stick to the script, then you should give me a copy first.* Sarah leaned in to listen to the voice of the Holy Spirit, or whichever of the mooks in the security center was talking into her earpiece.

"Laura is fine," she said, a little too quickly. The TV host smile was gone. "She is not being held against her will." *Thus spake the mook?* "I'm sorry, Mr. Walsh, but any other questions you have should be addressed directly to Ms. Trammler or the Bishop."

About damn time.

Sister Sarah turned on a sensible heel and headed for the stairs. She didn't even motion for me to follow. I guess our date was over. I had to step lively to keep up with her. We returned to the third floor, which had been set up as office space and a reception area for the mission's wealthy benefactors.

The corridor ended with a large door, stained to suggest oak. My guide opened the door and gestured for me to enter, turning to scurry away as I did.

The room on the other side was appointed in the classic early-twenty-first century, white-bread corporate conference room style: fluorescent lights, berber carpet, and a nauseating peach tint to the walls. A giant whiteboard took up one wall, while a window out onto the Missions took up another. The bulk of the floor space was taken up by an oak laminate conference table the size of a Coast Guard cutter. Sitting at the end of the table opposite me, backlit by the window, was Laura Trammler, looking just as she had in my dream.

If that wasn't disconcerting enough, she looked at me as if she knew me.

"Hello, Mr. Walsh." She rose from the table and began to approach me. Her voice was the same one I'd heard in my dream. For a moment,

I had a flash of a memory of falling into Mr. Blue-robe's smile. I grabbed the back of a chair and tried to keep my balance while my knees buckled.

"Hello, Laura." I barely kept the croak out of my voice. "It's good to finally see you face to face." I held out my hand in greeting, and she smiled as she took it, firmly. I could feel an unwelcome energy arc between our palms as they touched. It coursed up my spine and made my vision go white, and I could feel the room flip upside down.

The bright light began to strobe in my head, alternating between searing, white-hot pain and the most disturbing of images.
Blue robes.
Silver blades.
A mass of writhing, nude bodies.
A scared young man bound in chains.
I feel cold iron wrapped tight about my wrists and ankles, and cold stone against my back.

I came to in the conference room, barely standing, the back of a chair clutched tightly to my chest. Laura stood clear of me, poised to catch me as if I might collapse. I got my legs back under me and tried to stand tall, flashing the nervous young woman what I hoped was my most reassuring smile. She didn't look convinced.

"Are you all right?" she asked.

"Fine," I said as I tried to cover the quaver in my voice. "I'm fine. Sorry, I should be asking you that question."

I motioned her to sit, as much to move on as to save face should my body betray me again. She kept a chair between us, but still sat as close to me as she could. The unfocused eyes in my vision were now engaged. She looked into my own with genuine care.

"I appreciate your concern," she said. "I am well here. And happy. You have nothing to worry about."

Tell that to my subconscious. "What about Ethan?" I asked, pushing.

"He worries too much. I'm afraid our life at home and on the run has given him a bit of an overactive imagination. I'm in no danger here. I'm safe."

And what about your brother's safety? She was doing her best to come across nonchalant, but there was an edge to her smile and a slight quaver to her voice.

"I'm sure you think you're safe and happy here, but I'm sensing something otherwise."

"You don't believe me," she said with a disappointed sigh.

"I only believe what my own experience tells me is true."

"How sad. The Bishop had hoped you would possess a little more faith than that."

I doubt the Bishop gives a flying fuck about me. I decided not to argue the point.

"Faith never helped me finish a job before." I needed to regain some control over the conversation. "So, you've met the Bishop?"

"Oh, yes." She practically gushed, perhaps a little too much. "Bishop Leveque has taken great personal interest in my spiritual well being."

"And you trust him?"

"I have faith in him."

"Is that why you stay?"

Laura looked away, just briefly. The older-than-her-years confidence was betrayed by a moment of hesitation.

"I choose to stay," she said, finally.

"And if you weren't here?"

"I can't see that happening yet," she said, again with less confidence.

"Don't you have faith in yourself?" I asked. I'll admit, I was starting to get annoyed by the conversation we weren't having.

"Don't you?" she replied, looking me in the eye again.

Dammit, kiddo, I'm asking the questions here!

"Faith? No."

"Really? The Bishop led me to believe you make a living following hunches."

How the hell would he know?

"Yes. But, every hunch I've ever had has had some basis in what I've observed beforehand." *Never you mind how or where I make my observations.*

She was quiet again, but her gaze never wandered from my eyes. She was looking for something, but I was damned if I could figure out what.

"What's your hunch about me?" she asked.

I held her gaze. *What was my hunch*? I wondered. We sat in silence for several moments while I tried to read what was going on behind those eyes. There was that confidence-beyond-years that I'd already seen, but it was masking something else. Then, in the briefest of flashes I saw it. Fear. Fear and an unspoken plea.

"What's my hunch? I think you're a very confused young woman who's looking for answers to questions you haven't even thought of yet. I think the Bishop has told you many things he knows you want to hear. I also think you feel threatened by someone or something here, but you're not sure if that threat is greater than the one that waits for you outside these walls."

Laura gave me the thinnest of smiles, and I could see her relax a little bit, but only just. "All that from sitting here with me for a few minutes?"

"That and plenty of personal experience." I decided to push what little confidence I'd just gained. "I met Evil Margaret last night."

That got her attention. I saw the flicker of fear again, the same look I'd seen on Ethan's face. This time, however, the fear was shored up by that same earlier confidence. She searched my eyes, looking for some confirmation that I wasn't planning on blowing the whistle on her. I gave her the slightest of nods and a slim but hopefully reassuring smile. A flicker of thanks crossed her face, and then she returned to her previous mode of devoted acolyte. She reached out and took my hands in hers. I braced myself for another mind-fuck, but it didn't come. I relaxed for the first time since I'd come into the room.

"Look," she said, "I'm really touched that you care enough about my brother to check up on me for him. But, trust me, you don't know anything about my situation." She took her hands away again and began to rise. A small wad of paper remained behind in my palm. I looked a question at her, but now she was pointedly avoiding my gaze.

As quietly and subtly as I could, I unraveled Laura's little gift. There was a message, written in a small, tidy hand.

They're watching us. You're not safe here.

No subtlety there, no sir.

I tried to get her to look me in the eye again. "Do you want to come back with me for a visit with your brother?" I asked. *C'mon, kid. Take the bait.*

"I'm sorry." Laura was speaking to the floor, now. "I'm afraid that won't be possible."

The door to the conference room swung open.

"Is our guest giving you any trouble, Laura?" The voice was a rich baritone. Warm. It could almost have been friendly but for the slight clip of impatience hiding behind the bright syllables. And there was something else, too. Something I couldn't hear with my ears, but sat there at the back of my skull, tickling at my unconscious. I turned around to greet our interloper.

I was glad I'd already sat down.

The blue robe wasn't here, but I recognized the man nevertheless. He was smiling at me—a wolfish, cruel smile. I froze as the reptilian base of my brain screamed at me to run.

"We're fine," Laura said. "Mr. Walsh was just getting ready to leave."

No I wasn't! I can't bloody move! I was doing everything I could while sitting there to suppress any physical manifestations of the full on panic attack that was now settling in. I could feel an immense weight on my chest, holding my diaphragm in place, my breathing out of control. I wanted to stand up and run, but instead I tried to find my center and regain some balance. I wasn't going to show this guy, whoever he was, that I was spooked. Not an easy job considering my spine was starting to burn again.

Dear God, what the hell did I just walk into?

I managed to regain control over my breathing long enough to will my traitorous knees back into submission and stood up, eyeball to eyeball with the man who'd been haunting my dreams these last two nights. The unnerving smile remained in place on his almost otherwise serene visage.

"I'm sorry to see you leaving so soon," he said. "I was looking forward to spending some time with you, Mr. Walsh. You're something of a legend among our clients."

"Well, you know what they say," I said, trying not to stammer. "Kingdom of the blind and whatnot. I apologize, but I didn't get your name."

"I'm sorry, Mr. Walsh," he said. There was a triumphant gleam in his eye. "I'm Bishop Alexander Leveque. I'm the executive minister of New Light Ministries."

Fuck.

Of course you are.

"Perhaps another day?" he asked as he opened the door to indicate the way out.

"Anything's possible," I said as I hurried to the door. *Even if it's not bloody likely.* The Bishop reached behind me to throw the door wide, guiding me in the right direction with his hand resting in the space between my shoulder blades. I felt a jolt arc between our bodies, searing into my scars—something considerably more than static. I jumped at the shock and twisted to face him.

Time slowed to a barely perceptible crawl. There was that smile again—cruel, wide, piercing—the malevolent energy of it stabbing straight into my ribcage. My heart began to race so that I feared it would shatter my chest, while the electric charge along my spine began to spread over my whole body, the now all-too-familiar sensation of fire burning across my shoulders with an ever greater intensity. I was rapidly losing my battle with my wobbly legs, and I chose to surrender rather than suffer the inevitable damage of a complete loss, falling to my knees at Leveque's feet. I could feel his eyes on me, following my descent to the floor. Despite the escalating agony, I could not look away from him. His malicious grin continued to bore into me, and once again I could feel myself drawn toward him, hooked by the soul. Around me, the room began to spin and I found myself falling into those bright and all-knowing eyes. I tried to grab on to an anchor in the room, but all things physical fell through my grasp, and I tumbled headlong into the malevolent aura of the smiling cleric.

I find myself in a stone box, the sounds of screaming—not my own—surround me and I can taste the dank moisture in the air. The box resolves itself into a cell, as I feel the cold weight of iron around my limbs. Another man is curled up in the opposite corner, unkempt and half naked. His back is to me, and I can see the deep rivulets of the wounds on his arms and torso, bright blood red contrasting against brown skin.

Again the world spins around me. As it settles, I find myself surrounded by a circle of torches. Men in all too familiar blue robes hold them aloft, and they speak in unison in a language I cannot recognize. I take a step forward and meet a wall of air, my temples throbbing as I touch it.

Another spin, and this time I am lying flat on my stomach. My wrists, my ankles, and my waist are restrained. The fiery sensation along my shoulders and spine has returned, more intense now than ever.

Against my better judgment, I scream.

Below my field of vision is the hem of a blue robe. The figure standing over me begins to tug at my shoulders.

No. Not my shoulders.

What, then?

The burning pain intensifies and I scream louder, joining the chorus of misery keening around me. Someone is cutting into my flesh, and I can feel the wet, then see it—blood red and spreading out across the stone floor.

The sound of cracking bone drills into my skull and I pass out, bringing momentary relief from the excruciating pain.

I awake still facedown on the stone slab. My restraints have been removed. My shoulders throb and burn. In the periphery, I can see a blue robed figure replacing a frighteningly familiar silver blade to a rack on the rough stone wall. He turns to me. His lips are moving, but I cannot hear his words through the thrumming of my own amped up heartbeat in my ears. The face is not the same, but the eyes are unmistakable. He finishes speaking and flashes a vicious smile, intense in its cruelty.

His robe is covered in blood and a fine down.

I shook my head clear, the pain still burning, my heart still racing. The Bishop looked at me with an almost leer and held a hand out to me. I shuddered at the thought of any more physical contact with him, and that flash of dread was enough to bring me back to my senses. I scuttled backwards across the floor on my butt, fumbling to my feet as I passed through the door. I turned my back on the pair in the conference room and ran with as much speed as I could muster toward the stairwell.

I flew down three flights of stairs and came bursting into New Light's lobby, knocking over a startled security goon in the process and nearly taking myself out at the knees. I was barely clinging to the real world. I could see the lobby around me, but underneath it were flashes of the vision of my stone cell, and the shouts of New Light's patrons were blending in with the horrible wailing of that other dream world.

I stumbled towards where I was certain the door was, my arms out in front of me to bulldoze whoever or whatever got in my way. Ahead of me, the slight grey frame of Twitchy Carl came into view, his face a mask of joy.

"I knew you'd remember," he cried. I barely heard him speak, as desperate as I was to get out of this place. He stepped into my path and my outstretched arm caught him square in the chest, plowing him under my feet. Instinctively, I sidestepped to avoid getting caught in the tangle of Twitchy Carl's flailing limbs as he went down. I could hear him behind me struggling to get up, still crying out to anyone who would listen.

"Prepare yourselves, you wicked world!" he screamed. "His eyes and His judgment are again upon us!"

The images from my vision were taking control of my sight, and I felt my body demanding surrender. I made one final push for the front door, diving through it as the world began to go topsy-turvy. I hit the pavement outside face first, sending the waiting lunch line scattering.

The sidewalk felt cool and inviting, and as long as I had my hands planted on it, the dizziness and the searing pain felt bearable. A crowd began to gather around me, yammering away. I could hear someone calling the police. I rolled over onto my back to try and reassure everyone that I was going to be fine, but all that came out of me was a drooling slur.

Everything looked out of sync. My body felt rooted to the ground, and darkness threatened to overcome me. The crowd at my head began to part, and a commanding baritone with just a trace of a bayou accent was shouting over the heads of the mob.

"Move away, now! Step aside! Let me help my friend up!"

Friend. That was a nice word to hear. I could use one of those. Everything was starting to grow dim. I was going to be dead soon, I knew. It would be nice to have a friend with me.

The source of the voice floated into what was left of my field of vision. The last thing I saw as the world faded to black was the face of Mr. Ray Bans, bending over to try and help me up.

Friend. I tried to smile while babbling incoherently at him. *Next time, I'll bring donuts. I promise.*

I gave up trying to stay with the world and succumbed to the darkness.

11

In the darkness, sounds of mortal dread surround me, moaning and screaming in a perverse chorus. My own unvoiced screams threaten to drown out the sounds of the others in my head.

Slowly, very slowly, the noise begins to fade, and with the growing quiet my own calm increases. I feel less confined in the darkness, and the dank smell of standing water and human waste is replaced with more pleasing aromas. I can smell coffee, now, and something spicy lingering underneath the rich bitterness. With the new odors, light begins to pierce through my eyelids.

I was coming to. The ground beneath my body was no longer stone or pavement but soft and comfortable. I moved my hands about and felt the contours of a sofa cradling my aching body. As my eyes adjusted to the light, I risked opening them. The light stung them, but not nearly as painfully as I'd expected. My vision was not yet fully returned. I could see only vague shapes and blurs of color. There was a block-shaped blur across from the sofa, and above it a rounder blur.

I tried to sit up, taking care not to move too fast. My head and shoulders throbbed, and I felt a wave of nausea overcome me, forcing me back into a prone position on the sofa. As my head hit the cushion, the round blur spoke.

"Don't move too quickly, now," it said. "It is extremely difficult to clean vomit out of this carpet."

The voice was a rich baritone. It had an accent that I couldn't quite place. English, maybe. But African, as well, with a bit of the Gulf Coast thrown in. A unique voice. There was something familiar in the sound of it. I struggled to sit up again, wanting a better look, but my body was having none of it. The sofa would be my best friend for a little while longer.

"I didn't expect to see you awake so soon," the blur said. "Most people would have been laid out flat for at least twelve hours after the psychic ass-kicking you just took."

The blurs were beginning to resolve themselves in my eyes. The block-shaped blur was now a desk-shaped blur, a rich maple color. The rounder blur was now more person shaped, the blur where his face should be a few shades browner than the desk.

"Take it slow," he said. "We've got all day. Coffee's on when you're ready."

The promise of rich, caffeinated goodness was more than enough incentive. Getting my elbows under me, I half sat up on the couch and settled my eyes on my host. I willed my vision into focus, but my head was still pounding and my body ached with the effort. Soon, the round, brown blur came into sharp and vaguely familiar relief.

"Where am I?" I asked.

"The French Quarter," he answered.

Not the answer I was expecting. The few pieces of my brain that were awake turned my hosts words upside down and inside out, but couldn't make sense of them.

"How did I end up in New Orleans?" The pedantic reaches of my consciousness had decided to take over the conversation.

"Not New Orleans," he scoffed. "You're in my restaurant, The French Quarter."

My memory was beginning to flood back.

"Specifically," he continued, "you're in my private office, hub of all my nefarious activities." He flashed a broad, mocking smile as he said this, laying on the Coastal *patois* a little more thickly as he did so. My eyes were now fully functional. I focused on that smile, and on the young, vital face with the ancient eyes.

"Saturday?" I ventured.

"None other than," he said, leaning back in his office chair, ruler of all he surveyed.

Every city has its larger-than-life figures—criminals, celebrities, and permanent fixtures. Baron Saturday was one of ours. He had a reputation in the city as being one who was highly connected. Word on the street was that if it was happening in the shadows, Baron Saturday knew about it.

I'd met him not long after I'd begun my new career as "security consultant." A false trail tossed out by a would-be kidnapper had led to my staking out the service entrance of his restaurant one evening and one of his security crew caught me snooping.

"Baron Saturday was wondering," he said, in a tone that let me know in no uncertain terms that this was not a polite invitation, "whether you might not be warmer inside. Maybe with a cup of coffee?"

And so, I found myself face to face with one of the city's most notorious personalities. Saturday not only set me straight about his complete lack of involvement with the kidnapping, he eventually set me on the right path, and I recovered my missing person in record time. He'd been a valuable source of information ever since.

Baron Saturday wasn't his real name, of course. Nobody knew what that was.

"What *is* your name?" I asked him once not long after that first encounter.

The oddest look crossed his face, a mixture of menace and offense. It passed briefly, and then just as quickly he began to laugh at me.

"Baron Saturday is all you need to know," he had said.

He claimed he preferred to keep an air of mystery about him, and that taking the name of one of the voodoo loa added a patina of authenticity to the restaurant.

"Mystery and authenticity," he told me, "are the keys to success in business and in life."

The cops I knew were always trying to pin something on him, to connect the dots of the city's organized criminal culture back to the Baron. All trails eventually led to dead ends. Officially, Baron Saturday was just an extremely successful restaurateur. However, the rumors of his role as criminal mastermind persisted, and Saturday didn't seem too concerned with dissuading anyone of the notion. The hired muscle surrounding him only added to the mystique. The rumors certainly hadn't hurt business any.

Mystery and authenticity, indeed.

I looked across at his smiling face. The skin of his shaved head glowed under dim incandescent light, a single gold hoop glinted from one ear.

"You're lucky I've been having you followed," he said, rising to go to the coffee pot on a corner table.

"Not very subtle about it, either," I said, gratefully accepting a mug of the deep, bitter brew. "A well-armed, muscle-bound chauffeur in a shiny, black sedan is not exactly inconspicuous in the Missions."

"I didn't intend to be sneaky about," he replied.

"Why are you watching me? What's your interest in the Trammler kids?"

Saturday let out an amused snort. "I don't give a shit about your clients, Ray," he said. "I'm looking out for you. Word is the world's been turning upside down on you rather frequently of late, and I've got a lot riding on your not being dead any time soon."

"So, what, do I owe you a favor now?" Not for the first time, he got an odd look in his eyes as they met mine. The jovial entrepreneur mask slipped for just a second.

"You don't owe me anything," he said, suddenly serious. Then the mask was back. "I just need you to keep doing what you're doing," he said with a smile that managed to look both friendly and predatory.

"And what, exactly, am I doing?"

"I can't tell you that," he said, turning away.

"What?"

He turned back towards me, the serious look returning to his features. Saturday looked at me for a good ten seconds, and then sighed before turning away, again. "I have promises to keep. Some things you're better off discovering on your own."

"Saturday, what the hell's going on?"

Again, he turned to look me in the eye. "Raymond, I've been keeping an eye out for you for years, now. You've made a pretty steady habit out of staying well and clear of New Light Ministries. Why are you bothering with them, now?"

"I picked up a job from Ruth Penfield. The Trammler kids I was talking about. Younger brother gets dragged into the city by his older sister, who then dumps him on the streets while she takes up with New Light. He wants her back. I go to work."

The Baron nodded, then took a long sip of his coffee and studied me from over the rim of his mug. "What have you learned in the process?"

"The girl's free to come and go as she pleases, yet she seems beholden to the place. At the same time, she's scared shitless of whatever it is she's seen inside there, and I sense it's not just soup lines. She's paralyzed."

"She's a pawn," he said. "Bait."

I gawked at him. "How do you know this?"

"Give me some credit, Ray," he laughed. "I'm Baron Saturday. I know what goes on in this city."

"Are you telling me they've taken away her will? She's brainwashed?"

"I'm saying that your fate and hers are tied together. You're both in very deep, now."

"Don't be so damn melodramatic," I said, perhaps just a bit too harshly. "It's just another case, there's some misunderstanding going on, and it'll all resolve itself soon."

"Of course, Ray. You're right. It's all cut and dried. How could I be so silly? Your dream life is just smacking you around of its own accord." Saturday was looking at me now with a glare that could have stopped armies.

I never bought into his whole "secret master of the underworld" shtick, but there were moments when I'd seen him flash some real power, moments that could make anyone sit up, take notice, and pray they were never on his bad side. This was one of those moments. Right now, he frightened me more than anything else that had happened today. My heartbeat began to stutter.

"Just some bad sleep," I said, hoping he didn't hear me lying to myself. "A little too much to drink before bedtime."

"Mm-hmm. And how much did you have to drink before you went face to face with the Bishop this morning?"

"What makes you think anything happened with the Bishop this morning?"

"Because, Ray, I've been watching, remember? And I'm guessing that little psychic beat-down wasn't self-inflicted. Otherwise, André wouldn't have had to scrape up the gibbering heap that used to be you off the pavement and dump you on my sofa."

I stared down into my coffee. Saturday's look softened. "You're lucky you're not a vegetable, right now. So quit trying to tell me your life is just average-ordinary. All right?"

I nodded. I needed to stop pissing off the people trying to help me. It was time to start talking to my guardian angel like the fount of information he usually was.

"Saturday, what is New Light Ministries, really?"

"Everything it claims to be," he answered. "Nothing it appears to be."

"Quit being obtuse, dammit. No fair taking advantage of a man while the room's still spinning."

"I'm sorry, Ray. I'm treading into dangerous territory, here. There are some things you still need to discover for yourself, and I have promises to keep."

"Promises to who?"

"You'll learn that in good time, as well."

"What *can* you tell me?"

"You've already met the 'Bishop,' right? You've encountered what kind of power he's got, especially over you."

"It's all in my head, man. Lack of sleep."

"Ray," he interrupted, speaking sharply, "you have no clue how your visions work, do you? Why you're so in tune with souls who are lost or in trouble?"

"Empathy and a deep attention span?"

"More than that, Ray."

"What's this got to do with New Light?"

"For all intents and purposes, New Light's exactly what it seems. It's a shelter and a social service outlet. Their good deeds are very good, and the everyday grunts on the front lines deserve most of the praise and thanks they get."

"I sense a 'but' coming on..."

"*But*, over the last several years its internal administration and leadership have been taken over by, shall we say, other interests."

"And cue the dramatic organ sting."

"Ray, I am being so deathly serious right now."

"Serious, right." I tried to contain my growing sense of mirth over where this conversation was going.

"About a dozen years ago, the founding elders of New Light began dying off, one by one. Victims of violent crime, stress related heart attacks, nothing that seems unusual on its own, just everyday hazards of the work the Ministry does, right?"

"Why not?"

"Until you realize that within a year's time, every original member of the upper echelons of New Light Ministries was gone. Dead. And replaced by virtual unknowns. I've tried digging up everything I can on the new management, and I can't find a damn thing. Think about it, Ray. I've got connections in this town that run deep, and I couldn't learn item one about these characters."

"Frustrating."

"Damn straight! That alone was enough to make me suspicious. So I had André and the A-Team, here, start doing a little legwork."

"Did that make you feel better?"

"Not one bit. What I did learn scared the shit out of me, Ray. They're still letting the main mission run as usual. It's a convenient front and lends them some legitimacy. Meanwhile, they've acquired other properties throughout the city and have converted those to other purposes. Work a little less than holy, if you know what I mean?"

"I'm afraid I don't."

"Black magic, Ray. Big, bad, nasty rituals. Scary shit I haven't seen in nearly a lifetime." He paused, shuddering. "And I've had a long life."

By now, I was having the hardest time containing my growing sense of amusement at Saturday's story. The Baron was looking annoyed.

"Okay, I'll bite," I said with a chuckle. "What's their secret plan?"

"Don't just humor me, Ray," he said with a growl that would have warned me off if I'd had all my wits.

"I wouldn't dream of it. I can't wait to see where this goes."

"They're recruiting as many young adults as they can, just like your Miss Trammler, channeling them from the mission to their other locations. The chaos of that many young minds tied together is like one giant battery for their work."

"And that work is . . ?"

"They're trying to reclaim something they've lost."

"And what's that?"

The Baron paused for just a moment. His face held a mixture of fear and sadness I'd never seen from him before. Like he'd lost a prized possession and he feared what the thief might do with it. It was a palpable emotion. I could feel it boring into my own flesh, cutting off the good humor I felt just a moment ago. He looked me in the eye and let out an old, world weary sigh.

"Me?" I asked and tried to hold back a laugh. "You think they're looking for me?"

Saturday turned away, but not before I could see the beginning of an answer in his eyes.

"Good Lord, I set foot in the place once during my derelict years. Are they really that possessive?"

Perhaps the absurdity of my situation finally got the better of me. Perhaps I was tired and frightened, Maybe it was some mix of all of that, but I could no longer contain myself. I laughed. The sound came out somewhere between raucous guffaw and a tight, strangled scream.

Saturday fixed me with tired eyes.

"Good luck to them, then," I said. "I've been looking for myself for ten years with no answers in sight." The laugh continued to come forth from the depth of my soul, sounding more scream-like by the second.

Saturday's face clouded over, a touch of that real power that I feared emanated from his features. He was up out of his chair and across the room in a heartbeat, his fists clamped around the lapels of my jacket, jerking me up to my feet. The direct contact pushed me out of myself.

I am back in the cold, fetid stone cell. My roommate is still huddled in the corner, stripped to the waist, the wounds on his back oozing. I stand up and move as close as my own chains will allow me, curious as to my companion's identity and moved by some desire to lend some comfort. His skin is mottled and blood-streaked. His body had been large once, but there is still some power and vitality radiating from his now emaciated frame. Our captors have done their best to strip away his life, but I can tell it will take more than what these bastards can do. Then horrible recognition begins to dawn.

Back again in the dim office, Saturday released his tight grip on me. Settling on my feet, I felt the ground move beneath me and I allowed myself to sink into the sofa to avoid falling flat on the floor. Saturday's eyes never left mine, his anger subsiding. A look of genuine tenderness replaced the tempest in his gaze.

I stared at him, willing myself not to draw the obvious conclusion that was knocking at the door of my waking mind. Soon, though, the silence between us grew too heavy.

"Let me see your back," I said. Saturday nodded, then turned, unbuttoning his shirt and stripping it away from his shoulders. The scars glistened smooth and pink across his back, showing familiar patterns.

"Who are you?" I asked.

He looked at me as if he was about to speak, but instead he choked as the words caught in his throat.

"I don't understand any of this!"

"And you never will if you keep asking me," he said.

"Why can't you give me a straight answer?"

"I wish I could, Ray," he said, shaking his head. "I wish I could, but I quite literally cannot."

"Bullshit."

"Believe what you want, friend. You'll know the truth soon enough."

"How?"

"If you continue down this path, the truth will be unavoidable."

Saturday's words struck true at my heart. I had the same thought myself just this morning. My mirthful disbelief evaporated, but comfort did not come to replace the void.

"Who is the Bishop? Why does he want me?"

The Baron gave me an appraising look and seemed to come to a decision.

"You'll forgive me later," he said, "if we bend the rules a little, right now."

"Why not," I said, resigned to whatever nameless game it was that he was playing.

Saturday walked to his desk and kicked aside a corner of the rug beneath it to reveal a cutaway section of hardwood floor.

"Tell me," he asked, "have you ever heard tales of the Most Holy and Secret Order of St. John the Divine?"

I shook my head. Saturday bent down to remove the cutaway floorboards, beneath which was a small steel safe. He put his hand to the dial and began to turn.

"I'm not surprised," he said. "The Roman curia considered them a blight on the face of the church. An Inquisition crushed them into dust in the twelfth century. Rome burned their name away from every possible record. As far as the world today is concerned, it is as if the Order never existed. Not even the current Roman leaders know its name."

"But you do?"

The dial of the safe made a loud thunk and Saturday swung the door open. He reached in and removed a wooden box of antique stained walnut, thin and oblong, and walked it carefully back to his desk.

"One piece of evidence survives," he said with smug and obvious pleasure, "and I have it."

He clicked open the oaken box and removed a Lucite sheet, within which a tattered, yellowing parchment was set.

"The final letter to Rome from the field marshal of the Papal Inquisition tasked with the destruction of the Order's last refuge."

He turned the well preserved document towards me. It looked good for its age. A neat, tight Latin script filled the parchment from top to bottom, neat and unornamented.

"Why don't you give it a read?" Saturday suggested.

"I can barely speak English, right now," I replied. "I think Latin may be out of the question."

Saturday placed a strong hand on my shoulder.

"Not at all," he said, as I felt a rush through my body and my eyes began to burn. "You just need to remember how, is all."

I turned my eyes to the page. Miraculously, I began to read.

12

The first day of August in the year of Our Lord 1209

To his Holiness, Innocentus Tertius, Vicar of Christ, Bishop of Rome, the grace and blessings of the Lord, Our God, and his son, Jesus Christ, be upon you.

This shall be my last missive, for by the grace of God, my work here is near an end.

You will already have heard of the twenty thousand heretics—men and women, lord and serf, young and old—that were put to the sword by Arnaud at the town of Béziers. It was there that so many of the unholy had come to take refuge. After giving the good and the faithful the opportunity to leave unharmed, Arnaud ordered your soldiers into the heart of the town, first shattering the doors of the apostate church of St. Mary Magdulene, slaughtering Cathars and any others who stood with them. From there the cleansing continued throughout the town, until the end of the day, when Béziers was reduced to a wasteland. There were altogether another seven thousand heretics put to the sword or cleansed in the holy flame. However, we would soon learn our work was far from finished.

Already, Arnaud was prepared to move the army on to Carcassonne, where Trencavel was known to be harboring the last vestiges of the Albigensians inside the great walled city. Your most faithful servant was determined to finish the work, and yet the horrible stories that began to circulate among the devout refugees in our camp convinced us that our crusade near Béziers was not yet complete. The townsfolk spoke first of abductions–of children, of the young, men and women alike. They seemed to fear speaking any more despite our urging to continue their testimony, and looked askance at us, no longer sure who to trust despite the lives we had granted them. As the night wore on and the wine flowed, their tongues loosened, and they spoke next of beastly howls that filled what would have been otherwise peaceful nights; then, tales of creatures, beautiful and horrific, seen in shadows prowling the forests; and, finally, of blue robed men–Cathars, your Holiness, there can be no doubt–who acted as masters of the beasts, and who were known to these faithful as The Order of St. John.

That evening, as most of the army slept, a few of the brothers and I were determined to keep watch over our camp in the woods. If demons did prowl the forest, we would be there to see it. As those who took refuge had spoken, so we, too, heard. The cries of the beasts were full of rage and despair, and they surrounded the camp. So terrifying, so unearthly were these sounds that we could not have slept if we tried. The next morning, as our brother Arnaud prepared your troops to move on to Carcassonne, we sequestered a small portion of the force to move further south into the forest that we might track down this Order and end it.

South of Béziers, about two miles through the forest, our company came upon an old, disheveled manor house that had fallen into disrepair. While it seemed unlikely that any unholy order or any other creature would be housed here, the ruin did make for a good hiding place for the odd runaway from the previous day's campaign. I ordered two of your lieutenants to enter and try to flush out any stray vermin.

As soon as the men crossed the threshold, the hounds began baying and straining at their leashes trying to break free from their handlers, wanting nothing to do with the accursed place.

The howls of the dogs seemed to incite an infernal chorus in the surrounding woods. From within the ruined chateau and echoing around us in the forest came yelps and moans more terrible than the hounds' frightened cries, voices both human and otherwise–worse than any we'd heard in the night– piercing the struggling dawn light. The forest echoed with the sounds of fear and anger and loss, rich enough on their own to drive a man to madness. In truth, most of our company ran screaming into the woods, mad already, or near to madness. The hounds having run off with the cowards, it was left to my lieutenant and me to survey the ruins.

Your Holiness, would that I had followed the dogs so this missive might end here.

The chateau was a mass of rotting wood and plaster–but for the ghost of its old frame telling tales of its past life, the mass in the middle of the forest clearing could have been some demonic fungal growth, organic and unnatural all at once. The odor of wet rot and death was abundant within what remained of its interior, overpowering to such a fullness that my lieutenant began to retch and heave almost as soon as we had entered, so much so that I left him pallid and doubled over at the entrance with an order to pull himself together, and pushed myself further into the innards of the hell hole.

The maddening howls continued to rise up through splin- tering floorboards, growing louder and hinting at more pain and suffering; hinting at more evil. My lieutenant, his guts now somewhat under control, returned to my side, begging again and again for us to run until I at last struck the coward on his ear while pushing him forward into the damp and darkening mess.

What little evidence there was suggested we had entered what had once been the tavern room of a public house. Behind where the bar had once been was a doorway that looked much sturdier than the rest of the ruins–greener wood and fresher lacquer. Curious, and not at all wise, I walked towards it for a closer look. The unearthly sounds seemed to emerge through the portal, and I spurred my lieutenant on ahead of me, sword at the ready to dispatch whatever hellish creatures we might encounter as we passed through.

The doorway opened onto steps that led only downward, a fitting direction based on the noises that grew more intense as we began our descent. Two flights of wooden steps twisting back on themselves soon gave way to steps of stone, not laid out in blocks, but rather carved from the earth upon which the ruins lay, spiraling downward it seemed forever until we began to feel we might fast be approaching the gates of Hell itself. The air around us grew ever colder, ever more damp until the wet chill threatened to soak through our armor and penetrate the pores of our skin. My lieutenant began to tremble violently, but he could not have retreated if he wanted, as the passage we traversed was so narrow as to let only one body through at a time, he on point and my own self behind him determined to see this ghoulish mission through to its completion.

Further and further we descended, and still the maddening sounds of anger and suffering increased until my head was full of the diabolical noise to the point where I could no longer hear the Lord's Prayer that I'd commenced reciting as a talisman against the rising sense of doom. I began to sympathize with the more cowardly sentiments of my lieutenant, wondering if turning around would perhaps be the more prudent course. A mere moment before I thought I might turn my head to look back over my shoulder, our descent came to a sudden stop, as I stumbled into the back of my companion, his own descent halted by a thick oaken door, reinforced with iron.

The lieutenant turned to ask for orders, but by now the wild and angry howls had drowned out any chance of mere mortal speech. I signaled him to push against the armored portal, and I braced myself against the narrow walls to act as leverage for the attempt. My efforts were barely needed. Armored though the door may have been, it had not been secured. Thinking the gatekeepers foolish, I urged my lieutenant forward, this stroke of seeming luck filling me with an undeserved sense of bravado. I was too full of my own hubris and self-righteousness to sense the real danger that lay ahead.

Ahead of us lay a long hallway dug out of the hardened earth. Small pockets lined it on either side, cells carved out for the residents of this hellish menagerie, with oak and iron doors, much like the one we just passed through, closing them in. We could not see the creatures that lay behind them, but the unearthly howls were enough to dissuade either of us from becoming too curious. There was light emanating from a passageway at the end of the long path, and it was in this direction that I pressed my lieutenant forward, his sword drawn and held out ahead of him, just as I held my crucifix out ahead of me.

The beastly things behind the cell doors could sense our presence, and as we passed their screaming intensified. Some sounds were more fearsome than wild animals, while some sounded almost human, pleading with us like whipped dogs for release, or promising pleasures earthly and unearthly in exchange for their liberation. Despite the awful stew of terror and temptation, we pushed forward, intent on tracking down the masters of this abominable dungeon.

At the end of the corridor, near the light source, one cell was thrown open, its residents departed, their broken chains the only things that remained lying on the floor of the rough-hewn cave. At its center there lay a circle etched in the stone and embellished with symbols and sigils we did not recognize, but which filled us with a rising sense of dread, nonetheless- so much so that we quickly backed out of the cell and pushed forward towards our final destination.

The light at the hallway's end shown through yet another oak and iron portal, ajar just as the first. The glow radiated from a fire just on the other side, the flames casting and recasting strange color and shadow with their dancing. Voices–human voices–carried through the crack in the doorway. Again, I signaled my lieutenant to push through.

On the other side lay what may once have been a chirurgeon's workshop, or perhaps an inquisition chamber. Its contents were strewn about and shattered, and copious amounts of blood painted the floor and the walls. In one corner, a corpulent, blue-robed Cathar stood with his back to the wall, a defiant look in his eyes. At his right hand, a young girl, no more than sixteen, cowered on the floor, her belly swollen greatly with child. The firelight that had drawn us to this room came from two sources, the first being a fireplace like the one a smith might use in the center of the chamber, burning red-hot. The second fire was something else entirely, burning a pale green and seeming to rise out of a long and slender blade that rested in the hands of tall, pale man. The wielder of the sword possessed an unnatural beauty, at once mesmerizing and frightening. The two of us were frozen in our tracks.

He was clothed in a brief sackcloth, which hung to cover only what was necessary. The rest of his body glowed with the same green fire, and while at first I thought his flesh merely reflected the unearthly fire of the sword, on second glance it seemed to emanate from within him, the sword an extension of his own being. My hair stood on end, and I felt an unshakable desire to fall to my knees in reverence for I knew now that I stood in the presence of something nigh to holy. He stepped forward and pointed the rapier-like flame in the direction of the cornered heretic, who faced his fate with an unnatural calm, seemingly immune to the unearthly howls intensifying all around us, and to his own certain death fast approaching.

"Kill me," the Cathar barked, commanding his would-be executioner. "The work is too far along for even your kind to turn it back, Seraph, and my own survival is assured." The blue-robed devil glanced in the direction of the frightened mother-to-be.

"I have been your prisoner for so long, I have almost no memory of a time when I was free." The thing the Cathar called "Seraph" spoke with a voice both lyric and terrible, and I at last succumbed to the compulsion to sink to my knees as I heard it. His voice was a soul searing sound, full of loss and anger and still achingly beautiful in spite of that, and it filled the room in such a manner as to threaten to extinguish all light. The young mother turned her head away and would have clawed her way through the stone wall if she could. Even the heretic in his defiance winced to hear it. "If it were my will," the Seraph continued, "I would render some punishment worse than death."

The alien fire in his hands flared brighter.

"Be thankful," its wielder said, "that it is not my own will that decides your fate, today." And with those words, the Seraph struck. The verdant flame entered the Cathar's body, the point of the sword thrusting true through his heart, plunging in until he screamed, a heart-wrenching sound, and I watched, stunned, as his soul was drawn out of his body, channeled up through the Seraph's fiery blade. In an instant, the man's body was reduced to a dry husk. The Seraph withdrew the sword, and the Cathar's dry corpse sunk to the floor, no wound evident where the sword had entered, no blood shed. The beautiful creature then turned its attentions to the trembling girl.

"Hold, angel!" called a voice from behind us, and I turned my head to see the source of the intrusion into this holy and terrible moment. From over my shoulder, I saw a thin man, a Moor from his looks, holding his hand out in a halting gesture as he ran towards the glowing man.

"She bears his child," the creature rumbled. "He has magicked his seed. He will be reborn through her. I cannot let that stand."

"Nothing is predestined," the Moor replied. "The Order has destroyed enough. Let it end here, friend."

The Seraph considered these words, and turned once again to look at the girl, staring her straight in the eyes and seeming to be bore straight into her soul. The world held its breath in that moment, a few seconds stretching out into eternity until the creature seemed to come to some decision. He nodded slightly, and stepped back, the glow receding from his body and the blade, now certainly an extension of his own hand, dissipating into the silence of the now cramped room. The howls of the other prisoners ceased. The girl collapsed to the floor, supine and weeping.

Until now, all this had played out before my own eyes and the eyes of my lieutenant as though we were dreaming, or watching some strange passion play. Now, however, we became residents of the room. The Seraph looked straight at me, and though his otherworldly power had receded, his look still filled me with deep dread.

"You, brother," he said, addressing me, "have arrived in time," and saying this, he knelt beside the fear maddened young mother, his terrible aspect now replaced with something far more gentle. With little effort, he picked her up in his arms and approached me.

"There is a convent in Bordeaux that will care for her," he said. "Take her there, keep watch over her until she gives birth."

I nodded my assent. Your Holiness, what else could I do? But the angel was not finished with his instructions.

"Then kill the child before it sees the end of its first day."

The look of horror on my face was matched only by the gasp of the Moor.

"Angel!" he cried, but the terrible creature shot him a look that silenced him instantly.

"Release the others," he told the Moor. "They will finish the work your inquisition could not," he added, turning again to me. "I see your reluctance. Know that this child will grow to be the monster I have just passed judgment on. It is certain. The child cannot live." Then he reached out and took my head in his hands. I felt the green and holy fire enter my temples. "Its life, or yours," he finished, and I could feel my fate sealed.

I took the girl in my arms and turned to leave the dungeon. Ahead of me, the Moor had begun opening the cells down the corridor. I stood frozen in awe and horror as creatures beautiful and terrible stepped out of their prison and began to run for the surface. Your Holiness, I cannot begin to describe what I saw in that moment. We have catalogued all manner of unholy and unearthly creatures, but nothing in our libraries, no words and no woodcuts, comes close to portraying the evil I witnessed released into the unsuspecting world that day.

The angel sensed my dread. "Do not concern yourself with them," he ordered me. "They are mine to deal with, and I shall do so."

I did not doubt him.

My lieutenant and I followed the unholy menagerie back out through the doors of the ruins above. Dusk was settling, and the beasts had already disappeared into every corner of the darkening forest.

The Seraph and the Moor followed us out of the ruins and turned to part ways with us. Before fading into the woods, the angel turned to me one last time.

"Do not fail me," he commanded, the verdant fire flaring up around his body for just a moment before fading as the darkness swallowed him and his companion for good. I stood for a long time, shuddering.

Neither of us wished to make camp there for the night, despite the rapidly approaching night, and so we pushed on back towards the remains of the village, for even those ruins seemed safer, and there we bedded down for the evening.

The next morning, I awoke to find myself alone. My lieutenant had hung himself from a tree on the edge of town, and the girl had disappeared, whether abducted or run away I know not. I had failed the angel before I had even begun, and I knew he would come for me. This, Your Holiness, this I fear more than death. More than even Hell.

We are ignorant of the true nature of Heaven and Hell. I cannot live with the knowledge of what I have seen, and I cannot bear the thought of facing the Seraph once again. If we were all wiser, we would walk away from all concerns otherworldly and take up earthly work, for we are unready for the battle. We are pawns in the hands of creatures who care nothing for our lives.

This will be my last report, Your Holiness. Once I have entrusted this missive into the hands of the Inquisition's courier, I shall follow my lieutenant into Hell. It is a better fate than I can hope for. I fear what the destruction of the Order will bring about on Earth. Even more, I fear the Seraph. So should we all. I resign my commission.

Peace (if there is any to be had),
Fra Alexander Marcellus, papal inquisitor

13

I placed the letter back into its box with the greatest of care. Saturday took his hands from my shoulders and came around the desk to face me, replacing the latch on the box. A wordless minute passed between us as he searched my eyes for some inner change, and I returned his gaze looking for some clue as to what question I was supposed to ask of him next. I felt fuzzier now than before I'd awoken in his office. Something large was knocking at the door of my subconscious, and Saturday stood there, expectantly, waiting for me to answer. Something else barred the way, but I couldn't stand the quiet or Saturday's stare any longer.

"Huh," I said.

Saturday arched one eyebrow, sharply. "Huh?" He turned away from me and walked back to the floor safe with the box in hand. "I show you a rare historical treasure, something you *need* to see, and all you can say is 'huh?'"

"Saturday, what does it mean?"

"It means Leveque has managed to resurrect the Order. And since I'm damn sure I was the only one who still remembered it at this point, that scares the hell out of me. And pisses me off." He slammed the door of the floor safe shut, punctuating his last point.

"What makes you think that the Bishop has brought back this Holy and Secret Order? I mean, there's blue robes, sure, but that's a little shallow for evidence."

"It's the magic he and his flunkies are trying to perform. That little reproductive trick Marcellus mentions in his letter? That's a signature trick of the Order. A demon-assisted means of prolonging one's existence. That's one reason why he's collecting such a young entourage."

"Demons?" I barely held back a laugh, then I remembered that Laura Trammler was part of that collection. I didn't buy Saturday's whole "evil magic monks" theory, but if there was any chance that Laura was being exploited, sexually or otherwise, I couldn't risk discounting what Saturday had to say.

"Supposing you're right," I said.

"I can show you."

"When?"

"Tonight. There's a warehouse party just outside the city. It's a recruiting front for the Order. Come with me, and I'll show you what I'm talking about."

"When?"

"Midnight."

Midnight. I almost slipped into a coma where I stood as I thought about all the sleep I needed. It wasn't just the encounter with Leveque that had kicked my ass, but the lack of any restful sleep after a few nights of recurring nightmare. I wasn't entirely sure I trusted the tale Saturday was telling, and I needed sleep. Lots of it. I needed sleep, and a drink with Ruthie.

"I've got a lot left to do today," I said, not lying, but not honest.

"You need to see this, Ray," Saturday said. "I'll pick you up at eleven-thirty."

"You have no idea where I might be."

"I'll find you, Ray. Trust me. Baron Saturday knows all and sees all."

And with that he let out a laugh that was somewhere between mirthful and wicked. I shook my head, and walked out.

IN MY OFFICE over the check cashing emporium, the little red light on my answering machine was blinking—just one message for a change, the voice of Danny Knowles demanding a call back, ASAP. I pulled a change of clothes out of the bottom drawer of my filing cabinet and tossed them into an overnight bag I kept stashed in the corner, then sat down to call the Lieutenant.

"What the hell have you gotten yourself into?" he said, drawling into the phone without even a "hello."

"What've you heard?" I asked, warily. I hated to think that tales of today's adventures had already spread beyond the plush confines of Saturday's office.

"I heard you ask me to look into your runaways," said Danny. "Why, what *else* are you into?"

"Nothing," I said, probably too quickly. "I take it you found something?"

"I found your runaways' mother."

"Not Margaret Trammler," I said.

"Excellent guess."

"Who is she?"

"Margaret? I'll get to that in a second. Ask me where I found Mama Trammler."

"Where did you find Mama Trammler?"

"Funny you should ask. Lake County clerk's office."

"Clerk's office?"

"Yep."

"Which means?"

"She's dead, Ray."

I slumped down into the office chair and let that little factoid sink in. "Who was she?"

"The deceased is Elizabeth Trammler—Lizzy—younger sibling to our dear 'Evil' Margaret."

"So she's still family, then?"

"She's a blood relative. That's as much as I'll grant her." I could hear a storm brewing in his voice. "Took me a little more phoning around to get into the story, but I finally reached—get this—the society columnist for the *Lake County Register*."

"So we're talking money?"

"And how. The Trammlers operate one of the biggest shipping companies on the Great Lakes. I hope you're not cutting these kids a discount, 'cause, brother, they can afford full price."

"What happened to their mother?"

"Lizzy Trammler was the family's designated black sheep. A party girl. Never married. Laura and Ethan are the family's dirty little secret. Laura came first. Ethan followed several years later. Lizzy refused to put the kids up for adoption, and she died from internal trauma not long after giving birth to Ethan."

"And that's where Margaret comes in?"

"No legal establishment of guardianship was in place, so the kids were bound for the foster system if someone from the family didn't step up. By now, Margaret was *de facto* matriarch of the Trammler clan. She didn't think the family could bear the shame of making Lizzy's kids public knowledge, either by adopting them or letting them slip into foster care."

"So she kept them?"

"Kept them hidden away. Hired private tutors and found a physician who still makes house calls, if you can believe that. Those kids have been living like virtual prisoners ever since their mother's death."

"So that's why they don't want to go home."

"They've been locked up, alternately ignored and treated like a nuisance for most of their lives. I wouldn't want to go back to my cage, either. That's not the whole story, though. Here's where our society columnist friend started putting the pieces together for me. The grandmother died two months ago. Laura and Ethan are set to inherit their mother's portion of the estate, a trust fund that falls into their control when they each turn eighteen, but with mom gone, control of the fund goes to their guardian."

"Of which there is none."

"Until dear Margie pulls a few strings and gets herself appointed."

"So now, she's got control of the kids' funds?"

"Exactly. Only now, she's gotta keep up appearances for the court. She lets the kids out in public and tries to make nice, at which point they run off the moment her guard's down."

"So we've got money and family shame," I said

"A dangerous combination."

I sighed into the phone. "What do I do next?"

"I can't tell you," Danny said, "and I don't want to know what you're doing next unless it's legal and I can help rain all kinds of shit over evil auntie's parade."

I chuckled, but not with much humor. "I'll hold her down for you."

We hung up, and I grabbed my bag and walked the block to The Welcome Table where I knew there'd be a hot shower waiting. Twenty minutes later, I was sitting in Ruth's office with a clean body, clean clothes, and a pure heart. Young Ethan was safely tucked away with an afternoon snack and a volunteer tutor. Ruth came in and pulled out the customary scotch.

"Snort?"

"Dear, sweet lord, yes please."

"What's the good news?" Ruth asked, sipping her whiskey.

"Blanks are being filled in," I said, and gave her the quick rundown on the Trammler family drama.

"Didn't you promise Ethan no cops?" she asked.

"They're not involved yet, I'm just calling in a favor with Danny. He all but ordered me not to tell him what was going on."

"So, basically you've got the Lieutenant doing your job for you," she said, grinning.

"I've not been slacking off, if that's what you're suggesting. I had a very productive interview with our friendly neighborhood voodoo impostor."

"Saturday?" Ruth's eyes narrowed.

"The Baron, himself."

The look on Ruthie's face could not be described as friendly. She studied me carefully for a second. This was a common response whenever the subject of Baron Saturday and I came up. Ruth wanted to see "if any of the bullshit had rubbed off" as she put it. She shook her head, took a slug of the whiskey and got back to business.

"We can talk about that later," she said.

"Or not," I said, irked.

Ruth glared, but said nothing. We remained quiet for a moment.

"What do we do now?" I asked, changing the subject back to the matter at hand.

"We need to be careful. Margaret's still in town, waiting for my call. I don't think the kids know about the money situation —at least Ethan doesn't—and I definitely don't want to send either of them back into an abusive situation."

"And that's assuming I can pry Laura away from New Light."

"Any luck there?"

"They've got her too frightened to move. She all but told me she was in danger. And *did* tell me I was, too."

"But?"

"But I've got nothing to go to the cops with, yet. Saturday's got some ideas..."

"Doesn't he always?" Ruth's eyes rolled so far back she could probably see her own optic nerves.

"Can it. He's a little nuts, but he's got me convinced the danger is real and deep."

"I know, Ray. I just want you to be careful. There're two kids' lives on the line, here, and Saturday's interest in you just doesn't strike me as healthy. I know his information's been valuable to you in the past, I just can't help worrying he's gonna ask a return price some day that you can't afford."

"I get it, Ruthie. I'm out of leads, though. It's a direction."

"Just be careful. Don't lose sight of Laura and Ethan, all right?"

I hated it when Ruth went into hyper-protective parent mode. The irrational part of my brain insisted she was being too possessive of my talents, but I knew that wasn't the problem. For some reason or another, Ruth had bought into the Baron's lord-of-the-urban-under-world shtick and blamed him for being part of the blight that made the shelter necessary. This wasn't an argument I'd be winning any time soon. I nodded just slightly at her, but I couldn't hide the hurt tone in my voice.

"I need you to trust me," I said.

She stared at me for a long time, appraising, and then nodded, but only just.

"I need to get some sleep," I said.

I almost didn't growl.

Ruthie couldn't look me in the eyes anymore.

I got up and left.

Twenty minutes had passed before I realized that I'd been wandering the streets of the Missions without paying attention to scenery or destination. Scenes from a rather stressful day were crashing around in my head, and I was letting my sullen mood get the better of me. I'd started today with the singular mission of discharging my paladin duties by retrieving Laura Trammler from New Light.

Almost eight hours later I'd ended up with a to-do list of too-damn-many things that needed fixing, with maybe only two items related to the task I'd started the day with.

I needed to get Laura back to Ethan.

And now I needed to get Margaret Trammler out of the picture, somehow.

I needed to find out more of what Saturday knew, and I needed to get Ruthie off my back for consorting with who she assumed was the enemy.

Most of all, I needed to find out why Bishop Leveque pushed all my psychic alarms up to eleven. The thing I least wanted to do.

I shook my head to try to clear the mess out and found I'd wandered into the edge of downtown. On a whim, I dug Dr. Dealy's business card out of my pocket. I was a block away from her office.

I was taking a chance that the good doctor would even be able to see me. It was close to quitting time for most sane human beings, and this particular one was in high demand. Maybe I'd be lucky and she'd make some extra time for me.

Dr. Dealy's office was on the fourteenth floor of one of the taller bank buildings. She made the bulk of her living counseling the wool-suited set, assuaging the guilt and allaying the anxieties that were so frequently the side effects of a life spent fleecing the little guy. That she could afford the lease on her office was testament to the fact that there was plenty of guilt and anxiety to go around.

I rode the elevator up to her floor and stepped into the small but lush waiting room of her office. A fussy, college-aged man was sitting sentry at the receptionist's desk.

"May I help you?" he asked, eyeing me with a suspicious look. I looked down and realized that the spare clothes I'd changed into in my office consisted of a pair of paint-stained jeans, white tennis shoes, and a grey, pullover sweatshirt. Given the neighborhood, I was out of uniform.

"I'm here to see Dr. Dealy," I said. "I have an open invitation."

"I doubt that, sir."

Of course you do. This was going to require a different tactic.

"All right, maggot!" I tried to conjure up a reasonable facsimile of a drill instructor. "I think you've slacked off enough behind that desk!"

"What?"

"I'm gonna make you into a man, or send you cryin' home to momma tryin'! Now drop and give me twenty!"

"Sir, I need you to please sit down."

"And I need you to come vith me," I said, trying on my best Austrian terminator accent. "The doctor's life might be in danger."

"Excuse me?"

"Ve haff to get to the choppah!"

"I'm calling security!"

I smiled then, and batted my eyelashes at him.

"Please, my good man," I said, drawling like the belle of the ball. "Theah's no need to bring the sheriff into all this. Not on account of li'l ol' me?"

Front-desk-boy's eyes went wide, while I twirled an invisible parasol over my shoulder. I leaned in closer to the desk "Ah'm sure a nice young man such as yourself wouldn't want to cause to much trouble for a lady in such distress." As I spoke I sat down on the desk and started to lean in to the kid. By the time I'd finished talking I was practically sitting in his lap.

"Oh... kay," he said. I could see the gears skipping in his head. "Right. Miss, you just sit right down, and I'll see if the doctor's available."

"Much obliged."

The receptionist frantically punched at phone buttons. After a terse, hushed conversation, the door into Dr. Dealy's inner sanctum swung open and she stormed out into the waiting area.

The look she gave me could have frozen a wildfire.

"Didn't I ask you to call first?" she asked.

"I may or may not recall that being part of your instructions."

"Don't you have a damsel in distress to rescue?"

"Tried that," I said. "The day went kinda pear-shaped."

"So you decided to come downtown and abuse my intern, then?"

"Wasn't the original intention, but he looked like so much fun."

She glared at me some more.

"I had a debilitating psychotic episode while I was storming the castle," I said.

The doctor just barely kept her eyes from bugging out of her head, then she turned to her intern. "I'm very sorry you had to be here for this, Kevin. Why don't you go ahead and clock out."

Kevin nodded eagerly and rushed for his coat.

"'Bye, shugah," I drawled after him as he made his quick escape.

"Please don't taunt the Kevin," she said as she indicated the way into her office. "My interns are all so damn fragile to begin with."

I plopped down in one of a pair of almost too comfortable armchairs.

"OK, Doctor," I said, sounding braver than I felt in the moment. "Hypnotize me."

14

"Listen to the sound of my voice, and only to the sound of my voice."

Dr. Dealy's voice is all I can hear. She doesn't need to ask twice. I sit, relaxed, in the dimly lit room. I'm not sure how long.

"We'll start on familiar ground," she says. "I want you to sit down in a room where you feel most comfortable. Wherever it is you go to unwind, that's where I need you to be now."

Like the beginning of a play, the lights go up on the scene, and I find myself sitting in my living room, my third-hand, threadbare sofa beneath me.

"Are you comfortable?" she asks.

I grunt the affirmative.

"Good. Now, I want you to take a look around. Let everything soak in."

I turn my head from side to side. Everything's just as I left it this morning.

"Can you describe what you see?"

"There's my window out onto the city," I say.

"Is it day or night?"

"Night."

"And what else do you see?"

"Coffee table. Dirty breakfast dishes on it. Empty bourbon bottle."

"OK, keep looking. Keep talking me through the room."

"Cheap rag rug under the sofa and table. Warped floorboards. Galley kitchen and bathroom off to my left. Door to my bedroom across the way."

"Good. Now get up and take a walk around the room."

I do. The floor feels strange under my feet. There, but not.

"Take a good look," she says. "Something's out of place. I need you to find it."

I do a slow three-sixty turn in place, but I can't find anything out of the ordinary.

"I'm not seeing it," I say.

"Keep looking. Somewhere in this room there is something off. I need you to find it. It might be right out in the open, or it might be fuzzy. It might even be just an uneasy feeling, but there's something wrong here. What is it?"

I keep walking about the room, but nothing is standing out for me. I take a third tour around the room and am just about to give up and sit back on the sofa when it hits me. Something in the periphery.

"There," I say.

"What?"

I turn to look straight on at what I think I see, but it fades away.

"Wait," I say.

I turn away again and it flashes in my peripheral vision. Once more, I turn towards it and it disappears.

"Something near my bedroom door," I say. *"But I can only glance at it in the periphery. It's not there when I try to look at it head on."*

"OK," she says, "that's progress. Look in the direction where you think odd thing out is."

I stare at a spot on the wall about six inches to the left of my bedroom door.

"Now," she says, "let your focus go soft. Stop trying to see it and just let it be seen."

I try to relax my eyes, but they're not cooperating. My head aches with the effort it takes to wrestle with my own skull.

"It's not working," I say, trying not to whine.

"Stop trying to force it," she says. "Stand still and just let it happen."

I try to remember what a thousand yard stare feels like, instead. I close my eyes briefly and then, opening them, try to focus on a point a foot behind the wall. For a moment, I feel like I'm suffering from double vision. Everything on the wall splits in two like a dividing cell. My eyes rebel and I close them again, trying to shake off the pain.

When I open them again, the double vision does not subside. Then it hits me.

"Door," I say.

"Door?"

"Another door. There's two of them on this wall, and not just the one into my bedroom."

"Opened or closed?"

I look again. It hurts to look at it. The door is no longer in the periphery, but there's a dull, screaming sound in my head whenever I focus directly on it. I force myself to look through the pain.

"Closed," I say.

"All right." Dr. Dealy is sounding immensely satisfied. "Now, I want you to walk to the door."

"Hell no," I say. Even thinking about coming near it sets off a fire in my head.

"Ray," she says, the epitome of forceful calm, "this is what you've come here for. You need to look behind the door."

Again, I shake off the warning bells and the fire in my skull. I take a step. I'm walking through mud. My feet sink into the floor with each step as the floorboards suck me in. Some part of me doesn't want me to get there, but I fight my way through, finally touching my hand to the doorknob.

The dull scream gets louder. I think my eardrums may shatter.

"I think this is enough progress for one night," I say. I think I may be shouting at the doctor.

"One more step," she says. "Now open that door."

"Pretty sure that's the shittiest idea ever." I am definitely yelling now. I don't care.

"Almost there, Ray."

She's right. I'll be damned if I quit now. Certainly not putting myself through this, again. Carefully, I turn the knob and the door swings open.

The screaming and the fire stop.

Now, I'm hit in the gut with a wave of dread. It feels like someone's carved "here there be dragons" on the inside of my soul. I prefer the fire and the screaming.

I don't remember stepping over the threshold, but my living room is replaced by a big black box.

"What do you see, now?" she asks.

"Nothing."

"Look closer."

"No, seriously. Nothing. Big, black, empty box."

"Is there any light?"

I look around. There's a slight glow coming from somewhere. Enough of one that I can make out corners of the room I'm in.

"Very dim," I say.

"Can you tell where it's coming from?"

I try to focus on one of the corners and see if I can trace the scant light back to its source.

"*Maybe,*" *I say.*

"OK. I want you to walk towards the light."

"*Jesus, seriously? That is not a comforting request by any stretch of the imagination.*"

"Walk towards the light," she says again, this time with a little more force.

"*Fine,*" *I say, beginning to walk, "but if dead relatives invite me to a never-ending tea party I'm gonna haunt the shit out of you later.*"

I walk in the direction of one of the box's corners. I lose count of the number of paces I take, but it seems to go on forever. Eventually, I become aware of a shift in the light. I look down and see that I'm casting a shadow. In the dark.

I'm casting a shadow in the dark.

"*Doctor, I don't like this game anymore.*"

"Where's the light coming from?"

I look down at the shadow again.

"*My right,*" *I say.*

"Good," she says. "I want you to…"

"*Walk towards the light,*" *I say.*

I turn and begin walking again. The letters on the unwelcome mat in my soul start to jump up and down.

"*Want to just grab dinner?*" *I ask. No, Ray, do not ask the shrink on a date while she's using your brain like a playground.*

"Just keep walking."

I do. Now the unwelcome mat is jumping up and down while it's on fire.

"*Something's burning, again,*" *I say.*

"Good," she says, "you're getting warmer."

"*Not even remotely funny, lady.*"

And then I can walk no further.

Something inside me asks me—begs me—not to find out why.
Moments pass.
"What's going on, Ray?"
"I seem to have hit a dead end."
"OK. I want you to tell me what you've run up against."
NO!
Was that my voice? It was inside me and outside me at the same time. I felt as though I was suspended in panic—my own, and not.
"Ray?"
I breathe deep and try to find my center again. I've come this far, and I'm not turning back.
Slowly, I reach my hands out to try to get a feel for what's stopping me. My hands come up against cold. Metal. My fingers close around bars.
"A cell," I say.
Light intensifies as the words leave my lips. A pale, green glow begins to spread out from a point behind the bars. A hand sits at the center of the glow, and the eerie light reveals more bars.
And a shadowy human shape within them.
"Not a cell," I say.
"What, then?"
"A cage."
The person—I assume a person—begins to rise from a crouched position. My heart pounds, threatens to beat its way from my chest. Here there be dragons, I think as a wave of sheer panic crashes down over my head and threatens to drag me under.
There is something dreadfully familiar about this shape. Standing, its body is tense, coiled. The shadows cast by the pale green light make its face seem gaunt and haggard. Hair hangs, stringy and unkempt from its skull. I hear a low growl that starts somewhere in its bowels. A warning.
I begin to back away from the cage, never taking my eyes away

from the growling man-thing, hoping there is still ground beneath my feet.

"Ray," says the doctor, "you're starting to panic, again. What's happening?"

"I need to go. Now."

"What's in the cage, Ray?"

In a flash, the thing inside the cage is at the bars, grasping on to them, shaking them and howling—a sound somewhere between animal and human agony.

I fall over backwards and try to scrabble backwards to put as much distance as I can between myself and this thing, but I can get no purchase on the ground in my subconscious. The howling man fills my view. The glow from his hands is bright enough and close enough that I can see its face.

NO!

My voice this time. I'm screaming it over and over again.

"Ray," says the doctor, "I'm going to count to three, and then I want you to come back here into the room with me, OK?"

The man-thing shakes the bars so violently, I'm afraid it's going to break free.

"One."

It looks up at the sound of her voice and lets loose a angry yowl.

"Two."

It jumps down from the bars and refocuses on me. It raises its hands and aims the green fire in my direction. I want to look away, but my eyes are drawn to its.

"Three."

The dream-room dissolved in an instant. I was curled up in a fetal position on a sofa. My head ached and my mouth was parched. There was a ringing in my ears, and I could hear nothing else but the word "monster" being murmured over and over again.

"What monster?" The voice of Dr. Dealy drew me further back into the reality of my confines. I tried to sit up with great care, unfolding myself into a sitting position in the chair I'd sat down in when I first entered her office.

"What monster, Ray?"

I realized I'd been muttering the word since the doctor had called me out of my altered state. I clamped my mouth and my eyes shut and willed the answer to not escape my lips. I shook my head at her, instead.

"You need to answer the question, Ray."

I held out for as long as I could. I realized I'd been holding my breath the entire time I'd been holding in the answer. At last, the desire for oxygen outweighed the need for silence. I exhaled with a burst and expelled the awful truth, as well.

"I'm a monster."

15

She let me sit in the dim quiet for quite some time. I'd made it clear I wasn't ready to talk about it, so she handed me a couple of aspirin and a bottle of water and let me be.

I sat for a long time, not thinking much of anything, just replaying the image of that anger-contorted face—my face—howling with fury from within an iron cage. I didn't want to figure out what it meant. I didn't want to make peace with it.

I just wanted it to go away.

After a while, Dr. Dealy came back and sat quietly across from me. I tried to bury my head in my chest so that I could pretend she wasn't there, but after a while the sound of her quiet breathing drew my eye upward.

She had gorgeous eyes. They were an incredible shade of violet. I thought to myself that I'd like to get lost in them someday.

Just not today.

"Still don't want to talk about it," I said.

"It's all right," she said. "But, I do want to talk to you. You can sit there and be quiet all you like."

I crossed my arms and leaned back in my chair.

"What you saw," she said, "wasn't real."

I opened my mouth to protest but she held up a finger to silence me. I shut my mouth and leaned back in my chair again.

"There is no monster," she said. "There is only that part of you that you've managed to lock away for the last decade. What you saw is just how your unconscious mind chose to draw you the picture."

"It felt real," I said.

"To the extent that you were experiencing it with all your senses, it was. And, what you've walled up of yourself *is* real. But it's not a monster."

"How do you know?"

"Because you're not."

"How do you know?"

She let out a sigh that was just shy of exasperated.

"I've met a few monsters in my day," she said. "Bad guys. Really bad guys. You are most definitely not one of them. You're a pain in the ass, all right? But when Ruth Penfield tells me you're the closest thing to a paladin she's ever met, I believe her."

My cheeks felt hot. I hoped the lights were dim enough that she couldn't see me blush. We sat in silence for a while as I rolled those thoughts around in my head and tried to balance them with the still vivid image of my own near-demonic fury.

"It was so angry, though," I said, at last. "*I* was so angry."

"I would be, too, if I'd been locked away and ignored for so long."

I had to chuckle at that. Considering the resentment I still felt about my time being an invisible foot soldier in the Missions, I knew exactly what she meant.

"So what happens next?"

"We let you sleep on it, see if any meaning in all this bubbles up to the surface."

I gave her a rueful smile. I didn't think sleep was all that likely. I could still see after images of the "NotRay" rattling its cage, still hear the angry howls echoing in my skull. The good doctor was looking at me sideway, a puzzled expression in her eyes.

"You asked me to dinner," she said. "Why?"

I shrugged. "Panic," I said. "Something absurd to say that might take my mind off the terror."

"So you were being a smart ass?"

Yes and no. "Pretty much, yes."

"Good," she said, although there was a momentary flicker across her face that said otherwise. "It's not a good idea to have a social connection if we're going to continue working together like this."

"I get that."

"Besides," she said, "I can't stand you." She gave me a grin that would've had the Cheshire Cat resign his post.

"What if this paladin just walked you home, then, doc?"

The puzzled look returned. She glanced at her watch.

"It's late," she said. "Probably not the worst idea." She stood up and walked toward her office door. "And you can call me Josie."

It was midweek, and the downtown streets were nearly deserted despite the relatively early hour of the evening. Even under the street lights, the emptiness of the area was disconcerting. I was becoming hyperaware of just how alone I was, how dwarfed I was by the size of the city.

Josie led me on a fairly straightforward route through downtown until we'd walked outside of the corporate zone, then she took a hard left down a dim alley.

"I can see why you didn't turn down the escort," I said.

"My route's not normally a big deal," she said, "but it's later than I usually like."

Normally, this wouldn't have been too trepidatious of a journey. Walking through the ghost of downtown, however, made for a more dangerous situation. The criminal elements of the city's invisible army, those who were brave or desperate enough to venture beyond the arbitrary borders of the Missions, set up shop in the alleys and side streets of downtown on nights like this, searching for the next trick, the next score, the next mark.

The jittery young tramp startled us both, jumping out of a recessed doorway behind a convenience store. He wouldn't have looked out of place standing in line outside of New Light waiting for breakfast. Hell, I might have talked to him already and not known it. Tattered jeans and an oversized cotton sweater, all second hand, covered an unhealthily skinny body which, even in the unseasonably warm and open evening air, obviously had not been washed in days. Dirty, stringy red hair hung over his eyes, his facial features obscured by an eight o'clock shadow.

"Spare some change for a sandwich, mister?" he muttered.

I've been on the other end of this conversation before, and I've been acquainted with more than one street hustler in my time. The beginnings of the DTs were obvious on this one, and I knew a sandwich was the furthest thing from his mind. I enjoy a good drink now and then, but I don't want to be bankrolling anyone's addictions. My standard response to this situation is to offer to take someone to the nearest all-night diner and set them up with some ham and eggs. The truly hungry would gratefully accept the offer, while the drunks and junkies would usually walk away while saying unkind things about my mother.

I got ready to make the offer, but there was something about the look in his eyes that was telling me to disentangle from this engagement as quickly as possible. He stepped in a little too close, and I got a flash, just for a second, that his shakes were as much about nerves as they were about withdrawal. I decided to trust my gut.

"Sorry, friend," I demurred. "Can't help tonight."

Given my read of the guy, I was not surprised by the knife that appeared in his right hand. That one hand, at least, was now steady—calmed by his desperation while his nerves moved on to shake other, inner parts of him.

"How 'bout the lady just hands over her purse then?"

I could feel Josie take a defensive step behind me just as I was stepping forward to place myself between her and harm.

"Let's not get nuts, here," I said, trying on my most soothing voice—despite the rising fear I was feeling—while putting up my hands in a placating gesture. "Put the knife away, and I'll take you around the corner for a hot meal. How 'bout it?"

There was a brief, tense moment as our assailant's hunger battled it out with his baser addictions. I could see the dilemma in his eyes, just for a second, before addiction won out over hunger. Jitterbug came at me with the knife, swinging it towards me in a wide, arcing roundhouse motion. A bad move. He was obviously unfamiliar with the weapon.

I took a step at once forward and sideways, taking myself out of the knife's path and closing the distance between us. My arm shot out, my peripheral vision tracking the motion of his arm, and my hand met his wrist closing around it and locking it. His hand stopped in mid-motion as the knife continued its arc, falling uselessly to the ground. I turned his wrist in on itself, twisting his arm behind him while placing my other hand on his shoulder and yanking his arm upwards. Jitterbug yelped in pain and fell to his knees.

"Josie," I shouted, "get the cops!"

She hesitated for just a moment before heading back out the way we came. I planned on sitting on top of my new friend until the cavalry arrived. My adrenaline was up, and my heart thrummed painfully. My temples throbbed with pain as I tried to get ahold of my breath. My hand gripped more tightly onto Jitterbug's wrist, and I could feel a heat beginning to build where our bodies made contact. As the burning feeling intensified, I began to feel the dreaded and now all-too-familiar disorientation wash over me. The world in my eyes took on a greenish tinge, and the alley twisted around me.

A life flashes before my eyes—a life not mine, and yet still at once I seem to be living it.

I realize I am walking through the life of Jitterbug—Kyle, I know our name is Kyle, now—living it through him, vignette by vignette, as one being.

We are five, and our mother has brought home another new daddy. He is loud and he breaks things. He hurts us, and he hurts her.

We are twelve, and we are fixing our own dinner—cornflakes and sour milk—while we wait for our mother to come home again. She is out later and later. We're afraid that one night she'll never come back.

We are fourteen, and we're sitting in the manager's office at the drug store, waiting for the truant officer to arrive. We've just stolen a Coke and a bag of chips—the first crime of many to come.

We are fifteen, and living on our own. A girl we think we love gives us our first taste of meth.

We are eighteen, and sitting out our first sentence—thirty days for possession. No one comes to visit.

We are nineteen, and longing for the rhythm and security of the prison cell. We steal our first car, looking for a way back.

We are twenty, in and out of clinics and jail cells, and the drug has a firm grip on our life.

We are now, and this couple might have enough for our next fix. We'll hurt them if we have to, although we're frightening enough to the privileged mob where we haven't had to, yet.

It is tomorrow, and we're in a holding cell, awaiting arraignment. The DTs feel like they'll kill us, but no one hears our cries for help.

It is the day after, and we're in jail again. The withdrawal hits us hard, and we can't defend ourselves against bigger, stronger inmates.

It is a month later, and we are in the infirmary, the dehydration turning our body into a husk. All we can smell is death. We begin to dream of Hell.

We are out of time.

Once again, Kyle and I were living separate lives, suspended in the here and now. I felt myself torn—physically divided. Part of me, the part that I recognized as Raymond Walsh, felt pity for the boy. Sorrow, even. Within, however, I could feel the hum and the thrash of something else. Eyes closed, I could still see the image of the NotRay in its cage, and I realized it was not just a lingering memory. Not just a dream construct. This thing was raging against the wasted life before me. I heard a voice, harsh and insistent, calling out from within my core, at once me and not me.

His life has been weighed, it shouted, *and it has been found wanting!*

The part of me that was Ray didn't want to hear this, but the voice was insistent.

This poor creature's life must end.

I felt the burning rise up again, but it did not burn within me this time. Instead it came through me, glowing a pale green. I wanted to hold it back, to suppress the fire and let it consume the thing, instead. The me that was Ray did not want to cede control to whatever this *thing* was, but the thing in its cage demanded to be loosed. It wanted me to let the green fire course through my hands. It insisted I let the fire manifest as the deadly slender blade and consume the sinner. There was an ache of familiarity to this scene. I felt like I had watched this before, but I could not wrap my mind around why I felt this way.

Suspended in this gateway between city alley and nameless void, suspended in this moment, I had the chance to shed that which is Raymond Walsh—falsely constructed, limited, powerless—and let this other me come forth. End the hapless searching, perhaps. End the bad dreams and cold nights passed in strange alleyways.

All I needed to do was let the green fire take Kyle's life.

Simple, now, said the voice that was both mine and not. *One strike and it's over.*

The voice that *was* mine choked back the answer. He didn't deserve this fate. Could I do this? Then I saw the faces of Ruthie, of Ethan, of every runaway I've ever rescued, every member of that boundless invisible army who'd ever looked to the man—to the human being—that was Raymond Walsh.

Now! cried the voice from beyond me.

"No!" I answered, shaking.

In an instant, I was fully returned to the alleyway, still gripping tightly to Kyle. The green fire burned up and down my arms, and threatened to engulf the frightened young man. I looked into a pair of frightened brown eyes, then to his mouth, frozen in a silent scream. His greasy red hair was now streaked with a shock of white, and I knew then that he had experienced his own life in rewind and fast forward right along with me. Tears streamed down his cheeks.

I let go of his wrist, and his body collapsed to the ground. All the while the green fire continued to rise, seeking an outlet.

"I'm sorry," I said. "I'm so sorry."

He nodded, barely comprehending.

"I don't think I can hold this back much longer," I said, indicating the rising fire from my limbs. "You need to run before it takes us both."

The look on his face demonstrated that he did not understand. I could feel the energy insisting on a target. It burned brighter, lighting the whole alley. *That* he understood, and he scrambled to his feet.

"Run!" I screamed.

I didn't need to tell him a third time. He was out the other end of the alley in a flash.

There was a big blue dumpster opposite me. I stretched my arms out towards it, feeling something inside me pushing the fire away from my body and in its direction. There was a whooshing sound of ignition, and the waste bin disappeared in a satisfying green flash.

The alley grew dark again, and gravity insisted that I have a little kneel-down. I was alone with my thoughts. The only sound was that of my labored breathing, joined shortly by the sound of a police car's siren and the clacking heels of Josie, returning to the scene of the crime.

I stood up, brushing my knees and looking in Josie's direction.

"Too strong," I lied. "I couldn't hold him. Are you all right?"

She huddled in close to me, and I held on to her. I knew she could feel the quaking tension in my body, and her eyes were filled with a dozen unasked questions. I would have to answer them later. The first responder was now walking towards us.

"What the hell was that flash?" he asked.

"Damn kids and their fireworks," I said, hoping he wasn't going to dig too much deeper. In truth, I didn't have any better answer.

We spent less time with the police than I'd expected. After the rudimentary "name, rank, and serial number" routine, there wasn't much to say after giving our brief stories, my own heavily edited. Minutes later, we were walking back toward Josie's apartment. There was no acknowledgement of what had just passed, but we kept out of alleys for the rest of the walk as she huddled close to me, her hands on my arm. By eleven, Josie and I had reached the front door of her building.

"Here we are," she said.

"Safe and sound," I said.

We stood there for an uncomfortable moment. I knew she wanted to get the whole story from me, but I wasn't sure I'd believe me if I told it. I was still shaking on the inside. The thing that was NotRay was quiet for a change.

"It's been a day," I said, "and it's not over yet." I stepped back and started to turn away. "I'll phone your office ."

Josie's hand clasped on to mine as I moved away. We stopped there for a moment, hand in hand, time frozen. I turned back around and found her face inches from my own. She closed her eyes, and after a momentary hesitation, I leaned in for the kiss she was inviting.

Conflicting instincts took over. I wanted this. I hadn't been with a woman in... well, ever. As far as I could remember. *Could that be right?* My inner paladin chided me.

Not like this!

Not ever! This from another voice, stern and self-righteous. And cold. *Never with such a low thing.*

Josie pulled away.

"What's wrong?"

"It's been a long time," I said. It was partly true, at least. "And we're drunk on adrenaline, and..."

"Right," she said. She stepped back from me and almost tripped up the front step of her building in the process. "Right. We shouldn't let ourselves get carried away."

"Not at all," I said. I matched her backward step for backward step.

"This never happened?" she asked.

"I've already forgotten what we're talking about," I said.

"Wonderful. You'll call my office for another appointment, Mr. Walsh?"

Ouch.

"Will do, Dr. Dealy."

I could see her face fall as we retreated into defensive formality. Another uncomfortable moment passed as we stared at each other from ten paces away. Then, with an abrupt turn, Josie disappeared inside her apartment building.

I stared at the empty air she'd occupied moments earlier, trying to figure out what the hell had just happened. No good answers were readily apparent, though, so I turned on my heel and began the long walk back to my own place.

16

I had at least a half an hour before I was supposed to meet Baron Saturday for our little reconnaissance trip to the Order's warehouse party—just about enough time to change my clothes and rehydrate. Too little food and too much urban terror had turned me into a bit of a mess.

I headed into the bedroom to change into something appropriately stealthy, and realized just how exhausted I was by this evening's adventures as the siren call of the queen-size bed rattled the base of my limbic system, driving out all other thought. What could a twenty minute cat nap hurt?

Apparently, the evening had worn me down more than I realized. I passed into a deep and troubled sleep, images of what had passed between Kyle and myself in the alley replaying themselves on an endless loop.

I awoke feeling antsier and less rested than I did when I'd collapsed into the comforter, troubling questions careening around in my skull. Why did the thing that was and was not me demand Kyle's death? The green fire obviously emanated from within me, but what part of "me?" I'd searched so long for *who* I was but now I was beginning to fear that I was really in search of a *what*. Ruth and Josie both insisted that I couldn't possibly be a monster, but was my greatest fear about myself a reality? Ray— the person I was certain of at this point—didn't like the idea of what lay boiling under the surface. If who I was was a cold-blooded killer I was going to cling to the reality of Ray for as long as possible. The question was, could I? Was Ray Walsh enough to fight off the creature? *The creature.* Gods help me, I was beginning to think of it as something other than human.

Amidst the woolgathering, I began to get the sense I wasn't alone. There was the thing within me looming over everything, for one. But, there was a physical presence as well. From the corner of my eye, I could make out a broad silhouette in the chair next to my dresser, backlit by the ambient light coming through the living room doorway.

Slowly, I turned my head to get a better look, mimicking the movement of sleep as best I could so as not to appear hostile or threatening. Or possibly tasty. As my head came around, the bedroom's overhead light snapped on, searing my retinas and temporarily blinding me.

"Eyes," said the deep, accented voice of the Baron.

"Dammit, Saturday," I growled through the pain of the blazing light, "you're supposed to call that out before you hit the switch!"

"My apologies," he said, dripping with a false tone of obeisance. "Despite the smooth and refined persona you're used to dealing with, there are many cultural niceties of your strange land that I am still unaccustomed to."

"Fuck you."

"Ah, yes. You make an excellent point." The Baron stood up and began rifling through my dresser drawers, tossing random bits of clothing in my still-blind direction.

"How did you get in?" I asked, then thought better of it. "On second thought, I don't want to know. The better question is why are you here?"

"We had a date," he said. "Knowing your penchant for 'forgetting' and considering your not insubstantial adventure already this evening, I decided to lessen the risk of being stood up."

I'd ask how he knew about this evening, already, but I knew the answer would be something along the lines of "Baron 'MoFo' Saturday" and decided to forego the obvious. "You could have buzzed the door."

"And wake you up so rudely from a well deserved nap?" He turned towards me, smiling. "That would be rather crass. Now get dressed, we've got a party to crash."

THE CITY IS bisected, north side and south side, by a broad river valley that serves to hide much of its industrial doings away from those urbanites who did not wish to have their illusions of culture and civilization shattered. The Missions bordered along the north side of the river, bridging the gap between urban decay and ersatz-urbane gentility.

Saturday drove us over the viaduct, passing out of the Missions and into a sprawl of abandoned warehouses and factories. If he continued along the road back up out of the valley, we'd eventually pass more viable businesses and move on into low-rent neighborhoods before leaving the city limits for the comforts of suburbia. Tonight's adventure would not be taking us into *that* awful alien territory. Instead, we were driving up and down a network of alleys, passing amongst empty warehouses, searching for signs of a party.

Stripped down and abandoned buildings were rarely policed, as there was no actual property to be protected or served. This made the bare caverns of the disused warehouses perfect for all manner of questionable activity. A thriving counter-cultural community had filled the vacuum that was the broken-down industrial sector. Starving artists, wannabe music promoters, and impresarios of hipster guerrilla theatre took up residence alongside the up-and-coming merchants of poison and kink.

I felt the thrumming bass of our target pounding up through the floorboard of Saturday's coupe long before I heard it. Several passenger vans came into view, then the muted glow of the party's light show, and we knew we'd come to the right place. Saturday killed the headlights and engine and coasted down an alleyway, the low profile of the sports car effectively hidden amongst discarded crates and debris.

Saturday was out of the car and moving down the alley before I'd even unclipped my seatbelt. Over my shoulder, I could see him hugging the wall closely, somehow managing to keep his imposing profile in the shadows as he craned his head to and fro looking out for any party stragglers. As I exited the car, he signaled me to fall in behind him and keep to the wall. Seeing no one else about, he began to cross the lane towards the bass-shaken warehouse, stopping long enough to look back at me with an eyebrow cocked.

"Are you coming?" he asked, making his way across to the alley opposite, his eyes scanning upwards at the roof as he turned a corner out of sight.

Walking rather more blithely than I felt, I caught up with the Baron as he stood at the base of a fire escape. Making sure he had my attention, he pointed up, and then hauled a dumpster into position under the ladder and climbed atop with considerably more speed and grace than I would have expected from his large frame. He reached back to help me up. Quickly and quietly, we ascended to the roof.

The roof was a simple and flat industrial lead, with the one added bonus of a series of peaked skylights networked down the center, a glass spine for the cinderblock giant. Saturday motioned me over to the first in the series and we pressed our noses to the glass, our hands to our brows to cut down the glare of moonlight and give us a better view inside. If anyone were to look up, we'd be found out in no time.

Fortunately for us, there was too much fun to be had inside for anyone to be bothered looking in our direction.

That the glass of the skylights had not been shattered by the palpable wave of bass that had been threatening to separate my red and white blood cells since before Saturday and I had left the car was a marvel of engineering—by the warehouse's architect or the party's DJ I couldn't be certain. Despite the structural stability of the roof on which we were standing, my own heart had begun to match pace with the beat of the relentless soundtrack emanating from below. From our vantage point, I could see many bodies—some dressed in the now sadly all too familiar blue robes, others in various states of undress—jumping and writhing in time.

Around the edges of the impromptu dance floor, in almost shadowy corners, pairs of young bodies—along with some trios or more—entwined with one another in intriguing and often impossible poses. A full bar ran along one wall, and the light show glowed diffuse through a haze of smoke whose source was god-knows-what. All-in-all, while there were definitely illegal goings on below us, I didn't see anything worse than what one would find at a frat house party. I was beginning to wonder what had gotten Saturday's dander up so much.

I glanced up long enough to shoot a questioning look in the Baron's direction, and noticed he'd already moved on down the line of skylights, his eyes glued to the furthest one. Whatever had grabbed his attention held it firmly, as he didn't even acknowledge my approach. As I drew closer, he motioned me to get low next to him and have a look, all without ever actually looking me in the eye.

Hunkering down, I could immediately see what had so shaken Saturday. The skylight looked down on a section of the warehouse that had been cut off from the rest of the party room. There was even less light, and the wall between the two sections had obviously been built up thick enough to buffer the onslaught of noise from the other side. What little we could see was lit by braziers around the room's edges.

It was much less populated, with the Order's standard issue blue robes appearing to be the dress code. None of the fleshly display of the neighboring rave was evident but for one glaring exception. All focus in the room was directed towards its center where there resided a single nude body, either sleeping or unconscious and unmistakably female, reclining on some sort of table.

The hairs on the back of my neck began to stand, sending nervous jolts of electricity down my spine. Something about the scene below me was triggering a strong desire to flee. Were we being watched? No, the focus of the room was solidly fixed on the poor girl below us. Then I noticed the strange markings on the floor around her. They were too far down for me to get a clear picture of them, but as soon as I focused on them, I could feel an overwhelming urge to run home and bolt myself behind my bedroom door.

As my calves tensed to prepare and make good my escape, I felt a strong, steady hand on my shoulder holding me firmly in place.

"Don't start panicking on me, now," Saturday whispered.

"What the hell are they doing down there?"

"Sex magic," he said, matter-of-fact. "Like I told you before. The current incarnation of the Order has figured out how to channel all that youthful sexual energy for their, uh, alternative ministries."

I looked back down through the skylight. From a distance, it appeared the girl on the slab couldn't have been more than nineteen, if that. Then I thought of my meeting with Laura Trammler, and the mix of terror and enthrallment that I sensed from her. It could just as easily be her down there, and that thought alone was enough to quell the flight instinct and compel me to charge in single-handed to the rescue, creepy blue robes be damned. Only Saturday's steady hand kept me from doing something suicidally stupid.

"What now?" I asked.

Saturday glanced back over his shoulder at the scene below before finally looking me in the eye.

"Well, I've got good news and bad news," he said gravely.

"What's the good news?"

"I've got an inkling what our little cadre of disciples is planning down there, but all signs point to those dipshits not knowing what the hell they're doing," he said, pointing in the direction of the girl in the circle.

"And the bad news?"

"All signs point to those dipshits not knowing what the hell they're doing."

"And that's bad?"

"Have you ever heard the saying, 'A little knowledge is a dangerous thing?'"

I nodded.

"Well, you could level several city blocks with what these assholes don't know. If they lose control, we're all in deep hurt."

"Which brings me back to the question of what's next."

"Is it not obvious? We pay the dangerous little morons a visit."

"We just gonna drop in through the skylight?"

"Hell, no! You are partnered up this evening with a certified, high-caliber bad ass," he said with a self-satisfied grin. "We're going in through the front door."

With that, he got up and ran back full-tilt toward the fire escape. For a brief moment, I found myself wishing I'd followed Josie into her condo. Instead, I followed Saturday.

We scrambled back down to ground level and scurried into a shadowy alley across from the entrance to scope out security and make a plan.

"Only one at the front," Saturday said. "Not good protocol."

"They're probably not expecting a lot of hassle," I said. "Let's just walk in." I stood up and started to move out, but Saturday reached out a hand and stopped me, his palm at my solar plexus.

"Hang on," he said. "We have an audience." Saturday pointed to a shadowy space between a few dumpsters off to the side of the entrance. In what little moonlight there was, I could see a familiar shock of unruly grey hair. Twitchy Carl was there, trying to fade into the wall while at the same time desperately waving to get our attention. I buried my face in the palm of my hands.

"Friend of yours?" Saturday asked, obviously annoyed.

"President of the fan club," I said. "Let me deal with it."

"Please do."

I looked up and made sure Carl was looking me in the eye, then drew my hand across my throat, which I hoped was the universally rec-ognized symbol for "please stop letting the entire neighborhood know we're here."

Carl caught the message and nodded gravely. I looked to see where the doorman's attention was, and, seeing he was distracted by something further down the other alley, I gestured Carl to come over, quickly and quietly. The grizzled old bum jogged as briskly as his skinny legs could carry him until he came within range of Saturday, who grabbed him by the collar of his threadbare denim jacket and all too easily tossed him behind us into the darker recesses of the alley. I turned around and helped the old man to his feet.

"What're you doing here, Carl?" I asked, my voice barely above a whisper. "Isn't it past curfew at New Light? The Bishop's gonna wonder where you got to."

Carl blew a raspberry and shook his head with his signature twitch. "I'm a g-good soldier," he said. "I know how to get in and out without b-being seen."

"Let's hope so," I said. "Have you been inside?"

The old man shook his head and laughed. "Not my thing," he scoffed. "I just like to keep t-tabs on the boys in blue."

"Well," said Saturday, "why don't you keep tabs from here? Let the professionals do their work?"

"If the b-boss says s-stay away, sure thing," he said, looking up at me expectantly. I hesitated.

"Is he talking about you?" Saturday asked. "God help us."

"Stay here and watch," I said to Carl, ignoring the insult. "That's an order," I added—more for Saturday's benefit than for Carl's.

"Let's go," said Saturday, growing impatient. I turned to follow him, but not without flashing Carl a thumbs up, a gesture which he frantically returned.

"Now!" the Baron said, growling, as I ran to catch up with him.

Lesson number one in surviving the big city is to always give the impression that you know where you're going and look like you belong where you are. This air of confidence and self-certainty covers a multitude of sins, and had served me well in my painful transition from invisible foot soldier to respectable citizen.

As Saturday and I approached the front entrance of the warehouse, however, it became increasingly apparent that belonging, or even the appearance of belonging, was not in the cards. At least not for me. Saturday could pass through any situation by sheer force of will. I was the drag on this team. The party exhibited the calculated and well designed patina of hipster faux-poverty. I, however, had never been able to shake off the aura of the real streets no matter how dressed up or cleaned up I got. I emitted a signal that set off most bouncers' defensive barriers. Saturday was going to need to do some smooth talking to get us through without us having to make a scene.

The front door security man was a behemoth. With his arms crossed, he made a more than effective barrier to the door. The party organizers couldn't have done better if they'd strung the entrance with razor wire. Our approach had set off the alarm in his singularly focused mind. Saturday put on his "we're all friends here" face as he pulled up, nose to nipple, with the human portcullis.

"Can I help you?" the doorman said, the rumble of his voice clearly implying that help was the last thing on his mind.

"Nope," Saturday said as he smiled. And then he cold-cocked the bouncer with a blindingly quick strike.

So much for the smooth talk.

I winced as I heard the bridge of the doorman's nose crack under the Baron's hefty fist. The behemoth, outweighing Saturday by a good thirty pounds and against all logic, wilted to the concrete deck. Saturday caught him under the arms as he fell and dragged him to the side railing like he was a sack of potting soil, effortlessly tossing him over the side to the asphalt six feet below.

I stared at him, dumbfounded and just a little disturbed. He turned back to me, the friendly smile still stretched across his face, a touch of the wild animal heart beginning to radiate underneath it.

"Shall we?" he asked, indicating the now unblocked door. I was slow to respond. He caught the look on my face and the smile quickly faded.

"I'm sorry if I've offended your delicate sensibilities," he said. "Next time, I'll be sure to arrange for our lieutenants to parley first."

I continued to gape.

"The bruiser gets the bruiser treatment, Ray," he explained. "Time to go save the damsel."

I nodded as he turned into the front door.

Before we'd even set foot inside, my pulse had already taken on the rhythm of the bass, the beats threatening to hypnotize me and drag me into the party's heart before we had a chance to do what we'd come to do. What Saturday did next, however, made his takedown of the bouncer seem like an ordinary event.

"Good evening, *mes amis*," he said. He didn't shout, but his voice reached into every remote corner of the cavernous warehouse without him straining, filling the whole of the space with his theatrical bayou patois. The noise of the party could not compete, indeed was stopped cold by his polite greeting. The DJ's show screeched to a halt, and now every set of eyeballs in the place were pointed in his direction.

In our direction.

Awkward.

"Now," he continued once everyone's attention was assured, "most of you may not recognize me, but I'm sure you all recognize the name Baron Saturday. I'm the one who dropped that righteous hex on Bobby V six months ago." Again, that feral smile crossed his lips. "I trust you all remember what happened to Bobby?"

The quiet crowd grew quieter.

"Good. Now, my associate and I are here to rescue a sweet young thing from some very nasty, very stupid men in the room behind you. I recommend you leave as quickly and quietly as possible from the nearest exit before the fireworks start. And, if you're thinking about getting in the way, think about Bobby first."

Saturday paused a moment to let the impact of his warning sink in. There was visible cringing among the guests. I made a mental note to ask him about this Bobby V later, assuming we made it out of this adventure alive.

The crowd began to disperse, young hipsters heading for fire exits left and right. A clear pathway appeared, and I followed Saturday down the steps. A few blue-robed stragglers became apparent as the rest of the party-goers disappeared, staring at us warily from dim corners. For a moment, I allowed myself to think that we were going to get out of this without doing any more damage than the poor sucker-punched bouncer. That was wishful thinking, and a sloppy mistake. Luckily, I had an early warning system named Saturday.

"Ray! On your left!" And I turned in time to see a blur of blue robe streaking towards me. Some deep-buried instinct took over as the streak neared impact, and my arms shot out in a defensive posture, the now sadly familiar green glow engulfing them. As soon as blue streak came into range of the aura, it wrapped him in a cold, green web, and I braced myself for what I knew was coming.

We are on the streets, one of the invisible army. We make a good living panhandling, enough to fend off hunger, mostly. Enough, at least, to keep us away from more degrading pursuits. Still, like any soldier, we look forward to the day when we can muster out.

We are in New Light's bread line, breakfast shift number three. The blue robes are out in force, this morning. They tap us on the shoulder as we pass through the door. We have the honor of sharing a meal with the Bishop himself.

We are working on the other side of the bread line, now. We pity the invisible, and revel in our new found status. We stand in awe of the blue-robed faithful, and we tremble with anticipation for the day when we shall wear one, too.

We are dedicating our lives to the mission of the New Light. The Bishop draws blood from our palm as he chants deep and low in a language we don't understand, and we don the blue robe we have coveted for so long. Our brothers and sisters form a ring around us and chant a welcome up into the darkest recesses of the chamber.

We are blinded and in pain.

We are dragged out of the depths, screaming and scrabbling futilely at black soil.

We are surrounded by foul and worthless men.

We smell blood and dream of satiation.

We see women and feel the lust of flesh rise.

We are bonded to a fetid, humid body before we can take action.

We will yet satisfy all our passions. Human body be damned, we are yet still demon-kind.

The shock of this last image broke the connection with my assailant. We both fell to the concrete floor, spent.

Three? There was me, and there was my blue-robed attacker, but where did this other set of memories come from? Whose life was I witnessing?

As if to answer the unspoken questions, my assailant sprang to his feet, looking more hale than I felt, an animal grin across his lips and a look of cold fury in his eyes. His eyes seemed to shine with a life force that was not entirely his own.

The something inside me that was NotRay pounded at the walls of its fleshly cage, vehement. I know what this thing is—or what it does, at least. I could feel its name, but I did not have the memory or the sounds to speak it. The only word I could make out was the inner being's constant mantra.

Kill!

The now feral blue robe would be upon me in moments. My adrenaline was rising faster, and panic was settling in. I was disinclined to keep the inner creature at bay.

KILL!

I felt my body rise up from the floor, impelled by a power that was not completely mine. My arms shot out in front of me as my attacker poised to strike. I felt the still alien pulse of energy coursing through my center, streaming through my extremities. As the blue-robe leapt my hands shot forward, connecting with his solar plexus, the green aura passing from my body into his, then through it. The room grew still as it filled with a piercing, death-startled scream, followed by a soul-rending, tearing sound.

Blue-robe crumpled to the concrete. The green force continued along its trajectory, carrying with it a form that could possibly, with a fair bit of imagination, be called human. The body hit a steel upright on the opposite side of the warehouse with a wet, cracking sound, and fell ten feet in a broken pile on the floor. It collapsed into sickening convulsions on the cold concrete, trying to scream through rasping, agonal breaths until it heaved one last, shuddering gasp and lay quiet and still. Blue-robe lay at my feet, equally still.

The room stood frozen and silent, current antagonisms forgotten in the shock of the moment as the spirits of newly dead things filled the spaces around us.

Seemingly sated, the thing that wasn't me retreated back to the safety of its cage, leaving me to cope with the slow realization that my control was slipping, and that loss of control had led me to take not one but two lives. A small voice in my head suggested that a nice quiet state of catatonia might be a welcome relief right about now.

In an instant, the dam of shock burst, and the room exploded into chaos. I heard Saturday shouting wildly at the blue-robes to run, and blue-robes screaming in fear and falling over each other to follow the Baron's commands. I let the confusion wash over me, a security blanket clutched tightly as a talisman against my own shattered soul.

Now, the doors to the back room swung open, and the cadre of blue-robes poured out to investigate the furor. Sensing the fear in the room and witnessing the corpse of one of their own set them off. They split off by twos and ran at me and Saturday.

Without a thought, I dropped to the floor and felt the energy rise up once again. It surrounded me in a bubble that closed out the rest of the world and rendered the angry cultists powerless. I shut my eyes tight, and tried to wish the world away.

I AWOKE IN the warehouse cavern—I don't know how much later. The unnatural shield was gone and I felt the Baron's strong hand tap me gently on the shoulder.

"Come on, Ray," he said with no little urgency, "we need to be away from here."

Residual dread and nausea washed over me as I stood up and surveyed the destruction. Around me were blue-robes in various states of consciousness, heaped in corners and leaning against pillars. I could hear sirens in the distance.

"Who called the cops?" I asked.

"Not sure," Saturday said, "but they were bound to show up sooner or later, given the impression we made."

The wreckage of the party around us was a fairly strong testament to that fact.

"Samantha's fine, by the way," Saturday said. I looked up at him, puzzled. He looked off into a corner and I followed his gaze into a dim corner where a young girl sat cross-legged on a ratty sofa, wrapped in a blanket and trembling. "Our damsel in distress, Ray. The reason we let loose in here in the first place?"

I nodded. I knew that, but the events of the evening were quickly taking on the hallmarks of a dream. I wasn't certain we'd done what I'd thought we'd done. The greased eel that was my short term memory was slipping out of my grasp, until my mind settled on images of green fire and shattered bodies—human and otherwise. I looked around and noticed that the corpses had been removed. I shot a questioning glance in Saturday's direction, and he shook his head.

"Later," he said, and crooked his head in the direction of one of the exits, walking away as he did so. Less than surefooted, I followed.

An unmarked police car, lights and sirens blaring, screeched to a halt on the gravel outside the warehouse entrance, and a familiar Ken doll jumped out of the passenger seat before the car had even settled into a full stop. Lieutenant Knowles had his service pistol aimed in our general direction, and Saturday and I both stopped short with our hands in the air. Danny's partner killed the lights and siren, and I could see the growing look of recognition on the Lieutenant's face as his eyes adjusted to the darkness and he could at last see who he'd caught in his sights. His eyes rolled as he looked into mine, and then narrowed as he caught sight of Saturday. He aimed his gun at the Baron.

"Hi, Danny," I said as I pasted on what I hoped was a sincere looking smile, forcing myself to sound much more chipper than I felt.

"I know I said not to tell me what you were up to," he said. "Please tell me I'm not going to regret that decision."

"There's a girl named Samantha inside the warehouse," Saturday said, still reaching for the sky. "She was the victim of, shall we say, unwanted attentions."

"I wouldn't be too fond of your attentions, either, Saturday," said Danny still aiming at the big man's chest.

"Not us, Lieutenant," I said, my cheeks aching from the smile. "Cultists. Blue robed freaks." Danny raised an eyebrow at me, daring me to keep up with the strange alibi. "We're the good guys, here."

"Practically heroes," Saturday added.

Danny lowered his gun and holstered it, making a nod towards his partner. "We're gonna check this out," he said, walking towards the warehouse entrance. "You two, sit tight. I'm not done talking with you."

I sat on the concrete step as the detectives disappeared inside. Meanwhile Saturday, always looking to make new friends, leaned against the hood of Danny's car.

"This is an unwelcome development," Saturday said, somewhere between a purr and a growl.

"Don't sweat it," I said, sounding more confident than I felt. "Danny's a friend. He knows I'm not mixed up in the wrong end of this thing."

"Friend or no, the police will only complicate things now."

"Or," I said, "they could give us a hand shutting this operation down."

Saturday barked out a laugh—brief, cold, and altogether humorless. "The powers we're dealing with now are rather outside their jurisdiction."

I didn't like what he was implying, but I was still feeling fuzzy enough not to want to get into the discussion just then. Instead, we stared at one another, warily.

"Hey, boss." An insistent whisper broke the heavy silence, and an unkempt silhouette appeared at the head of the alley opposite.

"Carl," I whispered, jogging across the gravel road and trying to shoo him back into the shadows. "Get gone, buddy. We don't need the situation with the cops getting any more complicated."

"The girl gonna b-be okay?" he asked.

"Yeah, man. She'll be fine. No worries."

There was an odd look on his face, a mix of concern and terror, magnified by his signature twitchy facial tics.

"Seriously," I said, trying to calm him. "It's all good, okay? Now, get your carcass out of here before Danny decides to give you a night in the pokey."

Carl stopped twitching for a moment, then nodded.

"You need bus money, cab fare?"

He shook his head, still steady and silent.

"Okay, Carl, be scarce. I'll see you later."

Carl nodded again and took off out of the alley at a steady clip, disappearing into the pre-dawn shadows. I walked back over to where Saturday was still leaning against Danny's car. He still looked at me without saying anything, but now he looked more amused than annoyed. We sat just like that in affable silence for a long moment, until neither of us could take it anymore.

"How come you get a fan club?" Saturday asked, mocking.

"Fuck off."

"Well, I can't argue with that."

Danny's face appeared in the dim light around the warehouse doorway. "Ray," he said, with no little urgency, "I think you need to see this."

I stood up and followed him inside, leaving Saturday behind to continue polishing the car's fender with his rear end. Inside the warehouse, the atmosphere had begun to change along with the shift in the light outside. Minute rays of dawn had started reaching into hidden corners, but the cavern of concrete was no more welcoming for them. Danny's partner sat beside the blanket clad Samantha on the threadbare sofa.

"EMTs are on the way," he said to Danny as we gathered around the still frightened girl. The Lieutenant nodded.

"Give us a minute, will you," he said.

The other detective got up and headed for the door. Danny knelt down beside the girl. "Can I see that hand again?" he asked her with a great deal of gentleness. Samantha nodded and held out her left arm, palm up.

"We were doing a routine look-see," Danny said, pulling out the little black-light from his belt. "Guess what we found?"

He brought the beam to rest over the inside of Samantha's wrist and looked up at me, expectantly. I could feel the dread begin to rise before I'd even begun to look down. Slowly, I let my gaze drop to the spot under the black light. I knew what it was before my eyes had even adjusted—a glowing hexagon, six feather sides. I wanted to run, but I couldn't take my eyes away. I stood like that for an eternity, suspended.

"Did you know where you were headed tonight?" Danny said, breaking the spell.

I couldn't force words out of my mouth, so I just shook my head, numb.

"Blind luck, then?"

I nodded, and then managed some voice. "Other case," I said, barely above a croak.

"Fancy that." Danny snapped off the light. "Go home," he said. "Stay there."

I nodded, and began the long walk back to the warehouse door.

"I've changed my mind," Danny called after me. "You call me before you do anything else."

I staggered out of the door and nearly fell down the concrete steps before Saturday leapt off the hood of the car, Danny's partner glaring at him, and caught me before I cracked my head open. The Baron got my arm propped around his shoulder and practically dragged me back to his car.

Dawn would break soon, a cool, deep blue now visible over the horizon. Waves of fatigue flowed over me as my body came to the awareness of the hour while trying to block out the accumulated shock of the day just past. Saturday tore out of the warehouse district as the distant wail of sirens grew louder, and I stared out the window, eyes fixed on nothing.

17

I was conscious on some narrow level of the speeding movement of the coupe, and could feel some innate sense of direction, but the deeper recesses of my psyche were fully engaged with the sounds and images of bodies breaking and unearthly creatures—of terrified girls and strange, feathered shapes. The death of the blue-robed host and the demon that possessed him played on the screen of my subconscious in an endless loop—deaths hastened by my own two hands, cycling over and over again in horrific, minute detail.

Somehow in the midst of my catatonia, I made it home. Saturday set me up on my couch with a cold facecloth and a stiff drink. I looked around, but I couldn't find him. I was tired down to my soul, so I got up to seek the comfort of my own bed. I thought about dumping the drink, but the constant horror-show replaying in my head made me think better of it. I tossed the whiskey back and willed it to wash away unwelcome memories.

I didn't even bother stripping out of my sweaty clothes, but instead collapsed into my mattress, where I fell into a deep and troubled, restless sleep.

I sit at the bottom of a pit with only a dim light—enough to make out the shape of the cage next to me and the shadows of the gallery above. As my eyes adjust, I can see familiar faces looking down on me, silently judging my crimes—Saturday, wise, sanguine and unsurprised; Ruth, white-hot with anger, looking poised to kill me herself; Laura, her back turned and seeking refuge within the hems of a faceless blue robe; and Danny, whose eyes can barely meet mine, whose lips are turned down in a twisted mask of disgust.

I cannot bear to face any of them, and so I turn away from my jury trying to get a grip on my more immediate surroundings. The bars of the cage come into resolve, and I see now that I do not sit next to it. The bars surround me, the cage is mine.

Ours.

The creature in the opposite corner would look like me, if I'd had every last vestige of my humanity stripped away. Its eyes burn with cold fury—murderous and unforgiving—and its body glows a sickening, unearthly green. We stand eye to eye, but somehow it still manages to look down on me, a withering sneer of superiority on its thin, humorless lips. I am an insect under its foot, and it is ready to crush me. This is the thing I call "NotRay," the thing I have been harboring within me—a creature of pure vengeance and singular purpose.

I turn away from my horrible cell-mate and try to will myself through the bars, but its presence demands my attention. Fascinated and yet unwilling, I stare into the thing's eyes. The verdant fire intensifies, and I can feel myself being drawn into the unearthly light. I reach a hand out—to push away, or maybe to touch the fire—and I do not burn. The fire is warm, but comforting. I can feel layers of fear and dread falling away from my soul, my whole being cleansed in the unearthly light. All else is forgotten, and I give myself over to the fire, falling into it, the burning in my doppelganger's eyes enveloping me until there is nothing left but me.

We?

Us. Raymond, the other, and the holy fire.

Peace.

Bliss, almost. A feeling I thought I'd lost. No falling this time. Instead we—no—I float. Weightless. Careless.

Whole.

Then it ends in a flash of silver. A whisper thin blade arcs across my vision, and now I fall. Terror replaces bliss, and now the fire that engulfs me burns, and I plummet screaming into a chasm that looks eerily like a cruel, cruel smile.

I awoke bracing for an impact that never came, and I could feel my body burning. My eyes opened to sunlight filtered through green fire. Primal instincts took over my muscles, my reptile brain screaming of its fear of fire, and my body curled itself into an upright fetal position that somewhat mimicked sitting up.

I was engulfed from head to toe in the green fire. I could feel the residual adrenaline brought on by the previous night's visions pounding through my veins, making it difficult to get myself under control. I closed my eyes again and breathed deeply, in and out, trying to get my body to behave and my mind along with it. With each breath, my heart began to slow and my nerves began to quiet, until I started to feel some semblance of whatever it was that passed for normal within me these days.

Now, like in the earlier visions, the fire felt warm and comforting. Something about it brought relief rather than pain. Security. Somewhere, deep in the heart of my brainstem, I knew that I was in control. Relaxed, I reached down into my inner depths, into the cage where I tucked away this strange piece of me, and I turned the fire off. Simple.

I opened my eyes. The mid-morning sun was bright. Sometime in the night, I'd left the security of my apartment as my visions played out. I'd wandered into the depths of the Missions, somewhere on the edges between the broken down neighborhoods and the dead limbs of the industrial zones. I was sitting in an abandoned parking lot outside of a low, crumbling brick building. The blacktop was cracked and weed infested, and apart from the insects, I was the only thing in the vicinity that was breathing.

The unseasonable warmth of the autumn continued today, or perhaps I just still felt the fire. Either way, there was a cool breeze coming from the west, and it felt good on my skin.

All over my skin.

My heart sank, and I took another look down.

Naked.

Fantastic.

It wasn't the first time I'd wandered off mid-dream *au naturel*, but it was definitely the farthest I'd wandered. It was too long a walk home to take in my birthday suit. What to do?

Crouching low, I wove my way towards a gap between the buildings where a big green dumpster stood. I flipped the lid open started to rummage through the contents. Dame Fortune saw fit to smile on me, and I found the corner of a blue contractors tarp, relatively unmuddied, sticking out from between old paint cans and scrap lumber. I pulled up on the corner and freed the blue cloth from its confines. I took a nail-studded board out next and began to tear a hole in the center of the tarp, constructing a makeshift poncho for myself.

I shut the lid on the dumpster and felt myself freeze for a moment. Memories of the previous evening—of Kyle and the eerie green fire, of dead things, inhuman—filled my mind. I shuddered as images of broken bodies, and of Kyle's white-streaked hair played before me, then smiled—barely—as I remembered the unfortunate city dumpster vaporized in a flash of green light. I shook my head to force myself out of my stupor and turned to start the long, ersatz-clothed walk of shame home.

The image of the fire, however, played in a continual loop and slowed me to a dragging gait. I turned and looked back towards trash bin, a perverse glee filling my heart.

I faced the dumpster, arms akimbo, and allowed a smirk to cross my lips.

"This alley ain't big enough for the both of us," I said. The dumpster refused to budge at the sound of my slow and dangerous cowboy drawl. "You've been warned. Have it your way."

I shut my eyes and reached down into the soul cage where the NotRay resided. Its hand reached out through a crack in the door and we touched, verdant energy arcing between our beings and coursing through the tissues of my body. The surge was tremendous, and my hairs stood on end waving with the charge.

How was it that my body, this fragile, fleshy vessel could contain, let alone control, such power? The fire continued to rise until I was sure that I was about to be reduced to ash. But, my flesh did not burn and my body stood strong. For a moment, I was reminded of the story of the burning bush I'd read in one of the ubiquitous Gideon Bibles one found in the Missions: "the fire burned, but did not consume it."

But, while the fire did not consume me, in that moment I was overtaken by something else, some primal instinct. I could feel my body reaching out toward the dumpster, I was uncertain of whether or not the movement is of my own accord, and it did not matter. Rather than fret over the source, I allowed myself to revel in the power. I willed it to course up through my arms and into my fists and punched at my helpless target.

The fire leapt from my hands in perfect columns and met the bulk of the dumpster. The steel wall caved under force and heat, and the bin collapsed in on itself, fading impossibly to a point, and flashed green into nothingness, the air around where it once stood making a sucking sound, wind rushed by me, vanishing to a point at the end of the alley.

My breath was heavy and labored, practically orgasmic, and I caught myself grinning like a rabid hyena.

"Take that," I said to no one in particular as the asphalt jumped up and bit me on the ass, hard, knocking the wind out of me. I sat, stunned, attempting to kick start my lungs. The absence of power after release was as overwhelming as the power itself, as if my soul had been sucked out through my navel with a drinking straw. Was it always going to be like this? A big bang and a winded dirt nap? Average Ray one moment and human dynamite the next? There had to be a setting on this power somewhere between zero and eleven.

Breath heavy but under control, I dragged myself to my feet. The scrap of lumber I'd used to fashion my little tarpaulin modesty piece was still sitting where I'd left it and I picked it up to get a closer look at it. Time for an experiment.

I held the wood out in front of me like a blade, took a deep breath and reached back down into the soul cage. This time, instead of grasping onto the hand of the thing within, I opted for the briefest of touches, and I could feel just the slightest arc pass between that and myself. I held the short burst tight within my fist and allowed myself to return to the present space, my gaze still focused on the makeshift weapon.

Something shifted within me. *Enough mayhem*, it said. *Time to play nice*. Instead of a sword, I held the wood aloft and allowed the sensation of power to pass out of my clenched fist and into the board. It glowed briefly with the faintest of pale greens, then ignited at the tip, a fire that burned bright but did not consume.

I was in control. There was an immense and still not fully tapped power residing within me, perhaps part of me, perhaps not, and it lay—I was certain—fully within my control. My body shook with an unfettered terror at the thought, and I lost control of my limbs for just a moment, long enough to let the burning board slip from my grasp. It fell to the asphalt with a loud clatter, extinguished. Slowly, I turned around and crept out of the alleyway and out towards the street.

All my worries dissolved as I caught sight of my reflection in a storefront window and I was reminded of my current physical state. I needed to get back to my apartment. I needed to get some clothes. I needed to be invisible for the next twelve blocks before some concerned citizen phoned in a naked guy in a poncho. Fortunately, the Missions provided some natural shielding. I wasn't the oddest dressed denizen of the neighborhood this morning, and the more fortunate of the city had a remarkable talent for unseeing. There was a reason we bums called ourselves the invisible army.

Relaxing into my anonymity and feeling the afterglow of my earlier exercises, I decided to enjoy my walk home rather than skulk. Confident, I did my best to broadcast my presence to the world. The inner power, the SuperRay, was giving me a buzz. The hell with invisibility. I wanted to be noticed.

Look at me, said the thing with my voice. *Yeah, I'm naked and wearing contracting refuse. So what? I've got the green fire! I've got the power!*

No one looked.

So what?

Head high, I rounded the corner to my apartment building.

"They vote you prom queen?"

There was a Ken doll standing in my doorway.

"Didn't I tell you to go home and stay out of trouble?" he asked.

"Hello, Lieutenant."

"What the hell are you supposed to be?"

"I am king of the Missions!"

"Awesome," Danny said in a way that made me feel things were anything but. "Put some damn clothes on and come meet our new Jane Doe."

AFTER A SHOWER and some fresh clothes, Danny drove me out to a park along the downtown edge of the riverbank. The crime scene unit was in full forage within the yellow-taped boundaries around a small parcel of grass at the river's edge. The early lunch crowd had begun to gather a short distance away, held back only by a few patrolmen.

"Someone's getting sloppy," I said.

"No kidding," said Danny. "Five early-morning joggers had already phoned this in before the first unit got on the scene."

"Stamp on the wrist?" I asked.

Danny nodded and grunted, looking at me sideways. I decided not to take the bait, but I knew we'd be having a conversation about my evening adventures soon.

"Another female, late teens early twenties," he said. "No visible marks. Only thing different is the more public disposal, but I'd say it's the same guy."

A crime scene drone scurried out of the way as we approached the body. Her head was turned at an odd angle, and I couldn't get a good look at her face right away, but still there was an electric feeling at the base of my spine. The other thing that wasn't Ray was jumping up and down in its cage. Something felt familiar, and the bottom of my stomach dropped out from under me.

"I.D.?" I asked, not hopefully.

"None."

I sighed and walked around to the other side of the corpse. I stared at her face, willing it to be someone else's, but to no avail. The body returned my stare through the now soulless, lifeless visage of Sister Sarah.

My head sunk towards the grass.

"Know her?" Danny asked.

I couldn't make sound come out of my throat, so I nodded, not looking at him.

"Care to tell me how?"

I stepped away from the body, turning to look out across the river. A few moments later, Danny was at my side. We stood, the two of us, just watching the flow of the river until I was able to find my voice.

"Her name is Sarah," I said at last, my shoulders slumping. "She worked for New Light, part of the religious order, I think. As much as there is one."

Out of the corner of my eye, I could see the Lieutenant turn to look at me, one eyebrow raised.

"She was my tour guide yesterday," I said, answering the unasked question. "And she was very much alive when I left there."

"And how 'bout last night's—um—festivities?"

"She wasn't part of them, as far as I know. Then again, I didn't go there looking for her."

"Who were you looking for?" he asked, his voice taking on a harder edge. Stunned out of my reverie by his tone, I turned to look him straight in the eye.

"My client," I said, trying not to blink too much.

"I thought she was stuck inside New Light."

I nodded.

"Then why was she at the rave?"

"She wasn't."

"But you just said…"

"I said I was looking for my client. I never said I found her."

"And why would a good little missionary girl be mixed up in the arm-pittier parts of the underworld."

"She wasn't."

"Wasn't what."

"Mixed up in the underworld. The rave's sponsored and managed by New Light."

"New Light?"

"It's a recruiting tool," I said. "Sex and booze and worse. The primrose path."

Danny's eyes narrowed. "New Light?"

"You doubt?"

"The most respected charity in the city?"

"That respect gives them a lot of cover."

The lieutenant's eyes narrowed further, but he ceased arguing. "Well there's certainly enough of a connection now to prompt a second look." He knelt down in the grass and gazed over the corpse of Sister Sarah. "Tell me what she saw."

I knelt down by the dead girl's head and reached out. The inner thing was still buzzing from the earlier recognition and I could feel it trying to jump out through my fingertips to get at the residual memory within the corpse's skull.

The dark room again. The smell of mold and damp. Our heart is pounding so loudly in our chest we can barely hear a sound outside ourselves.

The dim light of the open door appears in the far wall, and the shadow of the creepy man fills the space. Fear gives way to dread. We are going to die soon. This can't go on forever.

"Hello pretty," its voice rasps.

The inner thing buzzes again. Rattles at our cage. Something is familiar.

The sound of metal scraping on cement. A tray appears in the dim light and a bowl on it. Grey mush.

"Not m-much of a last meal," says the shadow, "but times are tough."

Again, the voice sets the caged thing jumping. It knows something. I should know. My consciousness batters itself against thick-headed skull walls, trying to grasp at desiccated memories. Everything is slippery.

"Enjoy it as b-best you can," the shadow says, beginning to back out of the room.

We need a closer look. I try to will my mind-host forward, but cannot compel her to leave the safety of her corner. My quarry is getting away, and still the caged thing buzzes.

The door closes, and I fail to scrabble at the dirt floor with hands that are not mine. Darkness descends upon the room as the door clicks shut, and with darkness I begin to lose hold of my host.

The daylight of the park was a razor slash to the retinas as I succumbed to the forced break in connection. Damp from the grass had begun to seep up into the seat of my trousers. The NotRay was still buzzing and jumping in its cage, and I couldn't hear anything for the awful wheezing sound that filled my ears. Holding a hand to my heaving chest, I realized the sound was my own—a desperate gasp for breath.

"What do we have?" said the lieutenant, standing behind me and hovering over the body.

I held up one finger to ask for a moment. Knowles reached down to give me a boost back up to my feet. My body did not feel steady, and I wobbled as I got to my feet.

"You're shaking," Danny said. "You all right?"

"Fine," I said, waving off the attention.

"What did you see in there?" he asked.

"Not sure," I said, struggling to get out more than one word at a time. "Something familiar."

"But what?"

"Too dark. Couldn't see."

"Enough to shake you, though?" Danny nodded towards my still tremor-wracked hands.

Dammit, I thought harshly at the thing inside, *quit rattling the cage!*

I shrugged at Danny and turned to walk out of the park. I couldn't be near Sarah's body anymore. My nerves and my stomach were starting to feel raw.

"That's it?" Danny called after me, obviously annoyed.

"Call you if I remember anything," I said over my shoulder. The flight instinct was kicking in to high gear.

"At least let me give you a ride back to your place!"

"Need the walk."

Danny muttered something unkind, but I was too intent on escape to take offense. I walked quickly through the downtown streets with my autopilot engaged. The wheels in my mind were turning. Every victim of our mysterious basement killer had been connected to New Light. Each one of the girls wore the stamp of the Order's secret party. Each had *been* a girl.

Laura's face filled my consciousness. I had no indication that she'd been to one of these parties.

Yet.

Then again, I had no guarantee that she wouldn't be a guest on the stone table any time soon. Laura Trammler was running out of time.

Whether she liked it or not, she was getting out of New Light. Tonight if possible.

It was time to check in on Ethan, and then draw up a plan of attack for busting Laura out of New Light once and for all. For that to work, I was going to need to pull off the most death-defying feat I'd ever attempted—I was going to have to get Ruth and Saturday sitting down in the same room together without killing one another.

18

The unusual warmth of the autumn had only increased as the day progressed. Young twenty-somethings were out and about town in shorts and sandals, and even the invisible soldiers who were queued up in the bread lines of the Missions and were usually adorned in more layers than necessary in the depth of summer were stripped down a few layers and showing signs of a nascent sweat-sheen.

I found Ethan Trammler sitting on the front stoop outside The Welcome Table, enjoying the early reprieve from autumn and ostensibly studying some classic American literature with one of Ruth's volunteer tutors—but it was rather obvious, to me if not to the tutor, that Ethan's mind was somewhere other than the words of Mark Twain. His eyes darted back and forth furtively between the yellowing pages of the paperback and the lines of the hopeful outside of New Light's mission across the way.

Ethan looked up at me with a smile on his face, but the huge circles under his eyes and the premature creasing of his brow belied the emotional weight his small frame was still carrying. His tutor saw me and finally realized that her student was a lost cause for the morning. She stood up and disappeared inside the mission, leaving room for me on the stoop. I took advantage of the open seat and plopped down next to my young client.

Ethan's focus was now firmly aimed in the direction of New Light's glass and steel behemoth. I joined him in his vigil, and the two of us sat there without speaking for several long moments as the traffic and the late morning passed us by, until his weary little voice broke our meditation.

"She's still in there," he said.

"Not for long."

He broke his gaze away from New Light and turned his head towards me. I could feel dozens of silent questions radiating from his tired eyes.

"We're getting her out," I said, turning to look at him. "Tonight, if we can."

"Who's we?"

"Me, Rev. Penfield. Friends."

"How you gonna do it?"

"I don't know, yet. That's why I'm here. I need to talk to Ruth."

I could hear the gears cranking in Ethan's young mind. He turned his gaze back towards New Light, a mandala that focused his mental powers. For the second time that morning, we sat there side by side, quiet until at last his cognitive wheels has arrived at their destination.

"I'm coming with you," he said. No question was implied, no permission asked.

"Nope."

"I need to come with you."

I sighed and stared at the too-old-too-soon soul in the elementary school body. Ethan met my gaze, resolute.

"Look," I said, "I know you want your sister back. I want to get her back to you, too. You just need to wait one more night. I promise."

"I can help you."

"No, you can't. These are bad guys, Ethan. Really bad guys. They scare the living crap out of me, and I've seen a thing or two scarier than you have."

"I'm not a baby!"

"Didn't say you were."

"Then let me help."

"Can't do that. I promised I'd keep you safe, too, Ethan. How'd Laura feel if I got her free and clear and got you hurt in the process?"

That gave him pause. A battle between passion and logic raged behind his eyes. Poor kid. As if he didn't have enough to weigh him down. Passion won out, as the tears of frustration he'd been fighting back rolled down his cheeks. He stopped looking me in the eyes and stood up, throwing his body in through the entrance of The Welcome Table and slamming the door behind him. Chalk up another victory for me, Mr. Killjoy, a boy's best friend. Maybe I'll volunteer at a youth center when this is all over so I can use these powers more efficiently on larger groups.

Resigned, I followed my moody little client into the mission to seek out the advice of my old friend.

I've never delved too deeply into the life story of Rev. Ruth Penfield. Over the years of our friendship, she's given me cause more than once to believe that there was far more to the good Samaritan than the bleeding-heart mail-order cleric that the average denizens of the Missions knew.

Did I have questions about how she was so easily able to create a brand new identity for my once-invisible, amnesiac self? Sure I did. Was I intrigued by her unselfconscious knack for blackmailing businesses of questionable ethics into providing much needed resources to her mission and to my own unusual enterprise? Of course. Despite all my curiosity, however, I always felt that I was better off not knowing how Ruth pulled off her particular brand of magic. My naturally overactive curiosity was tempered by a devout belief in what she had once called plausible deniability.

However, this didn't prevent me from acting on my suspicions and tapping into what I assumed were her questionable resources from time to time. Today was one of those times.

Ruth looked up without speaking as I breezed into her office.

"It's time for a jailbreak," I announced.

"You're expanding your menu of services?"

"Consider it a new business venture," I said, plopping down in a chair across from her. "Care to make it a partnership?"

I've never caught Ruth napping before. The woman is almost always two steps ahead of me. This time, though, I swear her eyes were going to drop out of her skull, they'd gone so wide. She cracked open a bottle of water and took a healthy swig.

"Ray, I appreciate how badly you want to finish this job, but this sounds like you've passed the point where you should be calling in your friends on the force."

"I am," I said, "definitely walking into dangerous territory."

"So, make the call."

"Three things, Ruth."

She leaned forward on his desk, fingers tented, waiting for what I had to say next.

"One," I said, "I promised Ethan no cops, and I intend to keep that promise. Especially because, two, we're way beyond what the cops can handle, here."

"Beyond?"

"Cult activity, brainwashing. Black magic."

"Ray..."

"No, Ruthie, hear me out. The deeper I get into this, the more my mind keeps getting torn open. I've seen things, heard things. These guys wield some serious power, and it's not earthly power, either."

Ruth stared at me, daring me to continue.

"Just listen," I said. "Bishop Leveque holds onto some pretty awful, old secrets. Each time I've come near him or his inner circle, it's awoken..."

I struggled for the right word in that moment, not wanting to shut down an already tenuous conversation.

"Something," I hedged.

Rather than delve deeper into a losing argument, I decided to show and not tell. I held my hand up, closed my eyes and rummaged around in my blistered subconscious looking for just a brief connection to the strange fire within. I envisioned the psychic cage in which I held the thing at bay and, bracing myself, reached my arm through the bars to touch it. It raged for a moment, looking for a way out through the bars, but once my hand was on it, I found myself in control of the situation. This was, trust me, no small relief. The caged thing relaxed under my touch, and I found myself able to draw just enough of its power.

I allowed my focus to slip back into the room, looked Ruth in the eyes and held out an upturned palm. Slowly, and with some trepidation, I allowed the unnatural fire to envelop my hand. Ruth's eyes went wide, a mixture of fear and awe.

"Holy shit," she drawled, somehow turning the expletive into a three syllable word.

In spite of myself, I let a tiny smirk cross my lips. Curving my fingers, I shaped the fire into a ball and, with an effort of will, I allowed it to rise up from my palm and drift toward the center of the room. Surprised by my own success, I lost focus for a moment and it drifted dangerously close to Ruth's sofa. I could sense her tensing in panic before I found the willpower to rein the green glow back under my control. It hovered dead center of the room until at last, starting to feel some fatigue from my efforts and not wanting to torch the mission to the ground, I willed the fireball into dissipation.

"Holy shit!"

"So you said."

"That's one hell of a parlor trick!"

"That's no illusion. Last night I blew up a dumpster in a downtown alley with that stuff."

Ruth couldn't suppress a good-natured snort at the thought of that image.

"You would," she said.

I smiled as well, willing the images of last night's even more traumatic destruction back into exile. Ruth didn't need to know about that, yet, and there'd be time for me to deal with the fallout later when the Trammlers were safe and sound.

Ruth shook her head, went to her filing cabinet and pulled out her ever-present single malt. She poured herself a small shot and tossed it back without ceremony, and then sat back down at her desk to face me.

"What was the third thing?" she asked.

"You're taking this awfully well," I said.

"Ray, you've been in possession of some pretty remarkable gifts for as long as I've known you. I've known for a while that your knack for missing persons had more to it than some innate deductive powers."

I nodded.

"I'll admit," she said, "that whatever this new thing is scares the hell out of me."

"Scares me, too," I said.

"Good. But, it doesn't surprise me."

"Really? 'Cause it sure as shit caught *me* off guard."

"Self-awareness never was one of your super powers, Ray."

I chuckled, but without much humor. The truth stings.

"Now," she said, "what's point number three?"

"You're the lady with the shotgun."

Ruth did a double-take and almost choked on her own tongue.

"Okay, that's twice you've surprised the hell out of me today. When'd you learn that?"

"Years ago," I answered, grinning. "You need to remember to lock your gun safe before you send me off to round up spare light bulbs."

Her eyes narrowed. "Point taken," she said. "So, how do we do this?"

"We eat lunch, kill some time while we wait for my other special guest to arrive," I said. "Then we conspire."

Lunch with Ruth was cordial, but tense. Saturday was coming, and Ruth was not his biggest fan. I dreaded the potential conflict, and would have moved mountains to avoid it on any other day. However, the success of this evening's adventures were going to hinge on everyone's participation. If Ruth couldn't move past her barely concealed contempt for the shady restaurateur, then my rescue efforts were doomed before they were even brought to bear.

Even as I thought it, the atmosphere in the room changed. Small talk ceased, and all of the attention in the room was drawn to the door out into the hallway. Saturday was here, and his not inconsiderable personal aura preceded him by a good fifty yards. I could see Ruth tense up as the anticipation mounted.

"Let me talk," I said, wanting to diffuse the conflict before it ever got off the ground.

"Why the hell is he even here?" Ruth growled.

"He's got resources we need," I answered.

"Bullshit, Ray," she barely kept from shouting. "The so-called *Baron* Saturday is a bad joke, and you keep falling for it."

I bit my tongue before I said something sharp and regretful. I knew Saturday's larger-than-life public persona gave many people the impression that he was just fooling around. That's just how he wanted it. After all the help he'd provided me in the past, you'd think Ruth could see through the act, but she was too invested in her need to protect me. Maybe we could change all that, tonight. It was too much to expect, perhaps, but what can I say? I live in eternal hope.

The imposing frame of the Baron appeared in the doorway. If we hadn't been sitting down, his presence may have just tipped us over. For the moment, the room belonged to him.

Why do we need Baron Saturday? The earth bends to his will, that's why.

"Raymond!" he said, his voice a sonic boom. "I cannot tell you how pleased I am that you've decided to explore the unused portion of your criminal nature."

Ruth shot a pleading look in my direction, and I pretended not to notice.

"A kidnapping? Wonderful!" Saturday smiled, enjoying himself a little too much. "I'm honored to be asked to play a part."

His eyes scanned across the table where I sat and where Ruth was trying very hard not to look like she was cowering.

"So, then, I'll be the designated professional?" His smile grew wider. "You should have warned me this would be a remedial class, Ray. I charge more for that."

Ruth jumped to her feet. "Goddammit, Ray...!"

I quickly got between the two.

"He's yanking your chain, Ruthie."

"He should watch his mouth in my place!"

"And you shouldn't be such an easy fucking target!" I yelled.

Ruth's focus shifted to me, a look of pure bafflement in her eyes.

"Did you just swear at me?!"

"Yes, Ruth," I answered as gently as I could, "I fucking well did."

She let out a tremendous snort and shook her head as Saturday started to laugh. I couldn't help letting out a chuckle. Soon we were all doubled over laughing, the tension finally broken.

"Now then, my friends," Saturday said, calling everyone back into the room, "shall we conspire?"

A few hours later, we had a plan well in hand. We agreed that the back room of Saturday's restaurant would serve as a base of operations, a location a safe enough distance away from New Light.

"Eleven o'clock, then," Saturday said as we gathered ourselves to depart. "Wear something black and comfortable."

As we made our way toward the exit, the Baron caught my elbow. There was a sense of urgency in his grip. I turned to face him and felt an electric shock strike my soul as I caught a hint of the fear and concern that hid behind the bold and carefree front he'd put on for our benefit earlier.

"Have you thought about sitting this one out?" he asked.

"Thought hadn't even occurred," I said.

"Well it should." He said it with a force that nearly sucker-punched me.

"Look, if you don't want to do this," I said, "then why did you bother coming? Why did you agree to help?"

"I want to do this," he said. "I just don't think you should."

"It's my case, Saturday. My client."

"I know," he said. "It's also *your* fragile little head that's on the line."

"Look," I said, "if this is about my last trip inside…"

"I told you yesterday that you were coming close to the point of no return. I think tonight might be that point."

"Don't worry about me," I said. I was trying to hit back at Saturday with my own words, now. "Worry about Laura. About Ethan. I can take care of myself." I could feel the NotRay thing rattling in its cage as my own rage grew. There was a slight burning in my skull. "Things have… developed."

Saturday took a step back, the look of fear and shock now playing across the whole of his face.

"Ray…"

"Drop it," I said. A growl of something other than my own voice escaped my throat.

The Baron's shoulders slumped. When he looked back up at me I saw something in his eyes I'd never seen before—resignation. Baron Saturday had lost control.

"It's started, then," he said with a sigh.

"Something's started," I said. My own anger had begun to dwindle.

Saturday looked at me with a mixture of sorrow and relief.

"I think," he said, "after tonight I won't be able to protect you. Not like this, at least."

"I can take care of myself," I said again.

"I know," he said, as he reached out to put a hand on my shoulder.

A shock passed between us.

I am pressed up against a wall.

The wall. The thing that separates me from the rest of my history. I have hit my head against it so many times, but now it feels different. Hard brick has given way to sand and fissures. I dig my fingers in and feel the soft grit give way to my hands, so I begin to worry away at the crack in front of me.

I dig with fervor for several minutes until light begins to show through. I open the breach a little more until it is large enough to put my eye to.

Beyond the wall, I can make out, just barely, a road. My road, *a voice says.* My life. *It stretches out past forever. No matter how I try, I cannot focus on its origin.*

My eyes grow tired, and I hear voices whispering.

No, not whispering. Muffled. Loud but indistinct, their clarity marred by this wall. I turn my eyes in the direction of the sound, and through the narrowest portion of the fissure I have dug out I can see shapes, at once both indistinctly human and unmistakably familiar.

The Ray-shape and the Saturday-shape argue. The substance of the argument is unclear, but it's an argument. Angry gestures are exchanged. The indistinct memory of Ray is trying to force something into the hands of the memory of the Baron. At last, the Baron-shape takes it and storms out of sight as my own memory shape freezes.

　Then fades.

I grabbed the Baron's hand and tore it away from my shoulder.

"Fuck off," I said. "Just leave me alone."

Saturday had no response.

"You've been lying to me for years," I said. "We get Laura, and then we're done."

Saturday nodded.

I shook my head and left the shelter, slamming the door behind me.

19

I wandered the streets on autopilot for what seemed like hours, images of Saturday and green fire clashing together in the back of my skull. A coal of rage glowed in my heart, and I could feel the caged thing within me doing its damnedest to stoke the fire. I was only slightly ashamed to admit to myself that I let it do so.

Angry felt *good*. It wasn't a constructive feeling but it was a damned sight better than the fear and confusion that I'd wrapped myself in over the last few days. I reveled in the anger as I walked, letting it burn away at the fog in my skull.

I'd need to let it go, and soon. I didn't need the rage clouding my judgment when I went to rescue Laura. That wouldn't do anyone any good.

After a long walk, I found myself outside Josie's office building. It was past quitting time in the white-collar world, but I decided to take my chances that she might be working overtime.

The hallway lights of the fourteenth floor were on, but behind the glass entryway to Josie's office it was pitch black. A note on the door apologized for any inconvenience, and asked its reader to call the office tomorrow to reschedule appointments.

She hadn't even come in today.

The events of last night must have rattled her more than I imagined. The need to see her felt all the more urgent now. I needed to know that she was all right.

Yeah, complete selfless interest, that was it.

Back out on the streets, I retraced the route back to Josie's condo. My walk took me back through the fateful alley where Kyle had met the full force of the thing inside. Whatever the energy was that had pushed forth from me last night had left a positive silhouette on the wall—something vaguely dumpster-shaped surrounded by an ashy aura. I almost chuckled at the thought of the dead waste bin until I pressed my hands to the char on the wall and called up the image of the poor junkie, white-haired with terror. Any mirthful thoughts were banished.

I shook the pictures out of my head and continued on towards Josie's. Sense memory brought me toe to stoop with her front door, and I scanned ranks of buzzers for the one with her name.

J. Dealy

My finger hovered over the button for a moment as I hesitated. She hadn't gone to her office today. Was she too freaked out by last night's encounter? Would my presence be too much of a reminder?

Would she be angry that I'd balked at her advance?

Whatever. Get over yourself, man.

I pushed the button.

An eternity of a moment passed before Josie's static laced voice came back over the intercom, demanding identity. I announced myself, and held back from letting loose with a rambling story of the past eighteen or so hours. Another long moment ticked by before the sound of a buzzer welcomed me into the inner sanctum.

My heart was thumping at the thought of being one step closer to her, but I wasn't about to let emotion get the better of me. Not this time, at least. I walked up the eight flights of stairs while I tried to regain my cool and stitch my skull back together so I didn't dump its babbling contents on her doorstep first thing. Standing at her doorway, I took a few deep breaths—both to center myself and to recover from the long upward climb.

The door opened, and deep violet eyes were staring into mine before I'd finished knocking. We hovered there for a second, staring at one another and feeling the weight of the air between us. Then the second passed, and Josie's hands were pulling me inside as the door closed behind us.

Again, we stared quietly at one another, and I wondered how far I could dive into those eyes.

"I'm thinking about hugging you," she said.

"I like hugs," I said.

"I'm also thinking about punching you in the nose."

"I like hugs," I said.

"Those options," she said, "are not mutually exclusive."

I opened up my arms and offered a welcome into an embrace. Josie balled up her fists and I braced myself for option B, but instead found her flowing into my arms as she wrapped hers tight around my chest. Surprised by the intensity of her embrace, it took me a moment to return the gesture, but when I did, it felt right. Mostly.

"Is this appropriate doctor/patient interaction?" I asked, not half facetiously.

"We crossed the line already," she said as she pulled herself away from me.

"A momentary slip-up," I said. "Easily forgotten."

"For you, maybe, Mr. Memory Hole. I've been replaying it in my head all damn day."

"Hence the day of playing hooky from the office?"

She ignored the comment. "I've replayed it so much, I've decided I don't want to forget about it."

"Which means?"

"I don't want to be your doctor anymore."

"What did I do?"

"Nothing, Ray. Not a thing."

"I don't get it."

She glared at me and let loose with an exasperated sigh.

"I don't want to be your doctor anymore," she said, "because I would like, maybe, to try that kissing thing again without having to call in to work guilty. I would like to maybe have dinner with you, perhaps even a proper date." She took a deep breath. "And then," she said, "I thought I maybe might like to see you naked."

"Fair enough. So," I said, "no more professional relationship?"

"No, Ray. In this case I'd very much like it if we could tell professionalism to fuck off."

I smiled at the profanity. "Can doctors talk like that to patients?"

"Former patients."

"Former patients."

"Yes, Ray," she said as she flashed a megawatt smile. "I earned my very expensive doctorate and can say 'fuck' in three different languages. Maybe four."

Once more, we stood there saying nothing, smiling this time.

"Are you going to say anything?" Josie asked.

"I thought I was a charlatan?"

"Didn't say you weren't."

"Fair enough," I said. "I will admit that the naked kissing dinner idea has merit."

"Merit? You know, the punch in the nose option is still on the table, right?"

"It's complicated."

I watched her shoulders slump. "You're seeing someone?"

"I see many people," I said. "Never romantically, though."

She cocked one perfect eyebrow at me in an unspoken question.

"That's the problem," I said. "I had another vision thing. This was supposed to be a professional call."

Before she could protest, I gave her the short version of my last encounter with the Baron. I watched as the early buds of lust and a seasoned professional curiosity had a scuffle in her skull.

"Fine," she said at last as she walked toward her living room. "We table the current motion and deal with the memory hole first."

"So the doctor/patient thing is back on?"

She stopped in front of a chair with her back to me, then turned on her heel.

"I am a friend," she said, "helping another friend."

"We're friends?"

"I think so, yes."

"Friends who have naked kissing dinners?"

"Sit down or that motion'll stay tabled for good."

Josie's voice guides me.

"Let your mind wander back to where the wall begins."

Memory runs in rapid reverse.

There is the nocturnal adventure with Saturday, the soul-searing encounter with the Bishop. There Laura. There Ethan.

Every visit from my nightmare flashes by in an instant.

Meals with Ruth. Nights at the shelter.

The face of every soul I've found.

The face of every soul I've failed.

Every day on the street plays backwards, now. Cold nights and hungry days. The images grow blurry as my sense of identity dismantles itself through lost time, until at last we reach my earliest known memory, the first alley, the first morning, and the first question—the one that still remains unanswered.

"Who am I?"

The wall stands before me now, the crack where I left it.

"Tell me who you see," says Josie.

"I can see two figures standing face to face. Saturday and I are talking."

"What are they saying?"

I strain to listen, but have no more luck than I did before.

"I can't hear," I say. *"The wall mutes the sound and I can't read lips."*

"I want you to look away," says Josie.

"What?"

"I want you to stop looking for your past and start listening. Put your ear to the wall."

I take my eye away from the scene with some reluctance and place my ear to the breach in the wall. The muffled sounds grow louder but no more intelligible, and so I strain myself to hear, willing my ears somehow larger.

"...can't do this, right now." The figure that is me is speaking.

"You—we—really don't have much of a choice." Saturday's voice is intense, insistent.

"I'm tired. Drained. If I fight now, I lose."

"Then let's run."

"Tired of running, too."

"Listen, Ted, the Order is here. They've arrived in the city. They think they've found you, and it won't take them long to get themselves set up in such a manner where they can grab you at will."

Ted?

"Then I'll hide."

"You'll hide," Saturday says. His voice drips with disbelief. "A creature with your magnitude of power is going to hide from a secret society with an entire retinue of mages?"

"Which is why I need your help." I began to sound desperate. Shrill. "Take this."

"Ted. No."

"Take it!"

"Your signet?"

"Take it home. Say the words tonight. In the morning I'll forget myself. More importantly, I'll be hidden in plain sight right under the Order's collective nose."

"And if you can't? How will you defend yourself?"

"I'll find a way. I always have."

For a long time, I can only hear the two breathing.

"And what do I do?" the Baron asked.

"Guard the ring. Keep an eye on me."

"Always."

"And under no circumstances—none—do you tell me who I am. Ever."

"What if you need reminding?"

"Then I'll remember. If I have to. But I have to do it."

Another silence passes between them—us.

"I'm doing this under protest," says Saturday.

"Duly noted."

Then the world dissolves around me.

"You got quiet."

Josie hands me a glass of water as I sit up on the sofa in her living room.

"I was listening," I said. "Just like you suggested."

"Did you hear anything useful?"

For a moment, I considered telling her everything—the part of the story I'd left out. If there was a relationship in the offing, I preferred to have it without secrets. I took a deep breath and prepared to spew the whole enchilada, and then I tried to imagine what I'd think if I were just a normal guy and I was hearing my story for the first time. Hell, I'd *lived* the story and it made me want to run screaming from the condo.

"Heard lots," I said, and let the held breath sigh from my lungs. "Hard to say if it's important, yet."

"Y'know," said Josie, "you get a little more terse with your speech when you're avoiding the answers."

"It's between me and Saturday," I said, and hoped that put an end to the interrogation.

Josie glared at me for a moment, then her look softened.

"Fair enough," she said. She stood up and walked toward the kitchen. "Hungry?"

I lost my bearings in the speed with which she changed mood and subject. Josie poked her head back around the corner and mimed shoveling food into her mouth. "Do you eat?" she asked me in a tone more appropriate for a five year old, which is to say that in the moment she spoke to me at my own level.

"Hungry," I said. "Yes."

"Steak sound good?"

"It's the most beautiful word I've ever heard."

I heard a refrigerator door open and close, and the rustle of butcher paper on the counter. A second later, Josie walked briskly back into the living and room and past me.

"Those'll need to rest for a few minutes," she said as a fabric blindfold fell over my head. I pulled the offending textile off to find Josie's blouse in my hand. I looked behind me just in time to catch a glimpse of her in the doorway to her bedroom. She looked at me over her shoulder with a mischievous grin, unclasped her bra and disappeared into the room.

I, being a red-blooded American male—and also not an idiot— took the only reasonable course of action given the situation.

I followed her.

THERE WAS A level of aggression contained within Josie that I hadn't expected. She approached lovemaking with a singularity of focus, riding atop me as if there was a race to be won. Not that I was complaining.

I picked up my own pace, feeling an equal and intense animal urgency rising within me. The more my own ardor increased, the more I could feel the creature within me—the thing that was NotRay—attempting to break free. I found myself in a quandary of divided attention—focusing desperately on impending sexual ecstasy, all the while fighting a losing battle to keep the otherworldly interloper well and clear of what should have been a private moment.

It was a losing battle. As Josie reached her climax, my attention shifted fully towards her, and the creature broke through.

And I knew her.

Not just *carnally*. I knew *Josie*, the totality of her.

We are six, standing in the cemetery, unable to understand why daddy's not coming back.

We are ten, coming home from school to an empty house. The television is our best friend.

We are fourteen, and mama's been committed.

Fifteen, and the mean girls beat us up every day.

The years rush into consciousness at frightening speed, now.

First kiss. College. Boyfriend. Girlfriend. Graduation grad school research assistant newlywed failed marriage independent alone isolated alone cold alone successful alone alone.

Alone.

This moment.

Alone.

The bedroom came crashing back into my awareness. I felt as though a weight had been lifted from me and sat up to realize that Josie was no longer in the bed. In a dim corner of the bedroom, she sat huddled on the floor with the bedspread wrapped around her. She was shaking.

"Go," she said, her voice barely above a whisper and yet somehow still dripping with anger.

"You saw?"

"Go," she said, her voice rising to a near primal shriek.

"I didn't mean..."

"...to hurt me? Of course you didn't. No one means to hurt me."

"It won't happen again."

"What, exactly is *it*?"

How do I answer that question? I must have remained silent for too long.

"That's what I thought," Josie said. She stood up, keeping the bedspread wrapped tightly around her.

"I'm sorry," I said.

"I know, but that's..." she left the thought unfinished. "I need a shower. Be gone before I get out."

With that, she padded out of the room and I heard a door close behind her. I sat on the bed frozen with shame.

20

It was evening by the time I made my way to the French Quarter. I took a long slow walk from Josie's condo and tried to let the cool evening breeze slough off the waves of confusion and shame I felt.

I lost control!

I'd been so proud of myself this afternoon when I sat in Ruth's office and played silly games with the green fire. Of course—*stupid!*—the visions were connected to the other-than-human thing within me. I'd been so wrapped up in the chance to be with Josie I never even considered the possibility that I'd be bringing a third wheel along for the date, or that the third wheel was—*goddammit!*—me.

I had a lot left to learn about who I really was if I was going to have any chance at achieving something that even remotely resembled a normal relationship. And it looked like Saturday had all the answers.

Saturday.

There was another relationship I was going to have to mend somehow. His general obtuse approach to the mystery that was me had become a focus for all my frustration. I'd taken my rage out on him and now it turned out that his practice of *omerta* whenever I probed too deeply into my story was my own fault, or the fault of whoever I was—*Ted?*—before the memory scramble. I needed the Baron if I was going to learn who I was. Who I am.

Hell, I needed the Baron if I was going to live through tonight's little adventure. Laura Trammler still needed to be extracted from the clutches of New Light, and I had almost lost sight of that fact in the midst of all my personal drama.

Get over yourself, Ray! Do the job at hand, then *deal with the soap opera.*

The back bar inside the French Quarter was dim. A lone figure stood behind wiping at the inside of a highball glass at the far end. I bellied up to a chair in the middle.

"Bourbon," I said, calling out to the barkeep. "Rocks."

"Not the best choice before an evening of kidnapping," said Saturday. He turned around and pulled the wax-topped bottle from the middle shelf, dropped a few cubes in an old fashioned glass and poured two generous, Saturday-sized fingers of the sweet amber liquid. "However," he said, "seeing as tonight might be your last night on earth, I'm inclined to make an exception."

I took a long, slow sip. Saturday just watched me and said nothing else. I stared into the bottom of the glass, trying to read the omens in the swirling eddies of melting ice in the whiskey, but no wisdom was forthcoming. Finally, I looked up at the Baron. If he was angry at me over my earlier outburst he betrayed nothing. Angry or not, I decided the high road was the best course to take.

"I'm sorry," I said, not for the first time tonight.

A small, sad smile passed across his face.

"Ray," he said, "I've known you a long time. Longer than you know." He grew quiet again, pensive, and then I watched as the small, sad smile was replaced by the biggest shit-eating grin I'd ever seen. "I'm amazed you haven't torn me a new one sooner."

I started to laugh with him, but found I was blinking back tears soon after. I've made many people's lives a little hellish with my deci-mated memories and the side effects that come along with it. This day had been an example of the worst it could be. Forgiveness, from any corner, was sweet relief.

"Finish your drink," Saturday said. "We have to get going, soon."

As if on cue, Ruth Penfield blew into the bar. "One hour to D-Day and you two are already bombing your livers?"

"We're just toasting Ray's impending demise," Saturday said.

The woman behind us was a completely different person from the one I knew. Gone were the relaxed jeans and camp shirts of the Missions stern-but-compassionate den mother. Instead, Ruth wore a pair of pants obviously designed for field combat and dyed a jet black. On top, she wore an equally black t-shirt that fit snugly about her arms. I'd always thought of Ruth as a stocky woman, spreading out with age. Dressed for action, I realized that much of what I thought was fat had been muscle all along. Her biceps alone would make a body-builder envious. A tattoo on her forearm—a huge broadsword pierced through a skull—hinted at an interesting past.

"We're trying to run a precision operation, here," she said. "Be nice if you both could stay sharp."

I could tell by the twinkle in her eye that she was having us on. Underneath that mischievous glint, however, a different story was being told. Ruth was nervous, maybe even frightened. There was a twitch to her playful demeanor that told me she hadn't made up her mind whether or not she'd bolt before the rescue operation got underway.

"Relax," I told her, "I'm here, now."

"That's real comforting," she said, a sardonic drawl escaping her throat.

"There's always Saturday," I offered.

"Even better," Ruth answered. "Tonight we get to find out just how full of shit that con artist really is."

"No more full of shit than you."

As usual, Saturday called the entire focus of the room onto himself. He looked dangerous, to say the least, dressed all in black—coveralls, gloves, and a pair of calf high tactical boots. His chauffeur, André, had entered the bar and stood just behind him. The body man was wearing his usual black suit and skinny tie, but he looked no less formidable than his boss. The telltale outline of the customary nine millimeter under his suit coat had been replaced by a larger protuberance.

"Now then..." Ruth's voice cut through the momentary distractions. She waited briefly with one eyebrow cocked, daring us to ignore her. "It'll be one a.m. in twenty minutes time," she said once focus had shifted back her way. "Let's review the drill."

"Sir, yes sir," I said, doing my best Private Pyle impression and throwing up an awkward salute.

"Thanks," she said, not meaning it in the slightest. "At one, we load up in Saturday's SUV. André's driving.

"André waits outside, ready for the getaway. I sweep security, Saturday gets us inside, and Ray puts his talents to work."

"If it ends up being that easy," Saturday interrupted, "we should all be worried."

"It's a church shelter," Ruth answered, "a fancy one, to be sure, but it's not a Federal Depository. You wanna rally the storm troopers together, go right ahead, but I swear it'll be overkill."

I felt an uncomfortable twinge in my gut. My head agreed with Ruth, but something deeper was trying to get my attention, screaming through a concrete wall that Saturday was right. It *was* just a shelter. A piercing, forbidding, headache and hallucination inducing shelter— but a shelter. I quelled the urge to second Saturday's objection.

"You're still bringing the shotgun?" I asked.

Ruth looked over at me and I saw a most disturbing grin spread across her face.

"Oh, yes," she said. "She's all ready to go."

I caught Saturday looking at me out of the corner of his eye. He looked worried. It was a look I wasn't used to seeing from him, and I found his mood slightly infectious. Meanwhile, Ruthie had pulled her weapon of choice from out of the duffle bag she'd walked in with.

She slung the pump action shotgun over her shoulder. It had been freshly cleaned, and I could smell the gun oil as it cut through the ghost of bourbon that still haunted the back of my throat. The gun's blued barrel practically glowed, and its wood stock had been custom finished to match the blue-black of the steel. A glossy copy of a Varga pinup had been painted onto the ebony stock. Bettie Page.

"Say 'Hi' to the gang, Bettie," Ruth said, practically cooing. "We're going out on the town for once."

Saturday's eyebrows tried to crawl up to the top of his bare head.

"Behave, and we'll do this more often." Ruth nuzzled the gun. "Saddle up, everyone," she called out behind her as she reached the front door. "Time to save the princess, Bettie."

I began to follow the Reverend out the door. I could still hear her talking to the shotgun.

Saturday fell in step beside me.

"Is that normal behavior?" he asked.

"I wouldn't know," I said. "Committing felony mayhem is not on our usual list of things to do together."

"Ray," he said, "I've lived a long time, seen a lot of freaky things. I only tell you this so you'll understand just how serious I am when I tell you," at this he pointed his head in Ruth's direction, "that I am goddamned *disturbed*, right now."

I laughed. There wasn't much merriment to it.

IT NEVER CEASES to be a shock just how empty and alien the Missions become after the witching hour. In daylight it crawled with perpetual bread lines. Now, it was just past one o'clock in the morning, the streets outside New Light's mission were deserted, and the block had become a ghost town.

André pulled Saturday's SUV into an alley a block over, then killed the engine and lights.

"Keep the phone nearby," Saturday told him. "Be ready to swing in to the rescue when I call."

André nodded, barely, and settled back into the driver's seat as we exited the truck. Saturday led the way, taking us down the block and passing the front of New Light from the other side of the street. We walked on down the block, following in the big man's footsteps, passing right by the mission.

Ruth coughed, trying to get Saturday's attention, but the Baron just held his hand up for quiet. At the next block, he turned down an alley and into the shadows. Reluctantly, we followed.

"Two night watchmen inside the foyer," he said. "No one else in the vicinity. In about two minutes, one of the rent-a-cops will step outside to make a quick sweep of the front sidewalk. If we play this right, we can walk in through the front door."

"How do we slip by them?" Ruth asked, cradling Bettie with a gleam in his eye.

Saturday placed his palm on the shotgun's barrel and lowered the muzzle to the sidewalk.

"Bettie's backup," he said. "A last resort. Leave the mooks to me."

With that, he walked out of the alley and crossed the street, motioning us to follow him. Rather blithely, and without any pretense at sneaking around, Saturday walked up the street on the mission's side with the two of us in tow and casually approached the front door.

Just as Saturday predicted, one of the navy-blazered security goons swung open the heavy tempered glass of New Light's front door and stepped outside.

"*Bon soir,*" Saturday hailed the guard with a cheery voice. The mook looked in the Baron's direction just long enough for the damage to be done. Saturday muttered something in a language I didn't understand and placed his hand on the guard's head, thumb and pinky spanning his temples.

The guard froze, eyes glassy, holding the door open for us.

Convenient.

Saturday walked into the mission as if he owned the place, turning at the mouth of the foyer to look at us, a canary-eating cat's grin on his face.

"Dear friends," he said, "shall we make ourselves at home?"

As Ruth and I walked in the door, the second guard came running towards the Baron.

"Hey!" he shouted, his hand moving towards his radio.

Without looking, Saturday reached behind him, muttering under his breath again, and took hold of the poor guard's head. Mook number two stopped dead in his tracks, as frozen and as vacant-eyed as his partner.

Saturday cocked his head towards the center of the foyer and we followed him.

"Nice trick," I said. "Any reason why you couldn't have tried that on the doorman at the warehouse last night?"

"Didn't want to," he said. "Sometimes, a guy just needs a good punching."

"What exactly did you do?" Ruth asked, incredulous, as we made our way towards the security desk.

"Essentially," Saturday answered, "I paused them. Everything around them has become, as far as they're concerned, invisible. Their minds are trying to adjust."

"Uh-huh," Ruth said with a skeptical grunt.

"Most minds are very susceptible to suggestion. Easily clouded."

"So, what," she said. "You're like the Shadow, now, or something?"

"No," Saturday said, a mischievous smile playing across his lips.

"Not *like*. Or something." With that, he went about playing with the security computer.

Minus the clicking of the terminal keys, it was quiet enough to hear the wheels turning in Ruth's brain.

"No," she said. "No, don't even try to tell me..."

"I'm trying to work, here," Saturday interrupted.

"You are not the goddamned Shadow!"

Saturday looked up from the computer. "Who knows," he intoned in a spooky baritone, "what evil..."

"Knock it off. You weren't even sperm in 1940."

"If you're good, and we make it out of here alive, I'll show you my autographed photo from Orson Welles," he grinned. The security terminal beeped. Saturday put his hand up to stop the argument. "There's our damsel," he said. "Ninth floor. West wing. Number 936."

"We should take the stairs," Ruth said, irritation momentarily forgotten and back to business.

"Agreed." Saturday toyed with the keyboard some more. "I'm faking an alarm on another floor," he said. "That should buy us some time. Let's go."

Together, we rushed for the west stairwell. Well over our heads, the faint sound of an alarm went off. I worried for a moment that we might end up calling unwanted attention to ourselves, but Saturday hadn't steered us wrong yet. Now was not the time for second guessing.

The stairwell door was locked. Saturday tried to force it open, but couldn't get enough force behind his shoulder.

"Stand back," Ruth said, and swung the butt of her shotgun down on the door handle. There was an unmistakable sound of metal shearing. She nodded to the Baron, who charged the door one last time, nearly sending it flying off its hinges as the latching hardware gave way.

The slamming sound could be heard echoing up the shaft of the stairway.

"So much for quick, quiet, in and out," I said as we began our ascent.

Saturday moved quickly up the stairs for a man his size. I could barely keep up, but the adrenalin boost was a welcome addition to my body chemistry at the moment. Ruth brought up the rear, a good half flight behind us.

We could hear the alarm grow louder as we approached the ninth floor. The door at the landing was not locked from the stairwell side, and we emerged into a dimly lit corridor. We could hear the commotion growing several floors above us, while not a creature stirred on the residential level. Saturday's hack-fu had been a wise move. Scanning the door numbers in front of us, I made a quick mental map of where Laura would be and pointed to my right, indicating the corridor that met the one we were currently in, and then my left, showing which direction we should turn.

Saturday nodded, tapped Ruth on the shoulder, and the two of them moved quickly and quietly down the corridor, sticking close to either wall. Both of them moved with a practiced sure-footedness that they could not have learned from the daily grind of restaurant-owning and homeless-sheltering. They swept either side of the intersecting corridor, Ruth's beloved Bettie held out in front of her like a protective talisman, Saturday's Browning a natural extension of his own hand. The Baron looked back over his shoulder at me and nodded the all clear. With a deliberation that belied my lack of calm, I worked my way towards the corridor, taking the left turn and counting the doors until I came to Laura's room.

The adrenalin in my bloodstream kicked into overdrive, and I felt a soaring intensity in the rhythm of my heartbeat. This was it. Now or never. All I had to do was open the door. Somewhere in the gilded cage in my soul, I felt the beast who was NotRay straining at its chains. It feared nothing—perhaps even craved the conflict. How could I hold it back? All it wanted was to dispatch its duty. In the face of the creature's fury, I felt shame in my hesitation and gave some slack to its bonds.

At once my hand began to move, not of my will or my doing. I became a spectator to my own body, and I watched my hand touch the brass knob, felt the cold metal on my skin, felt my wrist turn as my arm pushed the portal forward. The door swung into the room, easy and quiet on well-oiled hinges. The glow of a flashlight arced over my shoulder and pierced the darkness ahead of me, revealing the girl.

Laura Trammler slept. She lay still, her breath a deep pulse. All around us, the sound of commotion grew. The alarm was loud enough now to wake the dead—and still, Laura slept.

A chill passed among us.

"That ain't natural," Ruth said.

Saturday grunted his concurrence. "Grab her and let's go," he said. "Security is not going to stay distracted for much longer."

The command in his tone brought me back to the land of the living, my fear and my struggle with the beast's chains momentarily forgotten. Conscious now, I stepped into the room and scooped the spellbound girl into my arms, carrying her out into the hall.

As if on cue, the stairway door we had entered flew open, and two navy-blazered guards stepped into the corridor behind us. Noticing our unwelcome intrusion and the sleeping heap of New Light resident in my arms, they drew their guns in unison and began shouting incoherent commands. Ruth stepped around me, raising Bettie to her shoulder, and fired a round over their heads. The muzzle flash sent the guards diving for cover.

"Go! Go!" she yelled over her shoulder, and I felt Saturday's strong hand nudging my shoulder, urging me in the direction of the next stairwell. "Bettie won't hold them back for long. Get down the stairs." With that, he pulled out his phone to order our getaway. As we turned into the stairway, I heard the roar from Bettie's other barrel.

Laura was now slung over my shoulder, still sleeping her deep and creepy sleep, as the three of us burst back into the still deserted, still quiet lobby. Over our heads, we could no longer hear alarms or commotion.

Ruth's target practice dummies had not chased after us, nor had any of the other security mooks made an appearance. For all our earlier panic, we may as well have walked down the stairs considering the current lack of alarm.

"Too easy," Saturday muttered, his head shaking.

"Don't complain," said Ruth.

"Too fucking easy," Saturday repeated. He looked at the phone in his hand. "Now André's not answering."

A look crossed his face that I'd never seen before. It was a look of worry, and this alien affect began to suck what little confidence remained out of our little hunting party.

"Saturday," Ruth said, pointing in the direction of the front door. There, under the dim glow of the streetlight was the Baron's SUV. Saturday's shoulders slumped with some relief.

"Smart son-of-a-bitch," said Ruth. "Heard the phone ring and came running. Why waste time talking, right?"

The three of us rushed for the door before the security team decided to change its mind about letting us walk out alive.

"Still too easy." The Baron voice was shaking.

We flung open the doors and jumped into waiting, running truck.

"Let's get back to the restaurant," Saturday ordered as I lay Laura's comatose body across the back seat. The engine did not rev. The vehicle did not move.

"Oh, shit," Saturday whispered, with a tinge of fear I'd never before heard in his voice. We all turned to look up front.

André's lifeless body slumped low in the passenger seat. The garrote that had squeezed out his dying breaths had been tied in a neat and perfect bow around his neck—an unmistakable message, an unwanted and grotesque gift.

For what seemed like an eternity, we all stopped and stared. None of us master strategists had bothered to plan for this eventuality. We did not know what to do.

The bullet ricocheting off the SUV's hood snapped us out of our painful stupor. Several more shots were fired, throwing sparks off of Saturday's thick, bullet-proof glass.

The Baron muttered a hasty, "Forgive me," under his breath, then threw open the driver's door and booted the freshly minted corpse of his right-hand man out of the truck, hopping into the driver's seat as he did so, and squealing the tires as he sped out into the pitch dark streets of the Missions after midnight.

For a long while, I stared out the back window, looking for the chase that did not come. It did not need to. The damage was done. I settled into my seat and looked ahead. Saturday was deathly quiet, but in the rearview mirror I could see the tears that flowed freely down his cheeks.

All the while, Laura Trammler slept.

21

It was after two in the morning, and too quiet in the back rooms of the French Quarter. Saturday had retreated to his private office before the SUV's engine was cold, leaving Ruth and me to carry the still catatonic body of Laura Trammler into the restaurant's back room bar.

Now, more than an hour had passed, Saturday was still in hiding, and Laura still slept. We'd tried to wake the girl as gently as possible, but Ruth insisted that without understanding the nature of the cause of her unnatural torpor, we needed to refrain from interfering.

"Besides," she reminded us while looking pointedly at Saturday's closed door, "your resident expert in all things unnatural has gone into hiding."

Before tonight, I don't think any of us had every given a moment of thought to the people in Saturday's employ, or to his relationships with them. André had been my shadow, an extra set of eyes for my mysterious guardian and informant, nothing more. Now, Saturday's grief over the loss of his body man had become a tangible thing. It weighed on both of us. Even the good Rev. Penfield, who would normally be the first to laugh off an awkward moment, and whose first instinct might be to drag the mourner out of his office and back to work, even she hung back, too affected to dare cross the man's threshold.

As time went on, however, we began to feel more and more desperate. Even without the loss of André, the rescue of Laura Trammler was a pyrrhic victory as long as she remained comatose. It meant Leveque knew we were coming, or at least suspected so. And that meant that while we'd liberated her body, Laura Trammler's mind was still firmly in the grasp of the Order.

And we'd brought her possessed self right into our midst.

"I know I've counseled caution," Ruth said to me, "but the longer this goes on, the more uncomfortable I get."

"I'm right there, with you."

"I feel sorry for Saturday, but maybe we need to get him back to work, get his mind off things."

"I'll knock on his door again," I said. "I doubt I'll be able to drag him out, though."

"Well, someone needs to give us a clue what the next step is, here," Ruth said. "Laura's out. Who knows what's happening to her mind in the meantime?"

I nodded. I had some ideas about what might be going on in the girl's head. None of them were particularly pleasant.

I rapped out a soft knock on the door to Saturday's office. No one answered. Then again, no one told to me to get lost either. I turned the door handle and found it unlocked.

The room was barely illuminated by the lamp on Saturday's desk. I could hear him talking in hushed tones, and as my eyes adjusted to the dim, I could see that he'd carried the office phone over to the couch. Saturday lay prone on the sofa. His eyes wandered briefly in my direction as I entered, but they would not meet mine and I could not see a reaction to my imposition on his space.

Undaunted, I shut the door behind me and leaned against his desk while he finished his conversation.

"I will," he said into the phone. "We'll talk soon."

He paused to listen to the other end of the line.

"You too," he sighed, and placed the handset back. He sat up and moved to put the phone back on his desk.

"André's mother," he said, softly, not daring to look me in the eye. "I owed it to her to let her know myself."

"Where's his father?" I asked.

Saturday looked at me in the eyes for the first time. His eyes were rimmed with red, visible even in the dim, and I could see a lump rise and fall in his throat as he choked back a sob. It was all the answer I needed.

"Shit, Saturday," I stammered, reaching out. "I had no idea. I'm so sorry."

The big man waved me off and crossed back to the couch. He let out a heavy sigh.

"André's not the first child I've lost," he said. Then he smiled, ruefully. "I've outlived them all, to tell the truth."

I let the silence between us ask the next question. He looked up at me again, and I could see in the shadows, just for a moment, how *old* Saturday looked.

"The price you pay for an unnaturally long life," he said. "Still, it never gets any easier."

"Couldn't have been easy, what you did back there."

"No."

"What about his body?"

"Taken care of. I called in a few favors."

We sat in silence for a little while longer, letting the tragedy of the evening hang between us for just a few more moments.

"If you need some more time..." I said, ending the short vigil.

"I'll be fine," he answered.

"It's just that Laura's still not snapping out of it, and Ruth's afraid to let me near her until we have a better idea of what's going on."

Saturday nodded, and gestured towards the door.

"Let's take a look," he said.

Back out in the dining-room-cum-triage-ward, Ruth kept watch over our young sleeper. She looked up as we entered, a mix of concern and mistrust battling in her eyes. The air hung heavy with conflicting emotions for a long time, until at last Ruth breathed a sigh, mistrust giving way to a look of sympathy. She nodded at Saturday, and a small feeling of relief entered the room. It did not displace the weight of the Baron's grief, but it left me with the sense that there was a way forward.

We approached the table on which the almost lifeless form of Laura Trammler still slept. The Baron ran through a quick check of our patient's vitals.

"Still alive," he said. "Still breathing, although just enough to keep her below consciousness."

He pried her eyelids open and looked in, then shut her eyes again and watched her face, his attention never wavering.

"No REM," he said. "No dreaming going on. She's floating somewhere between waking and sleeping states. It's as though her brain's shifted into neutral."

He stood back for a moment and studied Laura's prone body. Then, he walked around to the head of the table.

"Everything about this little adventure was far too easy," he said, then stopped for a moment, wincing to himself. "*Almost* too easy."

He looked around the room to make sure he had our attention.

"Obviously," he continued, "Leveque and the Order want to send us a message. I think they've sent that message along with Ms. Trammler, here. The question is, how do we go about playing it back?"

"And," said Ruth, "how do we do that without frying the patient's brain in the process?"

"If I'm right," said Saturday, "then Laura will return to us once we've heard what the Order has to say. She's served her purpose for them, and she's no threat to them, either."

Ruth looked sideways at him, her mistrust of the man returning.

"How do you recommend we get to the message?" I asked.

"Some of us," Saturday responded, smiling, "use our natural talents."

And with that, he placed his hands on Laura's head and closed his eyes. For a moment, everything was still. Then Saturday started showing signs of strain, a bead of sweat, then more dripping from his brow. His hands started to shake, and it almost looked as though his knees would buckle under.

In a flash, Laura's eyes flew open, an eerie glow showing where her pupils would be. She let out an unearthly scream, and Saturday was tossed backwards from where the girl lay. He hit the wall with a painful crack and crumpled to the floor.

Almost as suddenly, Laura's eyes closed again and she returned to her previous state of limbo.

Saturday struggled to sit up, but failed to get purchase on the floor. He looked in my general direction, his eyes unseeing, and pointed at me.

"It's for you," he wheezed, and then the big man passed out on the floor.

I made a move towards the gurney, but found Ruth's hand on my shoulder.

"Ray, wait."

I turned to look at her. "What, now?" I asked.

"I don't share Saturday's confidence about Laura's chances," she said. "Whatever's got her laid him out flat, and he supposedly knows what he's doing."

"So?"

"So? You're not Saturday. Who's to say what knocked him flat won't kill you? And Laura, while we're at it?"

"It's true," I said. "I'm not Saturday. But Saturday's not me, either."

"Ray..."

"Ruthie, whatever it is I am, whatever it is I've been holding back, it's tougher than Saturday. When it's in the driver's seat, I've seen and done things no mortal person could."

She raised an eyebrow at me, and I nodded, letting her know I wasn't kidding around.

"Besides," I said, "it's *me* the Bishop wants to make a point to. Check on the Baron. I'll see to Laura."

Ruth nodded and moved to Saturday's side. Meanwhile, I stood at the head of the table just as he had and placed my hands on Laura's head. Then, I reached down to the soul cage and touched the hand of the thing inside.

The room around me fades into nothingness.

In front of me, a set of teeth begins to materialize, and with them, a mouth twists into a now sickeningly familiar smile. Blue cowl follows cruel smile, and blue robe follows cowl. After a few moments, the robed and imposing form of Bishop Alexander Leveque stands before me, illuminated in a single spot, the source of which remains a mystery.

"Nice entrance," I say.

"I would speak with the creature who now calls itself Raymond Walsh," says the figure.

"It's me," I reply. "Now release the girl before I…"

"Let me express my fondest congratulations to you," it continues, not registering my protest, "for recovering some of your forgotten power."

This isn't going to be a two-way conversation, obviously. I should have known better.

"By now," it continues, "you've probably surmised that the only reason you now have Laura Trammler in your possession is because we wished it to be so. While Ms. Trammler has been a valuable addition to New Light Ministries, we find her connection to the creature Walsh to be of much greater worth.

"We've known the creature's true nature for some time. Indeed, we've been waiting for its return with growing excitement. We seek the return of the Seraph to our care."

Then the image of Leveque looks straight at me. I know it is a ghost image of the real man, that it cannot see me, but still I can feel those steely eyes boring into me, the wicked smile throwing me off guard.

"You are ours, Seraph, and with our help you shall soon relearn your true place on this earth."

I shudder, a mixture of terror and anticipation. The part of me that is Ray, the part that has dominated my person for as long as my shattered memory stretched, feels a rising dread. But the thing that Leveque and I know is not Ray, the caged thing in the core of my soul, leaps for joy.

Free! it cries, *that one word repeating over and over again, tearing at the edge of my consciousness.*

I could not fault the thing its excitement. After all, these are answers I crave, as well. The voice from within the blue cowl continues.

"You will come to us, Seraph."

In a flash, I know where he wants me to be, the information dropped into my head, unbidden. I feel a searing pain in my temples.

"You will once more take your place with the Most Holy and Secret Order."

As he says this, the circle of light begins to expand around him, until a second, smaller figure is illuminated in its edges. I peer into the dim light, trying to get a better look at this new arrival.

"Of course," the Bishop continues, "we understand that you may be reluctant. You've spent far too long hiding among your inferiors. Befriended them. You've grown weak and complacent, we know."

My blood begins to burn and I can taste the bile rising in the back of my throat.

"So," he says, "we've taken steps to ensure your safe return to us."

By now the light has increased enough that I can see the face of the new figure that has joined us.

Ethan.

"Return to us," the blue robed figure demands, "and the boy will be returned to his sister, unharmed."

With a crack, the light disappears until all I can see is the Bishop's cruel smile, a dagger in my soul.

"You have one hour."

With a wave of nausea, I returned to the bar at the French Quarter. My ears were ringing so that I could hear nothing else in the room. I doubled over, trying to regain control of my stomach, and soon the urge to vomit passed. The screaming, however, would not stop.

Slowly, I straightened up and looked about me, trying to gain a sense of what had gone on in my absence. It was then that I saw Laura Trammler, sitting up with her mouth wide open, an unmistakable look of terror in her eyes. A heart piercing wail was pouring out of her throat; the ringing in my ears not a ringing at all, but the sound of Laura's fear vibrating in my skull.

Without letting up screaming, her eyes met mine. If my encounter with the shadow of Leveque hadn't already shaken me to my foundation, the wave of dread emanating from the heart of Laura Trammler would have finished the job.

I knew what needed to be done.

I turned and ran from the room and straight out the door into the dead of night before my own scream joined in concert with hers.

I didn't even bother to say goodbye, and I didn't care much in that moment. I probably wouldn't be around long enough to regret that, anyway.

22

our in the morning, now. I had taken a gamble on the keys still being in the SUV's ignition, considering the haste with which we'd all run back inside the restaurant earlier, and there they still were. Always bet on the side of human nature.

I pulled the small black tank screaming out into the streets of downtown, trusting I'd have no traffic to worry about other than the random prowl car. I got control of my heart-rate and took my speed down to a reasonable five miles over the speed limit. I had an hour to get where I was going, and it wouldn't do to delay myself with a traffic stop. My connections with the force would only get me out of so much trouble, and any delay could be deadly, no matter how brief. I kept one eye on the road and one eye to the heavens, praying to whatever was out there that I would not be too late.

I'm normally a public transportation kind of guy. Bus route maps are burned into my memory. Behind the wheel of a car, however, I can get a little disoriented. I was hoping that I could rely on sense memory to get me where I was going. Saturday had done the driving the last night, and I was cursing myself for not paying closer attention when he drove there and for passing out on the drive home. I knew I was in the north part of the city. I pointed the SUV in the direction of the river and hoped for a bridge and a landmark by which to guide this boat.

I gunned Saturday's truck through the Missions and on towards the industrial wastelands on the south side of the city. The warehouse district was even more of a ghost town at this late hour. At least on my last visit, there'd been the beacon of the rave as a pole star. Now, there was no light at all, other than what shone from the LEDs on the front of Saturday's truck. I could see well enough by them, but that meant that anyone else hiding amidst the great brick buildings could also see me coming—a distinct disadvantage.

The deeper I drove into the warehouses, the more nervous I grew. I found an out of the way place to pull the SUV over, then killed the engines and the headlights. My hands were shaking, and I could feel the thing inside me in its prison itching to be let out, practically leaping for joy. I sat there in the dark and quiet, breathing deep and trying to regain some sense of control over myself.

Slowly, I stepped out of the truck and into the unlit grid of gravel pathways that ran between the warehouses. I was lost, I knew. I'd followed Saturday too blindly the last time I was here, and I despaired of ever being able to find my destination in time. I wasn't getting much help from my adversary, either. The Bishop, for all his professed urgent need of me, hadn't gone out of his way to provide door to door directions. Probably another test.

This looked like a job for the beastie.

Standing at an intersection, I closed my eyes again and reached down within to touch the thing, letting its power flow through my limbs and into my head, willing the energy to behave like an otherworldly tracking device.

I felt a tug at my solar plexus, drawing me in the direction of what I hoped was my target. I kept my eyes closed and surrendered to the power that drew me onward, turning this way and that, staying on gravel pathways the whole time. I must have walked for a good ten minutes before I finally felt the tug at my chest release, and I opened my eyes at last.

I found myself in front of a familiar warehouse facade—flat roof, skylights, and the concrete stairway on which Saturday had sucker-punched the doorman. This was the place. I took only a brief moment to be impressed by the trick I'd just pulled off, then I got the creeps again. Either my control over the beast's power was improving, or the creature's control over me was increasing. I wasn't sure which.

Not a comforting thought.

Shaking off the willies, I walked up the stairway toward the front entrance. No point in sneaking in. After all, they knew I was coming, and I knew they wanted me alive.

The unlocked front door groaned open as I pushed on it, and I walked onto the large steel catwalk that overlooked the warehouse floor. Inside was darker than out. I could make out basic shapes inside the great brick cavern, surfaces touched briefly by what little light there was seeped in through the door and the skylights until the door slammed shut behind me and took away most of the shadows.

I found myself wishing that I'd checked the glove box for a flashlight before I'd left the SUV. It was a hasty mistake I hoped I wouldn't regret later. At least I had a railing in front of me to guide the way downstairs.

Virtually blind, I felt my way carefully down each rise. The steel of the industrial staircase gave off soft, echoey pings as the soft rubber soles of my shoes touched on them. Empty as the warehouse was, even that noise was enough to fill the space.

Step by step I descended towards the warehouse floor. Amidst the echoing footsteps I heard the distinct whisper-hiss of a match being struck, followed by the sight of a pinpoint of light flaring from its head. The resulting glow illuminated the faintest outline of the fingers that held it and not much else. It was a beacon, nevertheless. I became the proverbial moth to the flame. No sense in dragging out the inevitable.

As my foot touched solid concrete at the bottom of the steel staircase, I saw the point of light multiply. The still-ownerless hand touched match head to candlewick, cutting through the oppressive darkness another fraction of a lumen.

"I admire your promptness," said a familiar voice coming from the direction of the floating match. I could almost hear the sadistic grin behind it, and the thing in the depths of my soul-cage leapt to its feet—out of joy or fear, or both.

"Didn't want to keep you waiting," I answered.

He laughed, a sound considerably devoid of any humor.

"A little late for that," he said. "But what's a few centuries among old friends?"

I kept walking towards the source of sound and light while my inner monster kept shaking in its cage, excited. Perhaps I should have been more wary.

"Still," said the Bishop, "In the grand scheme of things it doesn't much matter."

I had closed the distance between us a little more quickly than I'd anticipated. I came up nose-to-wick with a white paraffin pillar on a tall, wrought-iron candlestick. In the glow, I could see the vague outline of the Bishop's robe in its telltale indigo.

"Delighted you could make it," he said. "Welcome home."

With that, he flicked his hand with a gesture towards the candles, and I watched, frozen, as the pillar split, then split again until it had replicated in a circle around me.

"Nice trick," I said and stepped forward to move towards the now maniacally grinning cleric.

Someone hit me with an invisible brick wall.

I fell on my ass and could feel my head throbbing. Leveque was laughing full-throated, now.

I stood up, rubbing my aching forehead and dusting myself off. It was then that I saw the chalk circle drawn on the floor around the bases of the candlesticks. Inside me the caged thing thrashed in fury. I shook my head in disbelief. I was trapped in the middle of a bad horror movie.

"You have got to be kidding me!"

And Leveque only laughed the harder.

"Relax!" he said, his booming voice filling the cavern of the warehouse. "Settle down. Get comfortable. You're not going anywhere for the foreseeable future. You might as well keep yourself in one piece while we wait."

"Wait for what?"

"All in good time, my dear prodigal."

He stood there grinning. I wanted to punch his smug little face, but I didn't relish my knuckles getting chewed up by the invisible cinderblocks in front of me. Time to keep talking, keep calm. Time to change the subject.

"I want to see Ethan," I said.

"Oh, angel, really? I thought the mental frailty was all an act, but you really have become just a babe in the woods, haven't you?"

I could feel my hackles rising, and Leveque's cruel smile only grew wider.

"Ethan," he said, "is safe and sound in his bed."

"What?"

"Honestly," he said with a tone of faux-exasperation, "if I had known you were so easily suggestible, I would have dumbed down the plan to call you back."

I hung my head. *Stupid, Ray. Real stupid. Emotions already running in overdrive, and here you go just running off to play paladin without stopping to check for traps first.* And now I was the prize and no one knew where I'd gone. By the time Ruth or Saturday figured out what had happened to me who knew where I'd be?

In the midst of my self-pitying reverie, I found my attention drawn to the Bishop's chalk markings on the cement floor. I was standing on top of an intricate pattern. I tried to focus above it and get a better look at the whole picture. Six sides, herringbone pattern. The feathered sigil. The mark of death for three innocent girls.

Bastards.

Around the sigil between two more chalk lines were another series of symbols. I couldn't read them, nor make sense of them. The thing that was NotRay, however, began to vibrate again, prodding at me, trying to get my attention.

Something had agitated it about the circle, and it was not the same dread I'd felt from within when the circle had closed. Something about the markings deserved my attention, but what? I could not understand what the caged thing was trying to tell me. I needed to keep Leveque talking while I tried to decode the alien tongue being screamed into my subconscious.

"Why me?" I asked, still looking down, feigning shame.

"Why?" the Bishop said, his tone mocking mine. "Because finding you is my purpose."

"That's it?"

"Isn't that enough? You've forgotten so much that you've forgotten what it means to have purpose, haven't you? Forgotten what it feels like to be called?"

I allowed myself a brief glance in his direction, a prompt for him to go on.

"Your recovery for the Order has been the sole and driving reason for my existence."

"But why me?"

"You're our prize possession," he said. There was a bitterness to his voice.

"And now that you have, me, I suppose you'll be out of a job?"

Bitter look followed bitter tone. I'd hit a nerve, and wondered what might happen if I continued to gnaw on it.

"I mean," I said, "once I'm safely back within the fold there won't be much else for you to do, what with your sole purpose fulfilled."

Leveque growled and reached out to grab at me through the circle. Fortunately, the invisible wall appeared to work both ways.

"Careful," I said, "don't damage the prize."

The Bishop took a step back and a deep breath.

"There will still be use for me," he said, his voice barely rising above a whisper.

"You sound doubtful," I said, egging him on while keeping my focus on the strange marks.

"I've been part of the Order for centuries," he said.

"And have you never wondered," I asked, "in all that time why *I* was your all encompassing purpose?"

He snorted, a mirthless sound. "Ours is not to question why," he replied.

"Why do it, then?"

"Because I cannot do anything else!" All pretense of control left him as his voice reached a near primal scream.

Startled, I turned away from my ruminations over the chalk marks and looked at Leveque's face. The familiar cruel smile was still there, but there was a look in his eyes that could not back up the smile. Behind the mask of cruelty was something sadder, more desperate.

"Imagine being a child," he said, "if that's even possible for you. Imagine being carefree during the day and terrified of the night. Imagine nightmares that belong to someone else's life taking over your young mind at night, creeping into your daily consciousness. Death and blood. Deviant sex and aberrant creatures. I was six, and I had seen things in my dreams, waking and sleeping, that no grown man should ever experience.

"Imagine slowly losing your grip on yourself as the dreaming world begins to take hold of your life. Imagine all the turmoil of puberty coupled with a *real* crisis of identity. Imagine being purposely traumatized into the awareness that your life was never your own.

"My mother raised me alone in the confines of the Order. The monks doted on me. For my eighteenth birthday, they presented me with a special gift: a novice—a particularly delicious young runaway I'd been eyeing, I thought, surreptitiously.

"I raped her on the floor of a bare concrete cell and the floodgates opened. The man who was Bishop Leveque had replaced the scared, scarred little boy. Crisis gave way to purpose. I knew why I had been brought into the world."

He paused. I could not look at him as his story progressed. I felt my gorge rising and the creature in its soul-cage rattled with rage against his chains.

I could feel Leveque, now, standing over me. Whatever doubt had entered him had disappeared. Waves of malice rolled off his body and struck at my soul, further agitating the beast.

And then my eyes and ears opened. I knew what the thing inside was trying to tell me. It screamed loud and clear.

Wrong.

Wrong!

WRONG!

There was a mistake in the chalk sigils. Instinctively, I reached out towards the gap. It was open, but just barely. The concrete wall was now putty. The light from the replicated candles began to dim as I pushed my fingers through, but I could not push all the way out.

"Good," the Bishop said, crowing, as the cruel mask was replaced, covering his moment of vulnerability. "You've found the chink in the armor."

"I'm going to kill you when I get out of here!"

"You may well," he chuckled, "but you need to let the reality of your being come forth if you're going to get out. I'm not sure you can, anymore."

He was right, I knew. I could feel the creature screaming the same at me from within. It wanted to be free. In my anger, I wanted to let it be free.

I sat back and loosed the chains within, freeing the Seraph, the creature of vengeance. I felt a tremendous power course through my veins. My hand, now not my hand, pushed through the wall like it was paper. The candles began to fade, and a voice that was mine spoke words that were not.

"Your Emminence," it called out as our arm breached the wall and the spectral candles winked out, plunging the warehouse back into darkness. "Make a wish." I said, as I blew out the last candle.

23

ree!

We lingered, the thing and I, torn between the desire to celebrate and the urge to serve our purpose. We dallied with celebration for just a moment. Leveque would wait. There seemed to be some confusion, however, as to what we were celebrating—our release from the confines of the circle, or freedom from a much longer captivity.

My head hurt. Two distinct beings were occupying the same space, and both of them were me. Everything that was Raymond Walsh, the fabricated man, stood in that spot alongside the true nature of the beast—no, not the beast, the *Seraph*—that was the word. The me that was unearthly seemed annoyed by this fact. And Ray? I was glad to still be in there somewhere. I wasn't planning on letting go of myself that easily. We'd need to fight that out later, though. There was still a murderous cleric to run down. Leveque couldn't hide. We'd caught the scent of his many sins by now and could track the bastard for miles if we had to.

Given the head start we'd granted him with our little schizophrenic victory dance, I imagined he'd have bolted out of the warehouse and into the middle of the night. His presence, however, was still very strong here. As one body, the angel of vengeance and the once-homeless amnesiac headed in the direction of the warehouse offices.

We found him waiting patiently in the largest office, the one Saturday and I had peered down into just a few nights earlier. The stone altar was still fixed in the middle of the floor. Cold, fetid air entered our nostrils—my nostrils—and the angel recognized the mixed essences of fear and sex and brimstone.

"Welcome to your true home," Leveque said. "Welcome back to the Most Holy and Secret Order."

His mouth was twisted once more into that stupid, awful smile. We resisted the urge to smack it off of his face.

"The Order has chased you for centuries," he said. "You are rightfully ours—summoned, named, and held."

"We are nothing but our own." The voice was mine, but the words came from somewhere else.

"You have never been anything of the kind. You're a puppet. A tool. Nothing more. You were a soldier, a tool of the Divine, but the Divine abandoned you."

"We were taken! Ripped from our home!" Dream images of terrifying and never-ending fall played in my consciousness and I shuddered.

"And no one came looking?" the Bishop asked. "You've been free of our grasp for hundreds of years and you never went home? Instead you've wandered the earth like a gypsy with that damned Moor. Tell me, where is your commander?"

We searched our collective memory and came away unsatisfied. We hung our heads.

"We do not know."

A look of triumph crossed his face.

"A soldier without a commander is nothing," he said, a spark of triumph in his eyes. "It seems you are presented with a choice. Serve the Order—we who appreciate your true power—or live a life with no purpose, alone and anonymous."

We are not alone! I wanted to scream, but the Seraph held me back. Instead, we continued to stare at Leveque with a white heat. The Bishop seemed to mistake our silence for indecision.

"Of course," he said, "we could save you that last indignity and just kill you."

"We are free. We are our own." Leveque frowned and a look of near fury crept into his eyes. And then we let loose the final indignity. "We are not alone."

The Bishop looked us up and down. The room was deathly still.

"So be it," he said. "The patience of the Order has its limits."

He reached into the folds of his robe and the sound of sharp metal being drawn echoed throughout the room.

"You will be ours, now, or you simply will not *be*."

Leveque held the blade that had haunted my visions in front of him. I had my own reasons to fear it, but my other half was panicked, too. The urge to run was great, and I was not inclined to ignore it. But where to?

Without my bidding, our muscles contracted in ways I'd never felt before, our body coiling tight, then with a great leap we were hurtling up towards the skylight above us. We braced with a forearm over our head and pushed through the glass, landing on the gravel roof.

Below, we could hear the cry of Leveque's frustration and the tinkle of glass shards hitting the concrete floor. We stopped to catch our breath and brush stray glass away. We were scratched, but not cut. I'd probably be bruised in the morning, if we lived that long.

I looked back to survey the damage. We'd put a sizable hole in the skylight. I started to shake, realizing what had just happened.

"We can *do* that?"

Wicked.

It wouldn't take Leveque long to catch up to us on the roof. I wasn't sure what our plan was from here. Being out in the open was good, sure, and I had a funny feeling after the last trick we just pulled that we'd survive a fall from the roof better than the Bishop would.

There were only a few ways that Leveque could get access to the roof. We scrambled over to a corner opposite so that we could be ready. Biding our time, we started to experiment with the power I felt coursing through our veins. We flicked our wrist in the direction of small pile of gravel. A rough bolt of energy in a shade of now-familiar pale green leapt from our fingertips and struck the gravel of the roof's macadam with a satisfying crack, leaving behind a crater of fresh sand and scorched tar in its wake.

I giggled like a child, while the Seraph furrowed our brow in annoyance. I ignored its unspoken scolding and threw a few more arcs around the rooftop. We might as well greet the Bishop's arrival with a show of our real power. Maybe give him second thoughts.

"You begin to grasp the power you are letting go to waste," said the Bishop, emerging from a cloud of dust we'd just created. "It's a crime you're willing to throw all that away for some misguided sense of autonomy. Perhaps you've forgotten that self-determination never did work out all that well for your kind."

As he spoke, I could feel my own consciousness receding into the background. The world was starting to look and sound like I was watching old, scratchy sixteen millimeter films while underwater. We started to walk towards Leveque. Not my choice. The Seraph was definitely in the driver's seat now.

"Good," said the Bishop. "It's better to stop running. Come here and let me end your suffering, quick and merciful."

I could feel us reaching down into the depths of our soul. We were drawing on a great deal of inner strength, and I could sense the well was getting low.

We reached out our arm as we walked towards Leveque, and a pale green arc jumped between our fingers and the hilt of the Bishop's whisper-thin blade.

Leveque stopped short, letting out a rather childish yelp as his fingers unlaced from the hilt. The bolt sent the sword flying until it arched over the edge of the rooftop and plummeted from sight.

Every last ounce of swagger drained away from Leveque's body.

We stood there, facing one another. His shoulders shook as a pale green aura pulsed in our hands.

"We may have forgotten much over the centuries," we said, a humorless smirk spreading across our lips, "but you have forgotten, too."

A questioning look crossed Leveque's brow.

"You've forgotten how many times we've killed you before."

I could see the Bishop rapidly replaying memories in his head. We were watching the same episodes. Demon-cloned Leveque, always chasing, always dying at our hands.

With images of his death playing over and over, the Bishop turned to run. We were more than ready for this, however.

"You must pay for the lives of the girls that you have taken," we called out. Leveque stopped in his tracks and turned back to us, a look of confusion in his furrowed brow.

"I have killed no one," he said. His voice was pitched high with his fear. "Not this time." He sounded pathetic and small.

"Three girls are dead, all bearing the mark of the Order." Leveque's jaw dropped as desperately tried to assemble words. "Three innocent lives have been taken by your Order."

"Never murdered!" Leveque strangled out a cry. "Sexual magic to bind you to us, but never murder!"

"You lie," we said, "and now they must be avenged." We smiled, cold and humorless. "That is our purpose." Our hand reached out and released the arc that had been building in our hands. A pale green web spread out across his shoulders, and he fell screaming to the ground. On guard, we approached where he lay. Leveque was curled up on his side, twitching and sobbing like a child.

Something in our affect softened, and the murderous rage that had fueled us subsided. We knelt down beside the incapacitated man and reached out a hand to his head.

Two lives play out in a few brief moments. One, Leveque—all deceit and depravity. The other, the life that could have been, the soul that had been pushed aside before birth to make way for the scion of the single minded Order.

The soul had not died in the process, but had been shoved back into a submissive position within its own body, forced to witness— forced to live—every moment and every detail of the crimes and depravity of Bishop Alexander Leveque. Something is missing. We sift through the wreckage of a wasted life, and can find no evidence for the murder of the girls. He has been truthful. For once.

All that is left now is the sound of sobbing. In a cramped prison inside the mind of Leveque, a pale man-child cowers in a corner. The soul that might have been is innocent, but the child that never was has gone mad. His eyes are wild, and a jagged hole has been torn through his soul.

In an instant, we know that this is the person who lies at our feet, now. Leveque, in his cowardice, had receded somewhere into the background of this shared mind, leaving the ruined and near feral child behind in the grown man's body to deal with the consequences of a life wasted. All this we know within the space of a few heartbeats.

One inhale, one exhale. We were back on the warehouse roof.

The quivering husk of a man was now staring up at us, a pleading look in his eyes.

"End this," he begged.

We hesitated, uncertain.

"We would give you your life back."

"I want nothing to do with this life," he said. "I do not wish to live with the memories of what they made me."

Still we hesitated.

"He will return, soon. Leveque. He will not stop."

We nodded. Murderer or no, Leveque still had much to answer for.

"Quick, now."

Again, we reached down into the well of our soul. There was a little strength left, but it would be enough. We called forth the pale green blade, the instrument of justice. Of vengeance. As we had done a hundred times before, we struck straight and true through the sternum and into Leveque's heart. We could feel his life force draining away. His eyes shut as the life force continued to ebb. Slowly, his physical form was overtaken by the energy of the blade.

I could feel ourselves tiring as our store of energy ran its course. A wave of fatigue and nausea started to roll over us, and we could no longer maintain the blade. With a heavy sigh, we released control, dropping to our knees.

The pale green web dissipated into the night, leaving no trace of Leveque's body. I gasped for air. I'd been holding my breath the entire time.

I was tired, breathless, and the world around me was starting to look fuzzy, and the sense of the Seraph had receded. It was still in there somewhere, but I—Ray—was back in the driver's seat.

I heard the sound of someone behind me clearing their throat. I turned my head in the direction of the sound and quickly regretted the decision. My dizziness increased as my eyes came somewhat shakily to rest on a vaguely Saturday shaped blur.

"You're out of focus," I slurred. "You should do something about that."

Then the rooftop jumped up and hit me on the head.

I AWOKE SEVERAL hours later on sofa in Saturday's office. Daylight streamed through the windows, and I was surrounded by familiar faces who appeared to have not slept at all during night. I reached back into my consciousness and felt the Seraph's presence still decidedly there, but as a passenger. The tight soul cage that had contained this part of myself for the past ten years was gone, shattered with the angelic creature's release.

Slowly, I sat up with a groan that caught the attention of my assembled friends. Before I was completely upright, Ruth's arms were around me in a tired, grateful embrace.

"Saturday hasn't said much about what happened," she said.

"He wasn't there for much. I think he stepped in just in time to watch me hit the dirt." I looked over to where the big man stood, watching me intently in return. "How did he find me?"

"*He has his ways*," she said with a deep inflection, mocking Saturday's accented baritone.

"However he did it," I said, "I'm glad he did."

Saturday caught my eye again. He was still watching me. There was a look of warmth on his face that I was unaccustomed to. He caught me looking and smiled. Wobbly but determined, I stood up and walked over to my mysterious friend.

"Have you returned?" he asked. An odd question in almost any other context, but I understood what he meant.

"For the most part," I answered. "There are still significant holes in my memory, and I'm feeling a little schizoid." I turned my thoughts inward for a moment, feeling around for the thing within me, now part of me, no longer quite so fearsome. "But, I know who I am," I added. "*What* I am."

Saturday nodded, smiling. I could see tension releasing from his body. "We can work on the memory," he said. "We can work on getting you feeling whole, again." His brow furrowed, just a fraction, and I could sense he was holding something back.

I put a hand to his shoulder, and could feel in an instant what was troubling him. I remembered the wall across my memories only one evening prior and I willed it to tumble down. I could see the scene between us with clarity, now. I held my hand out, palm up.

"You have been a true friend," I said. "More loyal, maybe, then I deserve. I release you from your promise."

He shuddered, I could feel the lock I had placed in his mind so many years ago falling away. With a look of great relief, he placed a signet ring—my signet ring—back into my hands. Saturday bowed his head, just slightly.

"Tzadkiel," he said. "Welcome back, my friend."

I shook my head. "I'm still Raymond Walsh," I said. "Don't ask me how, but somehow I am both things. Ray Walsh isn't going anywhere for a while, it seems."

"That's good," Ruth said. She'd changed out of her mercenary uniform and back into her familiar shelter clothes. "'Cause if Ray's still in there, somewhere, I need him to help me finish the job at hand." She cocked her head over her shoulder, telling me I should follow her into Saturday's office.

The Trammler siblings were on the Baron's sofa. Laura sat up, wide-eyed but obviously tired, a cup of tea in one hand. Ethan was prone, sound asleep, his head resting in his sister's lap. She was watching his sleeping face, stroking his hair as she did. I kept quiet, not wanting to ruin the moment.

"Thank you," she said, looking up only briefly.

I nodded.

"We're not quite finished, yet," said Ruth. "There's still the matter of Evil Auntie to resolve."

Laura's hand stopped its movement, and she looked up at us in a wide-eyed panic.

"What are you going to do?" she asked.

"I've arranged for a short visit," Ruth said.

Laura started to open her mouth in protest, but Ruth held up a hand to cut her off. "A short visit," she repeated. "She won't be staying long, and if all goes to plan, you won't be leaving town with her, either."

Laura looked at Ruth, mouth agape. There was an unspoken question in her eyes.

"You're eighteen," she said. "Did you know that?"

Laura shook her head.

"Margaret was hoping you wouldn't," she continued. "Your mother's trust fund falls to you. I tracked down a very guilty physician and a very helpful county clerk. They painted quite an interesting picture." Laura just continued staring in disbelief. "Margaret's got some 'splainin to do," Ruth said as she chuckled.

By now, Ethan must have sensed that something was going on in the room, and he was beginning to raise his head, still half asleep.

"Good morning," said Ruth. "It's time to saddle up for one last rustle. So, would you all care to join me at my office? I think we're in for an interesting show. I'd hate for you all to miss it."

24

By noon, we were all sitting in the room where I'd first met Ethan just a few days earlier. He and Laura shared a settee, while Ruth and I sat across from them. We'd been joined by a social worker of Ruth's acquaintance, and a man in a slate-grey suit, who she had failed to introduce, although his suit and fussy attaché screamed "lawyer."

Danny Knowles was trying to hover out of sight. I hadn't expected to see him there, and he registered my look of surprise as I saw him. He returned my look with a hard stare, not cold but not entirely friendly either. Saturday had begged off the meeting, wanting to tie up some loose ends with André's mother.

At ten past the hour, "Evil" Auntie Margaret came breezing in, all brassy hair and Hermes scarf. She crossed the threshold of the room with an air of entitlement and arrogance, which quickly drained out of her when she saw all of us assembled there to greet her. I could see her desperately trying to regain her composure, as she painted on a rather insincere look of concern and relief across her impeccably made-up face.

"Oh my goodness," she cried. "Rev. Penfield, you did it!" She crossed over to Laura and Ethan with her arms spread wide. "I never thought I'd see my babies again!"

Neither of the siblings made an effort to stand up and meet her embrace. Instead, Ethan buried his head in Laura's shoulder while she glared at the brassy fraud with a look of absolute contempt.

Margaret stood there for a moment, waiting for the embrace that would never come, then dropped her arms to her sides. She turned to look at the rest of the room, looking into an assembly of unfriendly eyes. Ruth had purposely left her nowhere to sit, and she shifted on her feet uncomfortably, a much more sincere look of disdain on her face.

"What's all this about, then, Penfield?" she asked, barely suppressing a tone of fury.

"Well, Margaret, my dear," she smiled, "we've found your prodigals, as promised."

Margaret stood there, silently glaring at us.

"And we also found all the baggage they brought along with them," she said.

"What baggage?" she hissed.

Ruth nodded to the man with the attaché, who snapped open the case and began to methodically pull out a passel of manila files.

"A notarized copy of the testamentary trust established by one Elizabeth Trammler for the benefit of her children, Laura and Ethan Trammler, to come into the control of the elder child once she reaches the age of eighteen."

"Which she has not!" Margaret spit. Ruth's mischievous megawatt smile cranked up a few more watts.

"A certificate of birth for one Laura Elizabeth Trammler, dated eighteen years ago this past March," the man with the attaché said, ignoring the interruption. Margaret's face turned deeper and deeper shades of red with each word from the attorney's mouth. Her hands balled into fists. She was a few short steps from Ruth, staring daggers at her. I tensed, ready to jump in the way should she snap.

"And a signed affidavit from one Michael Farleigh, M.D., testifying to his role in a conspiracy to obfuscate the details of the birth of Laura Elizabeth Trammler."

Margaret let out a growl of frustration.

"Trust has passed to Laura," Ruth said. "As has guardianship of Ethan, for the time being."

I could read the waves of caged-tiger energy rolling off of Margaret's body. If it was possible to pace in place, she was pulling it off.

"Ms. Carmichael, here," Ruth indicated the city social worker, "has agreed to keep an eye on these two while they get settled. We've found housing for them here in the city."

"No," Margaret said, her voice rasping.

"Oh, I know," said Ruth, "it's an expensive place to live. But, what the hell? They've got the money." She looked over at the siblings who were now holding on to one another, smiling and crying. "Don't you?" she asked.

"I'll fight this!"

"You can try," said Ruth. "But you may be a little tied up."

"The Lake County DA would like a few words with you when you return home," the attorney said, matter-of-fact.

"Tomorrow morning." Ruth grinned as she spoke. "Your flight's in an hour. Wouldn't want you to miss that appointment."

I could taste the sour woman's rage. Margaret took a step towards the sister and brother, murder in her eyes, and I was up out of my chair in a flash to get between them and her. I put a hand on her shoulder, and the world went away.

Margaret and I stand alone in a void. Her mood shifts in quick succession from rage, to offense, to terror as she looks in our eyes, the Seraph and myself.

"There was a time," we say, "when we would have killed you without a second thought for what you've done to these children."

We can feel her body wanting to faint, but we hold on to her tightly.

"Apparently, we have developed a more nuanced sense of justice over the last few years living as a mortal. It is far worse to show you your future, should you continue to interfere with these two."

And so we do, dropping into her mind whole cloth an image of what her world will be should she continue to harass Laura and Ethan. We show her a social world falling apart, and the inside of prisons. We show her a life without the comfort of her family's wealth. And we show her what we are capable of, Raymond Walsh and Tzadkiel, one and the same—the embodiment of justice and vengeance. We show her what we will do with her if she does not turn away. It makes the other images seem pleasant. It is an image worse than death.

And then we let her go.

A few seconds had passed by in the room, but I could see the eternity that had passed through Margaret's mind. All eyes were on her and the quivering heap she'd become. All eyes were wide with surprise. In her terror, Margaret's brassy hair had been streaked with a stark, bright white.

Everything was dead quiet for a full minute. Then, Ruth spoke in a barely audible whisper, with the air of someone once accustomed to being obeyed.

"Your ride to the airport's waiting outside," she said. "Get out."

At that, Danny stepped forward, grabbed her at the elbow and began to usher her out of the room. Shaky, and obviously numb, the newly humbled Margaret Trammler walked out the door.

Laura and Ethan stood up, and the older girl took a peek out into the hallway to make sure that 'Evil' Margaret Trammler had really left the building. Assured that the wayward matriarch was actually gone, Laura turned to look at Ruth and me.

"Is it true?" she asked.

Ruth nodded. "You're on your own now," she said.

"Except for two or three anxious godparents who'll be looking out for you every second," I said.

"Ms. Carmichael will take you home, if you're ready," said Ruth.

"Home," Laura repeated, almost in a trance. "We get a life of our own, now? Seems a bit unreal."

"Welcome to the club," I said. "We meet the first Wednesday of the month. You're in charge of the sandwiches."

Ethan giggled, then ran up to me, wrapping his arms around me and hugging my waist.

"Sorry I was such a pain," he said.

"Never happened, kid."

And then Laura was hugging me, too. I looked over at Ruth, who seemed far too amused to see me surrounded by clinging kids. The elder Trammler kissed me on the cheek.

"What's next?" she asked.

"You figure out your new life," I said.

And then I figure out mine.

OUTSIDE THE WELCOME Table, Danny Knowles was waving to an unmarked police car as it pulled away from the curb.

"Curb to curb service?" I asked. Danny didn't look at me, but stayed focused on the receding car.

"I hate people like that," he said. "Think money makes them bullet-proof." He turned and looked me in the eye, unsmiling. "Think they're above the law."

I decided to play it dumb and smiled.

"Should have sent her off in a patrol car," he said. "Better than she deserves." He turned back to look out over the street. We stood there silently for a moment, and I found myself trying to imagine what sort of life was awaiting Margaret Trammler, former evil stepmother, when she returned home.

"Got called out to New Light last night," he said, still looking streetward. "Report of shots fired."

"Really?" I said, attempting nonchalant and not succeeding all that well.

"Really," he said. Danny turned to look at me. There was a look of betrayal in his eyes. "And I notice that Laura Trammler arrived with you this morning."

I shrugged. I wasn't ready to talk about last evening's adventures.

"Anything you care to tell me?" Danny asked.

"She missed her brother," I said, not technically lying. "Got tired of being separated."

"Lucky for you," he said. "Funny thing is, what with the murders and all, we had an opportunity to follow up on the connection you suggested between New Light and the warehouse parties."

"And I was right?"

"Didn't have to look too far before we started seeing that strange little symbol in every corner."

My eyes went wide. Even I'd missed that. Granted, I'd been a little preoccupied last night.

"Then of course there was the stockpile of guns and Ecstasy."

"Who'd've thought," I said, perhaps a little too smug.

"Yeah, you were right. They're the bad guys."

"So, now what?"

"We went to have a chat with the Bishop, but he was nowhere to be found. No one knew where he'd got to."

"Tipped off?"

"Maybe," he said, eyeing me strangely. "We've got a warrant out for him, but he's in the wind."

"So that's that?"

"We took in most of the leadership last night. The rest surrendered this morning. They all seem lost without their fearless leader."

"Cults don't survive without their front men."

"We raided their warehouse this morning."

I put on my poker face.

"Nothing but broken glass and scattered candle wax," he said.

I continued to hold my cards close.

"And one sword." My face almost slipped. "Covered in Leveque's prints," he said.

"What happens now?" I asked.

"DA opens an investigation," he said. "City social services takes temporary charge of the shelter."

"And Leveque?"

"We keep looking." I nodded. "Any idea where he may have run off to?"

I shrugged. We stood there looking quietly at each other for quite a while.

"André Dufresne found his way into the city morgue early this morning," he said. My breath caught, but I said nothing. "Baron Saturday's right hand?"

I nodded. "We've met."

"Anonymous dump," said Danny. "Strangled."

"Saturday know?" I asked.

Danny looked at me from the corner of his eye. "Didn't seem all that shocked when we told him. Either he knew already, or he's more of a sociopath than I thought. Maybe both."

"Is he in trouble?"

"At the moment, no. See, we found a black light stamp on his hand. New Light's."

Shit.

"I'm not gonna pry," Danny said, looking me square in the eye. "As far as I'm concerned you've done right by those kids. And if you managed to shut down a den of iniquity in the process, so much the better."

I snorted. "Den of iniquity?"

"Technical term," Danny said. "Fuck off." He was trying not to laugh, rather unsuccessfully. "Just don't leave me out of the fun next time."

I nodded. Danny reached into his coat pocket and pulled out a plastic bag. It was marked with an evidence tag. "Speaking of fun," he said, "Dr. Saito pulled this off of Sarah's body." He held out the bag and I took it in hand.

I held the bag up to the light, peering carefully. Inside was one hair—long, twisted, and grey. I felt a rock in the pit of my stomach.

"Go ahead and open it," Danny said. "I wasn't looking. I had no idea what you were doing." He turned to make a close inspection of a fire hydrant, and I broke the seal on the bag, reached in and let my fingertips rest on the single strand.

Unbidden, the truth of the thing drops into my head. I know why our madman seems so familiar. Tzadkiel awakes, and judgment is clear. We hang our head, saddened by what must follow.

I let go of the hair and breathed in deep, trying not to let my emotions show to the Lieutenant. He's in over his head, and I can't let him get involved.

"Anything?" he asked.

I shook my head, making a point of looking him in the eye. "Old man," I said. "His face was fuzzy. I'm sorry I can't help more."

"It's all right," said Danny. "Saito's sent a clipping off to the state lab for DNA examination. We'll get him, yet."

No, you won't, I thought. I had another long night ahead of me.

"I need to go help the Trammlers get settled," I said, looking for the quick escape.

"All right. Just call me before you do anything stupid."

I wasn't planning anything *stupid*, so I nodded and went on my way. Tzadkiel had a social call to make this evening, and Lieutenant Danny Knowles didn't need to be around for that.

25

nother midnight. I quietly mourned the passing of my sleep schedule, and feared what I was certain was the onset of night vision. After a power nap, I hauled my soul-weary carcass back down into the Missions. Near the border between here and the industrial zones there was a little stretch of alley they called the Rum Run, a string of abandoned buildings that served as ersatz shelter for the boozing crowd—usually men too drunk to be put up in any of the shelters.

I let Tzadkiel peek out from around the passenger seat long enough to guide me to the opening I was looking for. Rain damaged plywood covered a half circle window leading down into a disused basement—storage beneath what had once been a shoe repair shop and now had not been for over a decade. The angel in me thrummed and shook, tapping my internal compass in the right direction, better than any GPS.

I let myself be nudged deeper into the interior of the basement. The damp rose to meet me with each step, and there was a stench—not foul, not pleasant, but definitely strong—hammering insistently at my nostrils, coming from somewhere ahead of me. Rust. Wet dog. Spoiled food.

Sweat tinged with terror.

Something familiar.

Tzadkiel—I—grasped at a fuzzy memory, wandered around the edges of something past, but met only with frustration and fractions of answers. I shook my head and pressed on.

I found myself in an alcove, a dead end but for three doors. One in front, two on either side. I was drawn to the door on my right. The Seraph—no, *I*—felt a jolt as my hand reached out to unlatch it. The door swung inward with a slow groan, and I peered into the barely lit room. I held out my hand to let the angel-fire fill it with a green glow.

A damp, concrete cell, bare but for the tattered mattress on the floor, resolved into view. Borrowed images filled my head, the final sights beheld by three girls, now dead. A backlit door. A creepy old man. And something else.

This was the place.

I gave in to an instinct and reached out to let the memory of the room speak to me. There was a sense of terror, but not of death. The girls had been held captive here, but their lives had been taken somewhere else. I let the memory of the room try to lead me to where, but the trail ran cold at the threshold. No matter. There was more to investigate.

I touched the door across the alcove and it pushed in easily, it's inner mechanism torn away. The stench of dog and rust hit me like a wall. The inner passenger jumped at the sense memory and I felt my lips wrapping around the word.

Iron imp.

I shuddered at the image in my head. Almost lupine, almost reptilian, wholly neither; fur like steel wool, teeth like a nightmare. I'd killed them before, knew what their screams sounded like. I knew how they killed, too, feeding on fear and draining life force without ever laying a claw on their victims. It was an awful way to die. And someone had called that thing up from the depths to do his dirty work. I could feel the rage rising. The Seraph's nature demanded vengeance.

I was the only living thing down here at the moment, but I wouldn't be for long. He had to come back soon. He'd grown attached to the place, considered it home. I could feel it, flowing out of the remaining door—a sense of comfort. I pushed it open and walked through.

The last room was well cared for. Clean and dry and marked by personal touches. A faded photograph was lodged in a crack in the concrete, black and white, yellowed with decades of age. Two figures stood on a boardwalk in some faraway time and place—one short and dark haired, dressed in a police officer's uniform; the other tall and fair and slightly unkempt with a serious look. My doppelganger.

Shit.

I flipped the photo over to look for some identifying mark. There in black ink faded to brown: "Me and Ted. June 1968." A faint and nagging image tickled the back of my consciousness. A foiled kidnapping. A grateful mother. And some terrible thing shoved back into the darkness where it belonged.

I could see two officers—one with a brand new Yashica, an oddity—begging for a snapshot with the hero of the day.

Me and Ted. June 1968.

I smiled at the memory, but the feeling of fondness did not remain long. Someone or something was stirring out in the corridor, a slow shuffle with an accent of slight scraping. I sat down on the small cot against the wall where I'd found the photo. Soon, the shuffling ceased and the door was pushed open again. I could see the new arrivals silhouette framed in the doorway, a shape so familiar now having been burned into the retinas of a handful of frightened dead girls.

"Who's there?" said a small, frail voice.

I raised my hand and let the odd angel fire illuminate the room. The silhouette gave way to a small, grey haired figure. An old man, broken and lost. Twitching. For a long moment we lived in the silence, staring at one another.

"You came," he said at last. I said nothing. "It is you, right?" he asked. "Not the other one, the false mask? It's Ted, right?"

I didn't answer. Couldn't in the moment. A mixture of righteous anger and profound sadness choked back language.

"Tzadkiel?" It sounded as though he was begging.

"It's me, Carl," I said.

The old man fell to his knees in front of me. "Oh, sir!" He choked back a sob. "I thought I'd lost you! I thought you'd been swallowed up by that character you'd created. But I knew! Deep down I knew you'd never leave us, leave *me* for good!"

"I'm back," I said. "I couldn't stay away. Not with you calling for me the way you did."

Carl looked up and smiled, his usual tics momentarily under control. "You noticed," he said, a sigh of satisfaction behind the words.

"How could I not?" I asked. "That's a lot of death dedicated to one purpose."

"You were buried so deep inside the mask," he said, the usual twitch returning to his body. "I didn't want to take so many, but you were resisting the call."

"You didn't want to?"

Again, the twitch stopped. "Not at first."

"And then it became fun?" My voice had risen to fill the cavernous spaces of the basement.

"Don't yell at me," he said, voice rising to meet mine. "If you hadn't run away..."

"So it's my fault? The deaths of those girls are on my hands?"

"You had a job to do! You disappeared, hiding in plain sight. The city was falling apart."

"The city is always falling apart."

"Yes, and you were the one who held it together!"

"I was tired, Carl. In danger."

"You're immortal! An angel! You don't need rest."

"That's not your decision," I said, all of a sudden feeling again the bone aching weariness I spoke of.

Carl sat there, still on his knees, twitching and staring at me.

"I was hunted," I said, at last. "Old enemies were getting too close. I had to hide." My old, distant former friend hung his head. "You put me back on their radar with your little murder spree. You wanted me back and you almost killed me in the process!"

Again, we were quiet. The narrow concrete hallways rang with the lingering echoes of my last outburst, and the two of us sat there listening to the sound until it faded.

"You don't really care about any of this, do you?" I asked.

Again, Carl ceased his nervous tics, a sly smile crossing his face.

"Not anymore," he said. "Once I killed the first bitch from the Order, I realized I was doing your job for you."

"Except for the fact that none of those girls were part of the Order," I said.

"And I made sure they never would be!"

I could feel Tzadkiel beginning to shake with anger.

End this! it said.

"Proud, are you?" I asked, spitting the words. "Why? You never laid a finger on the girls." Carl hissed as though he'd been burned. "All you did was summon an imp to do your dirty work for you."

"Lie!"

"You let it get to you," I said, unheeding. "You listened to its whispers in your skull, let it justify murder, let it convince you that you were powerful."

"No!"

"But you were never in power. You were always the servant, never the master."

Carl's twitch had returned, much stronger now. He collapsed to the floor curled into a fetal position and shaking, huge gasping sobs bursting from his lungs.

"You didn't kill those girls to bring me back," I said. "You called the demon to do that." He nodded, still sobbing. "You lost control."

Carl gasped for breath and slowly got his lungs under his control. Still breathing heavily, he uncurled his body and sat up. "I found it," he said, his voice a rasping whisper. "It was weak, near death. Chained up in the room next door."

"Where you kept your victims?"

"Our little game," he said. "Oh, God! I thought if I could bring it back to health just enough its presence would bring you out of hiding."

"It turned the tables, didn't it?"

"Drained me to within an inch of my life," he said. "Forced me to serve it."

"You can't control a creature like that," I said.

Carl nodded.

"Where is it, now?" I asked.

"Somewhere out there," he said. "The last kill brought its powers back in full."

"Loose in the city?"

"Loose on the earth," he said, his face twisting into a look somewhere between horror and mirth.

I sat on the low cot and stared into the face of my old friend, now a ghoul, for a seeming eternity. Tzadkiel buzzed. I choked back an urge to strike the old man down there and then.

"If I turn you loose?" I asked him, fearing the answer.

"I will find it," he said, his voice careening between joy and despair. "I need it. It is all that is left of my life."

I nodded. Strangely enough, I could feel the Tzadkiel nature within me still itself for the first time since I'd arrived at this place. Carl tensed, only the faintest of tics passing through his body. I could see his leg muscles coiled to run, but still he paused. He stared straight at me, a pleading look in his eyes. The imp had taken much of what once was Carl as it brought itself back from near death, but there was still a little of my long ago comrade still residing somewhere in the crevices of his shattered soul.

"End it," he said, a sound barely rising above the sound of his labored breathing.

Again, I nodded, and let Tzadkiel out of the passenger seat. I opened my arms to my old friend and he fell forward into them. I wrapped the old man up in an embrace, clutching him to my chest. I closed my eyes to the green fire that rose up around us.

I am present to every moment of his life. Every triumph and every mistake. I see myself through his eyes, begin to understand— just a little—the desperation that drove him to his fall. His soul is shrouded in so much calcified sin, and I find myself desperately digging in deeper, searching for the small shred of life that might still be left. I need to find the last little piece of this man, my long-forgotten, ill-used friend, that is still the Carl who once was. In a far-off corner, I find it—one little sliver of light, the true man not completely lost. I feed it with the angel's fire and it grows, for a brief moment, like breath on embers, until the soul of the man that once was fills the space we share. Carl remembers. The light dims.

There was no sound in the room. He did not scream at the flames engulfing him. There was only the rhythm of his madly beating heart, then a quiet voice of contentment.

"Thank you," it said.

Then stillness.

After my own heart stopped pounding, I opened my eyes. I was alone in the damp little room, my arms still wrapped around my own chest now, fending off a rising chill. My face ran with tears.

I could feel a wave of satisfaction flowing from the part of me that was Tzadkiel.

Justice, it said.

"Fuck off."

I was tired and tempted to curl myself up on the cot beneath me, to fall into a long, healing sleep. Exhaustion fought with jangled nerves, however. I didn't need the memories of horror that lingered in this place to creep into my head while I dreamed. Instead, I tucked Carl's old photo into my pocket and made me way toward the broken window I'd entered through.

I began the climb up through the empty frame but found I couldn't complete my escape. My limbs froze and I felt a shudder pass through my body. Something that felt like a rock took up residence in my bowels.

Scared.

I felt scared. Terrified.

There was an unnatural tinge to this fear, and I could feel the Seraph struggling against it. There was no reason to be frightened, but someone—something—wanted us to cower.

My arms grew tired of holding onto the window frame, frozen. My grip gave way and I tumbled back down onto the dirty floor of the basement, cracking my head on worn concrete as I rolled across my back. I lay there stunned and looking at bright, pinpoint lights of pain careening around my skull.

Broken thing.

The voice surrounded me, filled me. It was melodic, practically singing, warm. It was grating and tasted like metal in the back of my throat. It made me want to run screaming. It made me want to lose myself in its embrace.

Broken thing, it said. *Why do you come here?*

From where I lay, in the periphery above my skull, I could see a shadow fill the doorway behind me, but I could not get a close look at the thing. Instead, the now too-familiar scent of sulfur and rust and wet animal filled my nostrils, calling forth fearful memories and the faces of too many dead girls. The Seraph raged within me, willed me to reach out and end the foul thing's life, but my own fear had mixed in with the terror ridden memories of the beast's other victims, and I found myself rooted to the floor, lying on my back frozen and vulnerable.

I SEE YOU ARE FAMILIAR WITH SOME OF MY PREVIOUS WORK.

I struggled to move and felt my shoulders chafing against the cement floor.

WOULD YOU LIKE TO SEE HOW IT'S DONE?

Before I could even form and answer in my head, I felt the imp get ahold of my head. I tried to scream, but found my tongue thick with nausea and fear. Meanwhile, all my attempts to move were translated into nothing more than twitching spasms throughout my body. The imp chuckled at my feeble efforts.

I'D TELL YOU TO STOP STRUGGLING AND RELAX, it said, *BUT TO BE HONEST YOUR CONTINUED RESISTANCE ONLY MAKES THE FEAST- ING SWEETER.*

Taloned fingers spread out across my skull.

THIS WILL ONLY HURT FOR A MOMENT. YOU'LL FEEL AN AGONIZING PIERCE, FOLLOWED BY NUMBNESS, COLD, AND THEN —EVENTUALLY—DEATH.

The thing's hand left my head, and for a moment I though I might be able to get up and face it, but it was a hope quickly dashed. Needle- like imp talons jammed into either ear canal, and my head was filled with a searing pain unlike anything I've ever felt. I thought I screamed

but I can't hear a thing from within this void.

Void.

I recognize this vision.

Shit.

"But I know, now," I try to yell into the nothing. "I remember!" My words are lost, soundless.

OOH. The imp is here. Somewhere. I can move my head, now, but I can't catch a glimpse of it. IS THIS WHAT'S INSIDE YOUR HEAD? I LOVE WHAT YOU'VE DONE WITH THE PLACE.

And then it's tasting me. I can actually feel it sampling my psyche, a rough, animal tongue licking at the inside of my skull.

A LITTLE LIGHT ON THE ESSENTIAL NUTRIENTS, THOUGH. LET'S SEE IF WE CAN'T FORTIFY THIS MEAL.

I feel the talon strike, feel it rend a hole in the nothing. Now I can see the point of light of my nightmares, feel the hook in my heart, feel the inevitable pull toward the light. The imp laughs again, and I feel the twitching in my body give way to a full-on scramble. I can move again, and I do, desperately trying to gain purchase on heaven-only-knows what.

AH, *the beast says,* THE EVER POPULAR FALLING DREAM.

The light grows out from its pinpoint as I approach, and I feel air begin to rush past me, feel gravity.

LIKE POTATO CHIPS. I CAN'T EVER EAT JUST ONE, BUT THEY'RE NOT VERY NOURISHING.

Again, I feel the needle of imp talons jabbing into my skull. I scream again, and this time there is sound.

BUT THIS IS NOT YOUR DEEPEST FEAR, IS IT? THIS ISN'T THE DREAD THAT MOTIVATES. THIS IS THE PAST.

In an instant, I am surrounded by the blinding light I've been falling toward. My feet are firmly on what I can only call ground, although I can make out no difference between what is beneath me or around me. I can see neither horizon nor boundaries.

THIS IS YOUR PRESENT.

I am surrounded by a circle of friends—Ruthie, Saturday, Danny. Even Josie is there. They all smile warmly, and for a moment I feel my terror give way to contentment—happiness, even. A small part of me screams out that this isn't real, that I shouldn't give in to the illusion. Somewhere inside, I know this, and still I don't care. I want this, the makeshift family and the safety that comes with it. I wave at Ruth and take a step towards her, then another, but I cannot close the distance between us.

Ruth never moves, but I cannot get close to her. I step quickly, now, moving into a run, still she remains distant. A wave of panic swells in my heart. Frightened again, I turn toward Saturday and try to get to him, with the same results.

I run in circles now, desperately trying to reach any one of my friends, but this wall remains between us. I try to call their names, but my voice is choked off again. As my attempts grow more frantic, the smiles on the faces of my friends disappear. In their faces now, I can read only disgust. Revulsion.

My breath catches in my lungs as I glimpse the ugly look on Josie's face, a look I'd seen not long before. Distracted, I catch my foot on something (on what? I'm running on void!) and I fall. With a silent yelp of pain, I grab my ankle, closing my eyes tight as I try to get ahold of myself and waylay the rising fear.

Slowly, I open my eyes and look up again. The white void is gone, and is replaced by a dank, dim room. I see the iron bars that encircle me, and I recognize the room. The Seraph's soul cage. My friends still surround me, only now their backs are turned.

They need to understand.

I need to make them see.

I jump and cling to the bars, trying to call out to them with a still soundless voice. I run from wall to wall, shaking the bars over and over, but to no avail. I grasp on to my prison and hang my head, defeated.

At last, a mirror is shoved into view. A rock forms in the base of my gut and I turn my head, not wanting to see what I know will be there, but a rough hand reaches through the bars and grasps my skull (is that a needle in my ear?) and forces me to face the proffered glass.

The face is at once human and otherwise. Feral. Angry. It is the face of the Seraph. It is my face.

The glass drops and shatters at my feet, while the hand on my head pushes me back and I look up into familiar eyes. My eyes, the eyes of Raymond Walsh. The person and not the thing.

Ah, says the imp, there it is.

Ray (me?) grins and his teeth are sharp. Malicious.

"Guess what?" he asks. He holds out a hand and the Seraph's blade takes shape. "We're a monster!"

Before I can shout out, he (we) grab hold of Saturday and lunge, piercing his body with the sharp, green fire. The Baron burns, screaming in agony. Then, quick as breath, we strike the others down.

BEAUTIFUL, *says the beast.* THIS IS A PAIN TO REMEMBER. SUCH A DELICACY, TO BE PRESENT WHEN YOU BECOME THE MONSTER YOU FEAR.

"NO!"

The voice that cried out was not the imp's. Nor was it entirely mine. Tzadkiel had found its way back into the driver's seat. We had stood up, and our hand was now wrapped around the throat of a jackal-like creature. We had lifted it off the ground and had it pressed up against a wall. Its fur scratched at our hand like a wire brush, but we managed to push through the pain.

"We are not a monster," we said. "Not now, not ever."

The iron imp growled, tried to drop words in our head, so we squeezed its throat tighter.

"What we are," we said, "is the hand of God. We are judgment and vengeance and we *never* destroy the life of the innocent."

We squeezed again so that we could feel the crackle of windpipe beneath our palm, ignoring the iron shards of demon fur that were cutting into our hand. A snarl curled across the imp's muzzle as it struck back at us with blinding speed, raking four needle sharp claws across our belly. Shocked more that hurt, we moved to cover the wound, let our grip on the imp loosen in the process, and watched as the thing ran out a door on the other side of the room, our hands reaching out to snatch it just a half second too late.

The imp was fast, but I found that with the Seraph in full consciousness that I could pour on a little extra speed myself. We ran, keeping as close to the beast's heels as possible and found ourselves careening down a narrow stairway, two steps at a time. It was at least fifty steps to the bottom, where we stepped into a shallow pool of water. The imp was trying to make its escape through the service tunnels below the city, and I heard it still sloshing off into the distance. I paused just for a second to hear which tunnel it had run down, then called up the last little bit of willpower we possessed, stirred in the last of the anger we were feeling, and took off after it, quadriceps pumping like pistons in overdrive. My muscles burned as we closed the distance.

I came to a sudden, splashing stop at another node of tunnel junctions. The sound of the imp's retreating footsteps had ceased, and I found myself faced with a choice of five other tunnels. I was standing in water that came up to mid-thigh, now, and the smell of city waste in the water had begun a relentless march up my nostrils to the less pleasurable regions of my brain.

Slow as I dared, I started to make a circuit around the junction, straining to hear any sign of the imp and desperately trying not to gag on the sewage I was smelling. The stench grew worse the longer I stood, new notes of filth and waste adding to the mix every second. Banana peel and molding coffee grounds, mixed with urine and acid rain. Then came the waste water from the city's endless parade of hot dog carts. Rotten eggs. Wet dog fur.

The alarm in my head kicked in a fraction of a second too late. As I registered that smell, the howl of the iron imp sounded above me and I felt its weight crash down on my shoulders, knocking my feet out from under me and sending me sprawling into the muck. My head was now beneath the brackish water, and the imp held my head my head under. I struggled beneath its weight, but I had lost all sense of direction and couldn't get enough purchase on the ground below to push up.

My lungs ached as I held my breath, and every muscle in my body screamed. Once again, I felt the needle talon of the creature pierce through my ear canal.

NO ILLUSIONS, THIS TIME, it said. *NO FEAR. JUST A QUESTION.*

The imp shifted its weight and I sat up gasping for breath and needing to vomit.

WHERE IS YOUR GOD? it asked.

I started to answer, but found the words choked back in my lungs. Then, I realized I had no answer.

NOWHERE, YES? The imp smiled, and the look on its muzzle lay somewhere between malice and pity. *AFTER ALL THESE CENTURIES, WHOSE JUSTICE HAVE YOU BEEN SERVING?*

An eternity passed between the imp and myself, and the walls of the cavern around us echoed with our ragged breathing.

"My own," I said at last. "I serve my own sense of justice."

POOR ANGEL, it said. *DIVORCED FROM ITS MASTER. IT'S FORGOTTEN WHAT IT'S SUPPOSED TO BE.*

The imp stood up astride my chest and extended its talons full.

WHAT MAKES YOU THINK YOU'RE ANY DIFFERENT, ANY BETTER THAN ME?

This time, I didn't need to think.

"Because I've lived here. Lived with humans. I've seen the worst they can do—and their worst should frighten even you."

The iron imp furrowed its brow, puzzled.

"And I've seen what happens when they're at their best, and at their best they're better than any angel ever formed."

The imp sneered. *YOU'RE A SENTIMENTAL HALF-WIT.*

"Quite possibly, but let me finish answering your question. I'm better than you," I said, "because all humans have ever been to you are food and a source of perverted entertainment. But I've lived as a human. I have all that human potential in me."

I reached my hand out towards the creature.

"And I still have the powers of a Seraph go along with it."

The imp's body jerked, and it howled for half a second before I twisted my hand and with it the blade of green fire that was now thrust through its body. I caught the creature as it slumped forward and with a thought released the flame, letting the body fall into the pool of filth.

"Justice," I said.

The Seraph within me wisely kept quiet.

26

It was two in the morning and I was wide awake. Try as I might, I just couldn't sleep easy. I tossed off the covers and got up to stare out the window, looking out across the Missions into the city beyond.

It had been a week since I let Tzadkiel loose on the world. A week since I'd had the falling dream.

I missed that.

Stupid, I know, but it had been something of a security blanket. The loss was giving way to some anxiety. There was comfort in not knowing who I was. Of course, I didn't know it was a comfort until I'd regained the knowledge. Now, there was recovery to work through.

A few days after we'd sent Margaret packing and set the Trammler kids up in their new home, the papers and the TV news were trumpeting the news about the mysterious disappearance of Bishop Alexander Leveque. No foul play was suspected. I was sure, though, that Danny hadn't ruled the possibility out entirely.

The other brothers of the Order of St. John had packed their bags and bolted from New Light ministries. The city had taken over, for the time being, and new management was stepping in just as the Lieutenant had said. Things were changing in the Missions.

"It's not the end for them," Saturday had said to me. We had been standing near the grave of André Dufresne, Saturday's son, sipping coffee a few days earlier. "The Order held us both as precious possessions for a long time. You've seen how much difficulty they have letting go."

"I know," I said. "We've been running from Leveque and the rest of them for centuries. We cut off the head. They keep coming back."

"Why should this time be any different?" he asked. "You should have destroyed them—him—for good back at the beginning when you had the chance."

"The girl was an innocent," I said. "You were right to talk me out of it."

Saturday looked at me sideways. "I turned you into a damn boy scout," he said.

"Which is why I hang out with shady characters like you," I said. "That and spiked coffee."

Again we were silent.

"How long do you think we have, this time?" I asked.

"Depends on whether or not Leveque pulled off his death cheating stunt again," Saturday said.

"He did," I said. I was absolutely certain.

"Who knows, then? A generation at least. Maybe two."

"No time at all for guys like us," I said.

Saturday nodded. We stood around sipping our coffee for a little while longer. The Baron had brought a hip flask filled with a good dark rum. Libations for his fallen child. The alcohol and warm liquid were a welcome ward against the growing cold that was finally starting to settle on the late autumn. The two of us sat staring at the plain grave marker.

"Dufresne?" I asked.

"His mother's name," Saturday said.

"What happened with you and her?"

"She got tired of growing old with a man who doesn't."

We sat in the comfortable quiet some more.

"How have we gone on together this long without my knowing your name?" I asked.

"Names have power," he said, "and I haven't lived as long as I have without being very careful."

"You know mine."

"Ray? Not your real name."

"Tzadkiel?" I said.

"Means 'God's Justice.' That's a damn job description, Ray. Not a name."

"If I ever heard your true name," he said, "I'd probably go mad."

"And if I ever heard yours?"

"I'd have to kill you," he said, a wide grin on his face.

He held up the flask and I held out my cup for another splash of the rum. We sat in silence again for awhile, until Saturday stood up and poured the remainder of the liquor over the soil in front of André's grave.

"How many have you buried?" I asked.

"Twenty-three," he said, sighing. "And, no, it doesn't get easier."

"Why do it then?"

"What? Fall in love? Try to settle down?"

"All of that, yeah."

"I'm still human, Ray. I'm terrified of being alone, and there have been several women in my life who've made me very grateful for the life I have, interminable as it may be."

I thought about Josie. I'd dialed her number a half dozen times before giving up on her answering machine. Then a week ago Ruthie handed me a note from her. All it said was, "Give me space." So that's what I was doing. Besides, I didn't know if I could every fully make amends. And even if I could I didn't know if I could stand the thought of losing control again, of seeing her brief life flashing before my eyes.

"But to watch them all die?"

Saturday stared at me with his old, dark eyes. "The fearless angel gets a taste of humanity and loses his shit?"

I looked away rather than let him see the acknowledgment in my eyes.

"Pain is the price we pay for the good stuff," he said.

I had no response for that, so we let our breathing fill the silence for a little while longer.

"Do you want to hide again?" he asked.

I stopped to think.

"How many times have we done this, now?" I asked. "Run and try to hide, only to end up fighting the same fight against the same enemies?"

"Dozens," Saturday answered. "More."

We stared into our coffee some more.

"It's different this time," he said, finally. "Isn't it?"

"I'm done running," I said. "I'm not hiding again. We've got our work cut out for us, you and I, balancing the Seraph and the man. But, I like things the way they are, right now. I think it'll be worth it."

And I meant it.

I've lived a long time. I might never know death. I am Tzadkiel. A Seraph—an angel of justice.

But, I'm also Raymond Walsh. Finder of the lost. Friend to the outcasts.

Neither of us are monsters.

I'll outlive everyone I meet, I know. But I'll deal with that when the time comes. Like Saturday said, the pain is the price we pay for the good stuff. For now, I'm here with them—Raymond Walsh and Tzadkiel, fates bound with the human race.

For now, that's enough.

Acknowledgments

This book was a long time in the making. It's worn a few different costumes during its long gestation: endless aborted first chapters, a full screenplay, an attempt at "serious" literature, and finally the urban noir fantasy you hold in your hands now.

I owe a lot of thanks to others who helped me shape the story of Ray's reawakening into its final form:

To the members of the "Finish the Novel, J!" Facebook group for cheerleading the early drafts.

To Erica Baron, Allison Farnum, Laurie Neely and other brave members of the "B-Team" who took a crack at the first readable draft.

To Patrick Webb and Pip Evarts, members of my writers' critique circle, who picked apart the later drafts.

To a pile of agent rejection letters for helping me build resilience.

To Erin Scott for amazing cover art.

And, most of all, to my wife, Jess, for love and encouragement, for honest reading and editing, and for the best print book design money can't buy. I love you.

About The Author

When Clark Kent duties don't keep him occupied, J.C McKenna nestles into his secret bunker high up in the mountain of Northern New Mexico. Safely ensconced there, he makes things up and then writes them down. Once in a while, he makes the brain scrawlings available for others to read. When not writing, J.C. is a professional cat herder and amateur banjo player. He shares a cozy little home in the mountains with his wife and a couple of neurotic animals. *Seraph* is his first novel.

INDEPENDENT AUTHORS LIVE on word of mouth and reader enthusiasm. If you read and enjoyed *Seraph,* please consider leaving a starred review on this book's Amazon and Goodreads pages. Meanwhile, keep current with upcoming books and stories at jcmckenna.com

Thank you!